THE PLAGUE YEAR

THE PLAGUE YEAR

A Novel

John David Wells

iUniverse, Inc.
New York Lincoln Shanghai

The Plague Year
A Novel

iUniverse, Inc.

For information address:
iUniverse, Inc.
2021 Pine Lake Road, Suite 100
Lincoln, NE 68512
www.iuniverse.com

ISBN: 0-595-31876-2

Printed in the United States of America

For Courtney

Here was a new generation…destined finally to go out into that dirty turmoil to follow love and pride; a new generation dedicated more than the last to the fear of poverty and worship of success; grown up to find all Gods dead, all wars fought, all faiths in mankind shaken.

—F. Scott Fitzgerald

CONTENTS

▼

WATTFORD COLLEGE
FALL SEMESTER
1995
CANNONVILLE,
VIRGINIA

Call her Jody, the killer.

Lately, her memories were a kaleidoscope of woozy drunken nights in cheap-ass, beer-sodden dormitories, humping and sucking total fucking losers in cramped, creaking bunk beds. She vaguely remembered struggling afterwards to remove a lard ass frat boy passed out on top of her, cursing like a spoiled actress for having to put up with yet another abomination of twisted erotic desire. And through it all, loathing the messy, disgusting, aspects of sex, like wiping sticky come from her lips and chest with a soiled towel stolen from a filthy bathroom.

Glancing at the insignificant, boring names listed in her book, she tried in vain to connect at least one person with a meaningful moment. But they all blurred together in a maelstrom of alcoholic haze. She ran her fingers over the pages in the book, stopping at the name of Maury Posten and Read what she had written beside his name.

Who the fuck was he? Maybe I had sex with him on a beach somewhere, or maybe at some stupid frat party. Maybe I went home with him after drinking all night at Spanky's. Come to think of it, I must have been pretty hard up to sleep with some guy named Maury.

She remembered hearing faint muffled sounds in the heat of a clammy night, like the low murmured tones of a distant stereo, wondering sometimes if the singer would approve of her having sex with someone while he was singing. One night she stopped a guy right in the middle of sex and asked him to turn Rod Stewart off the stereo. For some reason she could not have sex with anybody while hearing "Maggie May."

Most of the time she remembered very little about the evening. Yet at other times, she could recall the minutest details. Perhaps, he had a button missing on the cuff of his shirt, or a broken shoelace on one of his sneakers, or a tiny birth mark the shape of a cherry tree. She remembered different smells, especially after-shaves and colognes like Halston, Fahrenheit, Obsession, learning to stay away from any loser who wore something cheap and tacky like Stetson.

Jody had them carefully listed in chronological order. Sometimes she could vividly picture their faces in the midst of extreme sexual pleasure. Some of them would scream like ravaged beasts when they came inside of her. Others were the quiet, moaning and groaning type, perhaps calling her "mommy" or "my little pussy." Rarely, did they share any love or tenderness. She came across Barry Nelson's name. He was rough with her. He loved to tie her hands down with his strong athletic arms and pin her to the bed. He would stand over her and yell obscenities like: "*Do you like to fuck me, real good?* She wondered if Barry Nelson would go to hell for screwing her like that.

He was certainly going to die for it.

Scanning the list, she tried in vain to find one guy that she would be sorry to see die. She came across Jason Sparrow and the notation beside his name.

Did I sleep with him? Maybe we went out one night, but I got so drunk I can't remember if we slept together. I have a crush on Jason Sparrow, so I hope we didn't sleep together…but I can't be sure.

She noticed Henry Dobson on the list and tried to remember what he looked like. She thought he was a cute Pi Kappa Phi or maybe he was a player on the football team. He loved to stick his penis in her mouth, clasp his hands behind her head and jam his penis down her throat until she would start choking and coughing. Other times she would roll over on the bed and he would mount her doggy-style. She loved to prop her elbows on the pillows and lift her ass as high as she could and offer herself to him as a kind of sacrificial gift from the Gods.

She spotted the name of Doobie McDermott whom everyone said was a faggy bi-sexual art major from New York. She remembered him as a real loser who eventually went all gay because he "had to have his dick." He loved to perform oral sex on her and she always showered thoroughly before they went out. She wanted him to lick her as much as he wanted. She could picture him now kissing her and feeling her up, moving his lips from her mouth to her breasts, twirling his tongue around her swollen, tingly nipples until she was eager and ready for sex. Doobie would lower his head down her body, licking her, giving her hickeys on her stomach, spreading her legs very far apart, and eating her out with rapid fiery tongue action. He gave her many wonderful orgasms.

She gave him a taste of death.

She knew it was perverted and sick to keep a record of all her conquests, but it made her feel better, periodically spewing some of the poisonous venom building up inside of her. Her moods vacillated from self-absorption to self-loathing to a raging hatred of men. Sometimes all these feelings would merge together and she would vent anger so fierce that she felt she would explode from rage. Her only hope was to find a miracle cure for her insidious disease. She did not know how long she could last at this rate. She was rapidly losing energy in spite of the medicine she took every four hours. Her nights alone were spent tossing and turning in cold sweats and she always felt as if she was in the midst of a low grade flu. She was, however, pleased that she was able to keep her weight down. Jody hated fat people almost as much as men. She felt only emptiness inside her. When she thought about herself she would get sick to her stomach, like she was going to throw up. Her only good thoughts came from thinking about Jason Sparrow. She thought that maybe she was falling in love with him, but was not sure what the feeling felt like. She loved herself—that was easy. But loving another person made her feel very insecure, especially since she could barely remember going out with him.

When Jody was alone she felt as if she was in the company of a monster, ready to devour a helpless victim. She wanted to rip her own heart out and throw it into a lake of fire. She wanted to take a razor blade to her face. Her mind only brought her great pain. She wished she knew where this self-loathing came from. Maybe, she reasoned, it had something to do with her childhood. In her journal she wrote:

I was always such a smart girl, so full of youthful curiosity. My father was cold as shit and I could never figure out why he didn't like me very much. I can't figure out why anyone wouldn't like me. I'm the cutest girl on campus.

Jody knew this disease meant she would never make it as an actress. That is all she ever wanted to be. She lived in a fantasy world where the theatre spotlight was always upon her. She imagined all sorts of fans begging for autographs, directors calling her on the phone to offer new plays, and saw herself standing before hundreds of people receiving acting awards. She was always on stage, even when alone. She delivered lines from famous plays to the mirror when no one was looking. Currently, she was imitating the Southern women in the plays of Tennessee Williams. If it was not for these characters, she figured she would probably go totally insane. She knew her body was deteriorating, but she could not stand the thought of losing her acting skills. She not sure how much longer she could keep up the pretence of normality. She was becoming tired, so she made one more observation in her journal before retiring for the night:

It is a good thing I'm an actress. I cannot believe other people can not see through my constant charade. Why can't others see my condition? I'm so vulnerable and weak. I don't know how I will handle the forthcoming decline of my wonderful good looks and charming personality. How am I going to maintain a charming personality in the face of impending deterioration and death? Has anyone ever been a charming leper?

These men, these victims, are like blood to a vampire. They feed and enrich my crumbling spirit. Each conquest is like getting a shot of pure heroin in the vein. It's a rush, an orgasm, thinking about how they will be eventually like me—rotting on the inside from a horrible disease. I get goose pimples knowing all these mean-spirited bastards are going down with me. I am Satan's wife, anxious and willing to take all I can to hell with me. I am not going alone. You can be sure of that.

Tonight I made a count of my victims. So far, since I have become infected, I have amassed 18 names on my death list.

And my final year is just beginning.........

BACK TO SCHOOL

"Jody, you're not paying attention to me. I caught Suzi Banford, who as we all know is bulimic as hell, in the basement of the dorm, stuffing a Little Debbie's oatmeal cream pie in her face. I swear to God I saw disgusting white stuff exploding from her mouth like a giant zit. She turned around and saw me staring at her so the bitch tried to hide the evidence by pushing and shoving that cream pie down her throat. She looked like a pathetic hooker recovering from a blow job."

It was true. Jody was not paying attention to Constance. At this moment she was more concerned with the minutia of her physical appearance, carefully selecting a loose strand of strawberry red hair dangling in front of her face, examining it critically, and twisting it around her finger.

"What does she do with the vomit?" Jody asked, meticulously biting the end of one of her hairs.

"Huh?"

"What does a bulimic do with the vomit?" Jody repeated.

"Gross, Jody," Constance moaned. "What do you want to do? Start an investigation or something?"

Jody's main interest in life at the moment was the condition of her split ends. She was currently mesmerized by a new piece of hair pinched between her thumb and her forefinger.

"I was just wondering, that's all."

"I guess she throws up in the toilet," Constance volunteered, unable to comprehend why she was suddenly talking about the status of missing vomit.

"No, I don't think so," Jody said authoritatively. "Did you ever see her throw up in the toilet?"

"No."

"Well?" Jody asked, "Did you ever smell vomit in the bathroom?"

"No."

"Well?"

"So, I don't know. Create the Puke Police."

Jody's attention momentarily shifted from a stray lock of hair to one of her brightly colored red fingernails. She focused a disconcerting critical eye upon the fingernail and concluded that it was not totally perfect.

"I was just curious," Jody said to her left index finger.

"Well," Constance said, "It's disgusting and I don't want to think about it."

Jody tilted her head upward in a melodramatic display of petulant disappointment.

"I'm leaving," she said to the ceiling.

Constance was relieved to see her go. It was too early for dinner, so she decided to stay in the student union a little longer. She went over to the counter, ordered a Diet Coke and sat down in a booth near four male students playing an energetic game of ping pong. Her thoughts drifted to what she was going to wear to the *Hootie and the Blowfish* concert on Saturday night. Somewhere between a polarity of indecision to wear either black or blue jeans, Danny Alderman unexpectedly appeared before her cradling a mini-cam and microphone.

"Hi Constance," he said in a friendly tone.

"Hey."

"How was your summer," he asked.

"Great. I was at the beach."

"You look nice."

"Thanks. What did you do all summer?"

"I worked for my town newspaper. Nothing special, just obits and community affairs stuff. It was pretty boring, but I got some experience."

Constance took a sip of her Diet Coke and eyed Danny seductively. "Are you doing Sound Bites this year?"

"Yes," Danny replied. "In fact, that's why I'm here. Would you like to make a quote?"

"Sure," Constance said enthusiastically. "What's the first topic of the year?"

"Well," said Danny, adjusting the lens on the camera, "I'm afraid it's not too original. I'm asking people what they did over the summer."

"No, Danny," Constance responded, "I think it's a good beginning topic. You can get to the serious stuff later."

From the look on Danny's face, Constance hoped she hadn't disappointed him with her comment. She wondered for a second whether she was acting stupid or if he had noticed the final stage of an awful zit that, with the help of make-up, was mercifully beginning to fade from her left cheek.

"I'm afraid there isn't much serious stuff going on this year," he said. "You ready?"

"Shoot."

"Okay, stand up."

Constance set down her drink, and raised herself up from the booth. Danny faced her squarely, holding the mini-cam on his left shoulder. A red light flickered on the right side of the camera.

"Ready? Okay, here we go. Constance Stewart, what did you do this summer?"

Constance stared directly at the camera, flashing a wide, beaming smile.

"Oh, I had a wonderful time at the beach in Ocean City working as a waitress in a Italian restaurant. I also read many books on modern poetry and kept a diary of all my experiences as part of an independent study for Professor Wilson."

Constance drew a blank and couldn't think of anything else to say. Following an awkward moment of silence, Danny shut off the camera.

"Thanks, Constance. You've been a big help. I only need three more."

"Too bad, you just missed Jody Hershberger. She would have been good person to ask."

"Really?"

"Yes," Constance said, "She spent the summer in Iowa working for an acting troupe. I think she got a part in a Shakespearean play."

Immediately, Constance was sorry for what she had said. She found it very uncomfortable saying anything positive about Jody in front of someone else. She knew that Jody never said anything nice about her. Constance had grown tired of Jody constantly talking about the whole experience as if she had starred in a Broadway play or something.

"Are you and Jody rooming together this year?" Danny asked.

"Yes," Constance answered, slipping back into her seat and retrieving her Diet Coke. "Jody, Amy and I have an apartment in Lunsford Terrace."

"Amy Toeffler?"

"Yes."

"You should have a great year," Danny responded enthusiastically.

"Yeah…." Constance mumbled, momentarily losing her train of thought. Unfortunately, just talking about rooming with those two girls for a whole year made her stomach turn…. "Oh, yes….we're gonna have a blast. Where are you living?"

"Bradford Apartments. About two miles from campus. I'm rooming with Jason Sparrow."

"Sparrow? He's back?"

"Third time around He's been here so long I think they might name a building after him."

Constance thought about Jason Sparrow and couldn't quite place him. She wondered whether she had ever gone out with him. Maybe they hooked up freshman year, but she had trouble remembering *anything* that happened in her first year of college.

"Well," said Danny, picking up the mini-cam from the floor and hoisting it on his shoulder, "I need to find those other three people. I've got a deadline."

"Sure. Glad to be of help. When is the paper coming out?"

"Thursday."

"Great. See ya."

"Bye Constance."

Constance watched Danny walk over to the other side of the recreation area and begin talking to Salli Kroupa, a girl she despised worse than mismatched nail polish and shoes. Pangs of anger and jealousy rose up from within Constance as she surveyed the two of them together. Christ, she thought, why does he want to talk to that horse-faced bitch from Texas who's probably majoring in something stupid like "real estate management?" She probably spent the summer bored to tears, watching soap operas, and talk shows between giving blow jobs to filthy cowboys.

Irritated and getting hungry, she left for her apartment.

Constance entered the living room, glanced at the mirror on the wall, noticed her lipstick was slightly smeared, and spotted her roommate Amy lying on the sofa watching television. It was late afternoon, but Amy was still unshowered, lounging in her flannel pajamas, looking tired and pale, like a stale powdered donut.

"You look like death warmed over," Constance said.

Amy was unresponsive, staring blankly into space.

"I am dead," she groaned.

"You just getting up?"

"Yeah."

"Classes?"

"Blew 'em off. Last night I went out with Bobby Humphreys. We got like….I don't know….wasted."

Amy's voice, barely audible, trailed off into an abyss of lethargy. She slumped further and further into the couch, rolling herself into a ball of hangover aches and pains. Constance was used to these displays of withdrawal and boredom. But somehow at this moment Amy was really getting on her nerves. She felt like putting a blanket over Amy's head to prevent the inertia from rubbing off on her. Constance assumed Amy was falling asleep and was surprised when she spoke again.

"I gotta watch out for Bobby," Amy declared, still coiled in a fetal position.

"Why?"

"I think he sleeps around."

"Who's he sleeping with?"

"I don't know. Everybody, I guess. We went to the Palms and he hit on every girl in the place, right in front of me. He's a dick."

"Whatever," Constance replied, barely hiding her contempt for Amy. Constance felt Amy deserved to be treated without respect. What did she expect? She dates the biggest trash dick on campus, then complains because he can't keep his eyes off other women.

"Where's Jody?" Amy asked.

"I think she's in the theatre. Where else?"

Amy uncoiled like a tired snake in the sun, stretching her left arm slowly toward the coffee table in a struggling effort to retrieve the remote control. Having successfully obtained the remote, she began channel surfing through a myriad of television offerings, pointing and clicking every other second, unable to find anything to her liking. Constance wanted to strangle her. A dizzy parade of mind-numbing drivel flashed before her, assaulting her weary senses. She felt like she was in hell, eternally condemned to an endless succession of trashy talk shows; sit-com reruns, psychic friends networks, infomercials, home shopping marathons, badly acted dramas, insipid game shows, and corny, unfunny home videos advertised as America's funniest. *Was that Rolanda? Jerry Springer? Geraldo? Jenny Jones? Rickie Lake? How about that bubblehead Leeza?* Amy's careening search for a suitable show landed on Oprah. *Was Oprah still on the air? How was that possible?*

"Goldie's on Oprah," Amy announced with a gravity usually reserved for discussing national current events on public television.

"Again?"

"Yeah."

Amy was addicted to trashy talk shows, Diet Cokes, her boyfriend Chipper, cheating on Chipper, the mirror, prime-time soap operas like "Friends" and "Melrose Place," her horoscope in the newspaper, work out videos, dumb comedy movies from *Blockbuster,* clinque skin care toner, anything sold in *Victoria's Secret, Elle* magazine, *Little House on the Prairie,* light-headed pop psychology books like *Co-Dependency No More!* and Domino's pizza (delivered). Constance was bewildered by all this. It boggled her mind to think someone could watch Goldie Hawn on the Oprah show, especially since she has been on the show a hundred times.

"I wish she'd marry Kurt Russell," Amy interjected.

"What?" Constance asked.

"Goldie. She should marry Kurt Russell. I think they really love each other."

"Yeah…" Constance mumbled, totally unnerved by Amy and her dopey fascination with Goldie and Kurt. Goldie began talking to Oprah about her latest movie. As far as Constance could tell, it was something about two women who wanted to be beautiful forever.

"I did a Sound Bite for Danny Alderman,"

Amy looked away from the television. A commercial was on, so she paid attention to Constance.

"Really?" she asked, "What did he ask you?"

"What I did this summer."

"That's all?"

"Yeah, I told him about the beach, the restaurant, and my poetry course."

"Poetry?"

"I told you before. I took a poetry class with Tom."

"Is that legal?"

"What do you mean?"

"Shit, Constance, you're dating him. Isn't that against school policy?"

Constance sighed audibly. It was true: Amy had a modern talent for getting on her nerves.

"I don't know," Constance whined, "What difference does it make?"

Constance felt Amy was about to launch into one of her puritanical morality lectures, so she bolted into the kitchen to get a glass of iced tea. Sipping her tea in silence at the kitchen table, Constance wondered why they just didn't make a law against three college girls living in one apartment. It should be some kind of universal taboo, she thought, like incest or cannibalism. We will, she concluded, undoubtedly kill each other before the year is out. Oddly, the thought of cannibalism made her hungry, so Constance looked on the shelves for some food to eat. As usual, Amy had the most food, including a whole bag of Reese's Peanut Butter Cups, followed by Jody's row of assorted macro-biotic health food, and Constance's shelf which only contained a box of Uncle Ben's converted rice and a jar of Skippy's crunchy peanut butter. She decided to have a peanut butter and jelly sandwich. She opened the refrigerator door and discovered she was out of jelly. On the third shelf, next to a carton of orange juice, she spotted a jar of Smucker's raspberry jam. She figured it must be Amy's.

"HEY, AMY" She yelled, "CAN I HAVE SOME JELLY?"

"SURE!."

Constance managed to unearth two pieces of bread from the shelf and made herself a sandwich. She didn't think peanut butter and jelly and ice tea went together very well, but it tasted okay. As she walked back into the living room,

Constance could hear Goldie talking about herself and how much more "mature" she is now compared with her "Laugh-in" days. Constance chuckled to herself. *Come on, Goldie! Laugh-in was the best thing you ever did. Admit it. You're nothing but a ditsy, washed up, bimbo blonde.* The dumb blonde concept was often applied to Amy who, in fact, did her best to perpetuate the stereotype. She once spelled the philosopher Plato's name "plateau" and referred to the competitive nature of business as a "doggy-dog world." Deep down inside Constance was furiously jealous of Amy's natural beauty. Blessed with a lovely face devoid of mortal imperfections, large oval blue-green eyes, high Scandinavian cheek bones, velvety soft skin, long sinuous natural blonde hair, and a gorgeous toned body (made even more spectacular by breast implants), Amy paralyzed the college boys wherever she went. As Constance said herself many times, "She could stop a clock." And Jody, in a characteristically vulgar declaration, told everyone, "She could make a dead man come." Both Constance and Jody agreed on this one irrefutable conclusion: No woman could be real friends with a woman who looked like that.

For these three women, living under the intense microscope of the male gaze and competition for men of status and substance put them at painful neurotic, irrational odds with one another. Raw, pathological jealousy permeated every aspect of their lives and lived like a hovering, unspoken stranger amongst them, always poisoning any attempt to form a genuine friendship. Each woman knew about the curse, but did not possess the power to control it. Constance knew that her hips were too wide, her thighs too flabby, her breasts too small, and her waist too large. She found grievous fault with the minutest parts of her body, including her finger nails, toes, eyebrows, ears, and even the knuckles on her hands. Sometimes, in the middle of the night, lying alone and thinking about her fate, she would curse God and rail against her misfortune not to have been born with the perfect face and rail-thin body of a New York model. It made her blood boil to think Amy could command legions of male admirers without possessing a single shred of self-awareness and intelligence. For a long time, Constance thought Amy was completely devoid of any kind of intelligence until she found out she scored in the upper twenty-five percentile on her high school SATs. This infuriated Constance even more than reading male bashing books and watching lame TV shows. Constance concluded that Amy was so beautiful she didn't need to use her brains.

"Are you going to the *Hootie and the Snowfish* concert tomorrow night?" Amy asked, interrupting Constance's train of thought.

"*Blowfish*, Amy...It's *Blowfish*, for God's sake."

"Whatever....Are you going?"

"Yes, but I need to find something to wear."

Jody Hershberger abruptly opened the front door and waltzed in dramatically like she was running down the isle to receive an Academy Award. She quickly seduced the mirror, while adjusting her too-tight, red knit pullover, and throwing her shoulders back.

"Hi, guys! Guess what?" Jody gushed in award-winning effusion.

Amy and Constance, slightly stunned, responded in unison: "What?"

"Omygod, y'all. You don't understand! I got the part!!"

"What part?" Amy asked.

"MAGGIE, THE CAT!!!" Jody squealed.

Constance was taken aback. She had no idea who Maggie the Cat was. Wasn't there a Broadway show called "*Cats*?" Maybe they were going to put Jody in a ridiculous cat costume.

"GREAT!" yelled Amy, pretending to know who Maggie, the Cat was.

"THAT'S AWESOME!" Constance screamed, overreacting, but wanting Jody to think she cared about her acting career and she had a clue who Maggie was.

Once again, Jody stared into the mirror, smoothing out a wrinkle in her sweater.

"We begin rehearsals in two days," she purred to the mirror.

When she was in this kind of manic state, Jody's voice would rise and fall in fabricated moments of peak drama, her hands waving and gesturing in all directions. Her sparkling ice-blue eyes would dart quickly from person to person, checking out their reaction to what she was saying, hungering for attention and response. Jody never really got off stage. She was the queen of exaggerated movements and boy-crazy flirtation.. Her speech would consist of staccato charges of giddy excitement and sudden upsets over the most inane things, like, "OMY-GOD, Y'ALL—I JUST RUINED A NAIL!!!" or "YOU DON'T UNDER-STAND—THIS HUMIDITY IS MAKING MY HAIR SOOOOO FLAT!!!"

Constance wanted to say something else like: "You'll be great for the part," but she was afraid Jody might ask her a question about the play and she didn't want her to know she didn't know the character. To Constance, the part sounded vaguely familiar. Maybe it was the female lead in *Batman Forever*. Maybe she was a character actress in *Dumber and Dumber*. Didn't Madonna play a cat in a movie? She couldn't be sure.

"Hey, what are you watching?" Jody asked, absentmindedly nursing a stray piece of hair.

"Oprah," said Amy. "Goldie's on."

"Is Kurt Russell going to be on?" asked Jody.

"I don't think so," answered Amy…"but she's talked about him."

"Omygod, he's hot as shit," said Jody.

"You think so?" Constance asked.

"Sure. I think he has a big dick."

"Huh?…He's a dick?"

"No, no….said Jody, "I said, I bet he has a big dick."

"Really?" Constance asked, "How can you tell?"

"He just looks like he's got one, that's all."

Constance tried in vain to think what Kurt Russell looked like. Was he in *Diehard?* Maybe he was the one in *Pretty Woman.*

"Constance did a Sound Bite this afternoon," informed Amy, who, like Constance, was not interested in discussing the size of Kurt Russell's penis.

"Oh?" said Jody. "What did they ask you?"

"What I did this summer," Constance replied.

"Did you tell him about all those beach boys you slept with?" Jody asked.

"No," said Constance, clearly annoyed. "I told him about the restaurant and my poetry class, and by the way, I didn't sleep with anyone this summer."

Jody ignored the comment, walked over to the mirror and looked at herself. This time she was apparently pleased with the results.

"I'm getting my hair cut this afternoon," Jody said to herself in the mirror.

"Short?" asked Amy.

"Omygod, no. I'll just have Rudy take off a few inches. I need to look good for this play. Remember, if a girl needs a hair cut, she may need a shave!"

For a few seconds Constance stared at Jody admiring herself in the mirror. Constance had to admit to herself that Jody was probably the cutest girl in the school. She possessed naturally wavy, shoulder-length, strawberry hair, dazzling blue eyes that sparkled brilliantly when the stage lights struck her. She always wore bright red lipstick that contrasted beautifully with her crystal blue eyes and stunning red hair. Her complexion was flawless with a fine line of tiny freckles dotting the bridge of her nose. The moment she walked on stage your eyes would immediately focus on Jody. She did not simply take up space on stage; Jody dominated the stage, making you forget that there were other people in your field of vision. She accomplished her dominating stage presence without benefit of a knockout figure. Jody was only five feet two inches tall, small framed, and light-boned with doll-like thinness and average sized breasts.

Jody was also the most ambitious person Constance had ever met. It had been said by more than one person that Jody would do anything to be successful. Every thought, movement and gesture was orchestrated for the sole purpose of advancing her acting career, one way or another. Jody was adorable on the out-side, but a vicious competitor on the inside. Now that she had been awarded this part, she was going to be even harder to live with. Jody continued to admire her-self in the mirror, ignoring the other two girls. Constance looked at the televi-sion. Oprah was replaced by one of the Brady Bunch girls having an argument with her brother about who was going to get the newly renovated room in the attic. Amy began complaining that her new class schedule interfered with *The Young and the Restless*. Meanwhile, Jody picked up a copy of *Cosmopolitan* on her way to the bathroom and suggested that Constance read the article, *"How to Improve a Boring Sex Life."*

Constance, feeling nauseated, started to leave the room to call Professor Wil-son. As she was leaving, Amy spoke to her without diverting her eyes from the television. "Are you going to the President's speech tomorrow?"

"What?"

"The President…he's giving a 'Welcome Back Students' speech during convo-cation hour."

"No way. He gives the same dumb speech every year. Are *you* going?"

"No, I'm going to Charlottesville tonight. The *Goo Goo Dolls* are playing at Trax and the ZETE guys are having a party afterwards. I won't be back til late."

"What do you think I should wear to the *Hootie and the Blowfish* concert?"

"Oh, go casual," Amy said, "Just wear jeans and a sweater. All their fans dress like slobs. You'll be over-dressed if you wear something too nice."

"Yeah," I guess you're right. I'll find something."

Constance retreated to her room, exhausted from the tiresome interplay with her roommates. She plopped on her bed, picked up the phone, and dialed Profes-sor Tom Wilson.

"Hello. Hey."

"Oh, hi," said Professor Wilson, "What's goin' on?"

"Nothing. What are you doing?"

"Getting my courses together. Classes are only a week old and I'm still not organized."

"I like your courses. They're fun."

"Oh, my goodness, don't ever let that information get out," Professor Wilson joked good-naturedly. "I'd get fired for not boring them to tears."

"Did you read my journal?"

"Yes, it's very good. You have a talent for writing. Are you taking short story?"

"With Sloan?"

"I think he's teaching it."

"No way. He's crazy."

"What do you mean?"

"He's just nuts, that's all. He doesn't give tests. He doesn't even use a book.."

"You don't need a book to learn how to write."

"Well," Constance countered, "He's still nuts. Besides, he hits on me."

"Sloan?"

"Yeah…good ole married-with-children Sloan."

"I thought he was happily married."

"I guess most English teachers are screwed up in one way or another."

"Thanks."

"Don't mention it, but you're right. I guess the point is to learn how to write short stories. Who cares if he has a crummy marriage and wants to sleep with me."

"That's a nice delicate way to put it. What are you doing tonight?"

"Nothing, really" said Constance, "Amy is going to Charlottesville, but I don't feel like going. That frat scene is getting old, or maybe I'm getting old."

"You only have a couple of good years left."

"Very funny."

"Why don't you come over?"

"Sounds good to me."

"About eight o'clock?"

"Sure."

"See you then."

"Bye."

Constance hung up the phone. Seconds later, Amy bounded into the room, simultaneously performing a series of jumping jacks as part of her latest aerobic routine. She ignored Constance, preferring instead to head for the closet, and started rummaging through her clothes for something to wear.

"Looking for something?"

"I need an outfit for tonight."

"Don't pick the blue sweater. It's new. Amy, you have a whole closet full of clothes." "These are all too big."

"What do you mean *too big?*"

Amy's eyes roamed forlornly over the rumpled pile of clothes she tossed on the floor.

"I think you're a size bigger than me. Look at these jeans. I think they're too baggy. Do you have any black leggings?"

"No."

"Maybe I should wear a skirt and blouse."

"Don't touch the paisley one. It's too nice."

Constance glared at Amy. This is what hell must be like, she thought.

"Did you decide what to wear to the *Hootie and the Crowfish* concert?" Amy asked.

"BLOWFISH!!!" Constance yelled. "IT'S BLOWFISH—NOT CROW-FISH!!!"

"Whatever. Who gives a shit?…I mean, Hootie gives a shit!"

"No, I don't know what to wear. I guess just a pair of jeans and a sweater."

"What are you doing tonight?" asked Amy, slipping gingerly into a forest green Anne Klein skirt.

"I'm going over to Tom's."

"Don't you want to come with me? We're gonna have a lot of fun."

"No, thanks. Those guys at ZETE are a bunch of dicks."

"I know. But they know how to party. It's free beer and I'm gonna get wasted."

"Go for it."

"Is this alright?" Amy asked.

Amy had settled on an oversized look, matching a pair of green print leggings with a bulky L.L. Bean tan knit sweater. She did not need a tight outfit to look good. Constance had to admit to herself that she looked stunning.

"Yeah," Constance muttered, "You look fine. Go get 'em—by the way, when are you seeing Chipper again?"

"Next weekend. We're going to the *Foo Fighters* concert."

"Never heard of them."

"You're kidding?"

"No, I guess I'm getting old."

"Well, you should go out more often. I don't know what you see in Professor Wilson."

"He's mature."

"How old is he?"

"I don't know. What difference does it make? I'm not going to marry him, or anything."

"I wouldn't date anybody I didn't considering marrying material."

Constance's level of patience was wearing dangerously thin. She wanted to say that if she thinks Chipper is marrying material, then she could find her a bed at the local nut house. Chipper was a going-nowhere dumb jock who was majoring in "Sports Management" or something equally stupid. She wanted to remind

Amy of all the guys she has cheated on with Chipper. She felt like saying, *"Are you going to marry that Phi Delt who cut you a line of coke last weekend after you fucked his brains out in a Range Rover?"* But it was no use. Common sense, rationality and logic were all wasted on Amy, who lived in her own fantasy world of self-absorption and deception. Constance knew there was no changing Amy's view of the world or her attitudes about men, women and relationships.

Suddenly, Constance detected a perceptible temperature change in the room. A sickening sweet smell permeated the room, as if an ill wind was blowing tiny sugar crystals into the atmosphere. She took a deep, nauseating breath. Her head was swirling from dizzy vibrations. The room seemed to be revolving around her, like an out of control, speeding merry-go-round. *Did Amy bring something into the room? What was going on here?*

Constance staggered over to a chair and collapsed, gazing cross-eyed at the ceiling. She was feeling terribly woozy and disoriented.

Amy rushed to her side.

"Hey, are you alright?"

"…What…?"

"Are you okay?"

"Yes, I'm alright. I'm just a little dizzy. I haven't been eating well lately."

"Do you want something? A glass of water?"

"Yes, please."

Amy went to get Constance a glass of water, but by the time she returned, Constance was passed out cold.

Jody was talking to Cody Ransom in the dining hall, whom she thought was just paying average attention to her, and he told her to watch out for Sue Terry because she had been spreading rumors about her, telling everybody she had been sleeping with a lot of guys, including Tad Christian, a lousy-as-shit actor with bad breath that she knew she wouldn't sleep with in a million years. As she was waiting in line, she also spoke with Bill Convers, who was paying serious attention to her, and he told her that he loved redheads and her new haircut looked cute and Jody said, "Thanks, big guy." He also asked her if her if she was going to be in a play this semester and she got the chance to tell him she got the lead in *Cat on a Hot Tin Roof.* She thought he was impressed, but she couldn't be sure. "What is Amy doing?" he asked and she said she thought she was going to the *Foo Fighters* concert. Jody wondered if he was interested in Amy because she was blonde and had bigger boobs than her, but she figured it was okay because she didn't have the waitress butt that she had. But it really didn't make any difference because he had a cute-as-shit girlfriend who was really nice, except for one crooked tooth, but a gorgeous body. On her way to her table, she got the chance to flirt with Carlisle Wilbon before talking to Helen, the snotty bitch from Texas across the hall, and was stupid-as-shit, but Jody was really nice to her, saying, "I love the new print above your sofa." Helen pretended to appreciate Jody's false compliment and said she had to go study, which was a lie, but that was okay with Jody because she didn't want to talk to her anyway. Taking a seat by herself, Jody was relieved when Harriet Simpson came by and sat down next to her. Harriet began discussing the faculty in the theatre department and how screwed up everybody was. Jody told her that she thought Bill Bartkowski sucked as a director, but he could act if given the right parts as a character actor. (Not the lead, of course, because he was too short, bald and dumpy). Harriet said she thought Alice Prince was a good actress and Jody felt a pang of jealousy.

"Well," Jody said, "She's okay, but don't you think she's a little affected in her delivery?"

Harriet admitted that Alice might be a little too forced with certain accents, particularly wealthy Southern belles. Jody agreed with her and asked her why she thought Lyle Winslow dyed her hair red, and Harriet said she didn't know. Jody was hoping Harriet would say that she dyed her hair to look like her, but she didn't say it, although last week Harriet told her she was a better actress than her. Harriet said she thought there were too many dykes and queers in the theatre department, and Jody agreed, although she got along with all of them, except Meredith Kelly who was always trying to hug her in the green room. Harriet wanted to know why Professor Byrd didn't come back and Jody said, "How should I know?" Scott Brady, who once paid attention to Jody freshman year, cruised by the table and gave Jody a look like he was interested.

"He's a dick," said Harriet.

"He's a dick?" Jody asked.

Harriet explained his dickness because he dumped her at a party for some ditzy freshman who already had two abortions. Jody was going to remind Harriett that she also had two abortions, but whatever. Harriet continued saying she might go see the *Cranberries* and Jody said she liked them, but they sounded too European, even though she had no idea what she meant by "European." Then, Roy Leavell, who was hot-as-shit, passed by Jody, stopped, then came back and asked her how she was doing. She flashed her best, flirtatious smile and told him all about the Maggie, the Cat part and he said he would come to the show. She thought Harriet became jealous because he talked to her most of the time.

Roy left and then Amy came by and bummed-out Harriet and Jody because she started talking about Chipper and how he was going to take her to the fall formal, rubbing it in that she had a date and they didn't, but Jody wasn't worried because she was definitely going to get a date for that one. Harriet also did not care about the fall formal because she had decided on Thursday to be a lesbian. Amy launched, moronically, into one of her mindless monologues, informing the girls about what happened on *Melrose Place* last night. Jody reeled in her chair, moaning and muttering, like who gives a shit? Finally, Amy asked them what they were going to do this weekend and Jody told her she was busy with rehears-als. Harriet lied and said she was going out with James Carrington, a dumb-as-shit soccer player, who once screwed a freshman on the President's lawn and threw the used condom on his porch. She didn't want Amy to know that she was going to a gay sorority party and hit on Emily Bergamo, a rich, but not too snotty sophomore from Alabama. Amy began lecturing the girls on co-depen-dency and how they were too dependent on men for their self-esteem and per-sonal growth. The term "personal growth" had become Amy's new religion, although she had no idea what the term meant. Jody figured she thought it meant firmer, washboard abs could save your life. Lately, it did not matter what the sub-ject they were talking about. It could be talking about vegetables, cars, hair salons, TV commercials, sex—anything. Amy would some how interject "per-sonal growth" into the conversation. Jody told her she thought her amateur psy-chological analysis was dumb-as-shit and she didn't' give a damn about co-dependency. Besides, she would never let someone like Amy tell her anything about my personal growth because she's never been on stage.

Amy, who continued to get on everyone's nerves, began talking to Harriet about a book called *Men Who Can't Love* and Jody looked away, bored, unable to focus on anything, until she finally spotted Carl Weldon, who was a good kisser and she thought he deserved to live. But somehow the sight of him hitting on a skanky freshman chick in pink paisley leggings and a too-tight yellow sweater gave her an uncontrollable rage. Feelings of hatred and disgust sprang from the depths of her being. It was time to be on the move. She left Harriet and Amy and went over to the table, pretending to want a cigarette.

"Hey," she cooed, "How about giving a poor girl a cigarette?"

The freshman bitch gave her a dirty look, but Carl reached into his shirt and produced a Marlboro Light.

She awarded Carl her most seductive pose (The one she would use in the play; Southern Belle, teasing, and coquettish).

"Got a light?" She purred, leaning over in Carl's direction, wishing she had worn a blouse that showed more cleavage.

"Sure," he said.

Carl offered her a light from his cheap bic lighter. She took a deep breath, sighed, flitted her eyelashes, and blew smoke in the direction of the freshman.

"Thanks…dahh…ling," she crooned, "You're sooo…wonderful. I'm a princess. Why don't you come up to my palace sometime?"

She could tell Carl was impressed with her dramatic flair. She whispered in his ear to meet her at the union at ten o'clock.

He said, "Okay."

After giving the freshman a dirty look, she returned to Harriet and Amy. Constance had materialized from somewhere. They were talking about what they were going to do this weekend. Amy was droning on about going to see the *Foo Fighters*.

"The *Foo Fighters* are a lame group," Jody interjected.

She was ignored.

Then the conversation drifted to the subject of soap. Amy thought Ivory was the best brand because it didn't have a lot of lotions and stuff in it. Constance thought Almay was the best because it was inexpensive and good for sensitive skin. Jody said I thought Lever 2000 was the best, hands down.

Constance said Lever 2000 was too harsh and Jody said, "How do you know?"

She said she used it before.

"When?" Jody asked.

"I don't remember," she said.

Jody began to suspect that Constance had used her soap.

"Did you use my soap?" she asked.

"No," Constance said indignantly, "I didn't use your goddamn soap. Why would I use your soap? I have my own."

Jody didn't believe her, but she couldn't press the issue because she had no proof she used her soap. Jody thought to herself that if she Caught Constance using her soap, she would rip her tits off.

"There she is!" Constance suddenly shouted.

"Who?" Everyone yelled at once.

"Vomit girl!"

"Omygod, it's queen yack!"

"Patty Puke!"

Jody looked across the dining hall and spotted a tall, thin, model-type girl with large round eyes, high cheek bones, and long blonde hair carrying a bowl of ice cream to a table.

"You mean she's bulimic?" Jody asked.

"Yeah, that's her," Someone yelled.

She looked like a normal girl to Jody.

"What do you think she does with the vomit?" Jody asked everyone at the table.

A deafening silence ensued. The kind of silence that screams boredom and restlessness at the same time. Someone—Amy—finally filled the vast hollowness of their existence.

"I think Lou Carter has a small penis," she said.

Of course, everyone laughed and said in unison: "How do you know?"

Amy, clearly embarrassed, said she heard it from a freshman which was a better than average lie.

Constance chimed in with: "Sarah Crews has probably not slept with a hundred guys, but I bet the figure is close."

"You mean Sarah Screws? mocked Holly Dunbar, trying to be as sarcastic as Constance.

Harriet said she thought Joe Tyson might be gay or bi.

Jill Stratford, a loser from Minnesota, agreed that Joe Tyson was gay because she saw him dancing the Latin hustle with a surfer dude in a totally gay nite club called "Gatsby's."

Jody said she thought Tonya Small had herpes because she saw her with a gross blister on her lip.

After a few minutes of putting down the freshman, they all left for different destinations. Jody went home to her apartment to get ready for her late date with Carl Weldon.

Danny Alderman walked into Billy Sample's office with a noticeable lack of enthusiasm. Billy was the editor of Broadside, the campus newspaper. Although younger than Danny, he possessed the wizened, cagey instincts of a veteran newspaperman. Danny found him hunched over his computer, squinting uncomfortably through his ill-fitting glasses. Danny liked working with Billy. He felt Billy was a no-nonsense, no bullshit kind of guy. He reminded him of those frenetic, camera-waving guys in the 1940's black and white films who wore rumpled cheap suits with press cards sticking out from the brim of their hats.

"Did you finish Sound Bites?" Billy asked without glancing from his computer.

Looking around for a place to sit down, Danny carefully removed a bundle of old newspapers from a dusty, beat up leather chair.

"Yeah," he replied, slipping into the chair.

"How did it turn out?"

Danny knew it was no use hiding his disappointment from Billy. They had been working together for a couple years and they were not in the habit of fooling one another.

"Well, to tell you the truth, it's pretty vacuous. Nobody cares what people did over the summer. It'll be old news by the time it comes out."

Billy stopped typing, looked up from his computer, and reached for a cup on his desk.

"Coffee?"

"No thanks."

"Don't worry about it," Billy said. "It can't be worse than this piece of crap I'm writing. Any ideas for next issue?"

"No, not really."

Billy arose slowly from his computer and walked over to a weathered, stainless steel coffee pot across the room. He poured himself a cup of coffee.

"I don't know what's happening," he said, staring blankly out the window. "It's not the best of times. It's not the worst of times. It's the...whatever of times."

"Yeah, whatever is right," said Danny.

"Maybe you could do something on national politics?" Billy suggested.

"I don't know..."

"Look. Forget it. Don't worry, you'll come up with something. You haven't missed a deadline yet."

"What's on people's minds these days?" Danny asked.

"Hell, I don't know...money...sex...themselves."

"Maybe something will come up."

"Don't worry about it," said Billy. "It's been two years and you've never failed to find a topic."

"I know. Thanks for the encouragement. Guess I'll split."

"Hey, don't leave yet! This came for you today."

Billy handed Danny a plain manila envelop.

"What is it?"

"I don't know, but it's addressed to you, no return address."

As he was crossing the main quad of the college, Danny saw his roommate Jason bounding out of Hazard Hall, one of the women's dormitories.

"Hey, Alderman!" Jason belted.

Jason ran frantically up to Danny, gasping for breath.

"Hey, buddy. What's up?"

"I just came from Billy's office and handed in a Sound Bite."

"You mean the one you were working on? What you did this summer?"

"Yeah."

"That's not a bad topic."

"I've got political theory at one o'clock."

Jason slowed down to Danny's pace, still breathing heavily. The two students walked side-by-side across the driveway leading to the President's house, passed the Harry C. Lewis library, and turned the corner at Blanchford Hall, one of the men's dormitories.

"I missed my econ class," said Jason. "I'm just getting up."

"Did you spend the night in Hazard?" Danny asked.

"Yeah, Patty Dowd and I hooked up."

"Is she a freshman?"

"No, sophomore."

"Oh, you must be going for older women now."

"Very funny," said Jason. "Listen, I gotta run. We're putting together a Dress-Like-You-Work-On-Wall-Street party for Birchshire Hall."

"Sounds real important."

"Hey, watch the sarcasm! It doesn't become you!"

Jason sprinted off toward Birchshire Hall. Danny leisurely strolled beyond the quad, passed Devon Hall through a narrow tree-lined lane, and entered the back of the student union. It was named Scott Recreation Center, but everyone just called it "the union." No one was around, except for two students shooting pool. Danny grabbed a stool at the counter and ordered a Coke from the waiter.

He began thinking about the courses he was taking this semester and idly wondering how difficult they might be. As he was lost in thought, a young woman emerged from the restaurant area, taking seat next to him. Danny did not notice her. He was in the middle of worrying about political philosophy of the western world. Moments passed. He began an additional worry that his Sound Bites were beginning to bore him and he was longer concerned with campus issues. Why should he care? He was going to graduate in the spring. Let some energetic freshman pick up the baton. He was beginning to doubt his ability to become a good journalist. He turned slightly, feeling the presence of the girl. He glanced around the room, as if waiting for someone. It was she who first spoke.

"Aren't you Danny Alderman?" the girl asked.

"Yes, how did you know?"

"I did one of your Sound Bites two years ago. You asked me if we should have more rock bands on campus."

"Oh? What did you say?"

"I said we should get the best entertainment we could find, considering all the money we put out for tuition."

"I'm sorry, but I don't remember you."

"That's okay. I'm Emily Patterson."

"Hi…"

"Are you still doing *Sound Bites?*"

"Yes. I just handed in the first one. It's 'What did you do this summer?'"

"What did people say?"

"The usual stuff—worked for my dad—went to the beach. Nothing earth shaking. No one did anything worthwhile as far as I can see."

Emily brushed her long, auburn hair back from her face, staring directly at Danny.

"What's worthwhile?"

"I don't know," Danny said, "Feeding the homeless. Saving the whales…I don't know…"

"Why all the sarcasm? Don't you care about those issues?"

Danny took a sip of his Coke, then reversed the process, blowing bubbles through the straw. He could feel himself sinking into one of his cynical, morbid moods that griped him so often lately. He thought he was completely direction-less, without any faith in himself or his future. *God, let's face it. The world sucks. Doesn't this girl know that? She must be a totally naive do-gooder. Probably recycles and takes her library books back on time.*

"Danny…?"

"Oh, I'm sorry. I was just thinking about something. I have a terrible habit of spacing out."

"That's okay. No problem. I was just wondering if you cared about any social issues."

"I'm just a reporter. Saving lives is not for me."

The girl swiveled in her seat, hastily turning away from Danny.

"Yeah, whatever. Nice to see you again."

"Hey, wait a minute! Listen, I'm sorry. You caught me at a bad moment. I'm having a bad day."

"I have to go…"

"No, wait. I'm just upset about my job—this whole 'what you did this summer' thing.' I didn't mean to sound like a complete ass."

"You did a pretty good job."

"I'm sorry."

"Look, it's none of my business, but it seems to me that you're being too hard on yourself. What's so bad about asking people what they did over the summer? You're not a terrible reporter because you asked a question that was not jumping off the front pages of major newspapers. Besides, don't be so tough on other people. People just want to have fun or make some money over the summer. What's wrong with that?"

"I don't know…helping people should be a part of their lives, that's all."

"Who do you think you are? Mother Teresa?"

"Hey, I'm no saint, that's for sure. I'm just a frustrated reporter. I'm not out to save the world."

"What are you out for?"

"Myself, I guess. Like everybody else."

"Are you that cynical?"

Danny reached for a menu and began to pretend to scan the offerings. Who was this girl? Am I being psychoanalyzed by this person? Maybe this was some kind of psychological experiment. Maybe I was one of her subjects, doomed to wind up on a final report: 'Today's Students: The Lost and the Alienated.'

"No, I'm not that cynical. I just don't know what the hell I'm going to do with my life. What can you do with a political science degree?"

"How about law school?"

"I couldn't take all the crooked lawyer jokes."

Emily didn't respond. Instead, she went over and played a song on the juke box. Momentarily, the plaintive, soft country sound of *Truckin'* by the Grateful Dead came wafting from the speakers behind the bar.

"So what's the next Sound Bite?" asked Emily, returning to her seat.

"I don't know. Nothing seems to be happening."

"I think there are a lot of things happening."

"Like what?"

"Jesus, what kind of a reporter are you? Do you expect an issue to jump off the wall? You have to dig for news. Do some investigative reporting. Remember Watergate?"

"You mean pull a Woodward and Bernstein?"

"You're a reporter, aren't you?"

"I just do a lousy column asking people for their opinions."

"Stop being so self-deprecating. It's not lousy. It's a good idea. You just have to look deeper. There are things going on."

"You still haven't named one."

"What about the new road to upper campus that doesn't go anywhere?"

"I heard it's part of a master plan."

"I don't see much of a master plan around here."

"Now who's being sarcastic?"

"Okay, you got me there."

"Anything else?"

Emily thought for a moment, absentmindedly stirring her soda with a straw and listening to the song she played.

Dallas, got a soft machine

Houston, too close to New Orleans

New York, got the ways and means

They just won't let you be…..

"Okay, why did the administration fire Professor Byrd?"

"I didn't know he was fired."

"I heard he's not back."

"Maybe he quit." said Danny.

"Professor Byrd? I doubt it. He's been here for a long time. Besides, I had him for modern drama last spring and he was very enthusiastic about the plays for the coming year."

"I could look into it…any more ideas?"

Emily sipped her soda and started singing along with the song:

Sometimes, the light's all shining on me

Other times, I can barely see

Lately it occurs to me…what a long strange trip it's been………

"What about faculty raises?" Emily asked. "I heard the faculty hasn't received raises for the past three years."

"Where did you hear that?" asked Danny.

"Professor Mason told me. We were at a reception for Junior Dad's last year and he was very upset about the whole thing. He said faculty morale was really low."

"Well," said Danny, "That might be worth looking into. Anything else?"

"Not right now, but I'll let you know if I think of something."

"Thanks."

"Listen," she said, "I have to go to class. Keep working on your column. Something will come up."

"Okay, I will. Nice to meet you, again!"

"Bye!"

Danny watched the girl intently as she walked toward the main exit of the student union.

He turned to finish of the last of his Coke. Suddenly, he had an idea.

"Wait!!!" Danny yelled.

He bolted from his stool and ran up to her.

"Hey, I just thought of something.. You already talked to Professor Mason. Why don't you interview him for Sound Bites?"

"I don't know how to operate a camera."

"That's okay. The interviews are transcribed for the paper anyway. I can get a picture of him later to put with the interview."

"I'm not a reporter."

"I have a feeling you have a knack for this sort of thing."

"Okay, I'll do it."

"You will?"

"I just said I would, didn't I? I gonna run."

"Thanks."

Emily turned and disappeared through the doors of the union.

Following political theory class, Danny returned to his apartment. His roommate, Jason, was perched on the kitchen counter watching television.

"Hey, man, what's up?" asked Jason.

"Nothing. I just got out of political theory."

"Any good?"

"I think it's going to be okay. We're gonna cover Marx, Hegel, Machiavelli, people like that."

Jason, in his usual frenzied state, unexpectedly sat up, leaped off the top of the counter, and in one graceful fluid motion, flew into the air like a bird, landing directly in front of the refrigerator. Danny watched the feat, granting Jason the respect usually reserved for professional athletes.

"Hey," said Danny, "You should turn that skill into an Olympic event, Counter Top Flying For Beer."

"It's my love of beer that provides the motivation!" exclaimed Jason.

"What are you doing tonight?" asked Danny.

"I'm going to the *Foo Fighters* concert," said Jason.

"I liked their first CD…Listen, you haven't heard anything about professors not getting a raise, have you?"

"Are you kidding? Professors don't talk about that shit."

"Well, one did. Professor Mason told someone that they have not gotten raises for the past three years."

Tilting his beer skyward and eagerly downing a huge gulp, Jason appeared to look for an answer in the bottom of the can.

"How could they not get raises when our tuition keeps going through the roof?"

"Precisely," said Danny.

Opening the refrigerator door to get his own beer, Danny noticed their food supply was down to an old can of Cheez Whiz.

"Hey, do you know anything about professor Byrd not coming back?"

"The old guy in theatre?"

"Yeah."

"I haven't heard a word. He's not here this year?"

"No."

"Maybe he quit."

"I don't think so. I asked Allie Foster about it in political theory. She told me she knew he had tenure. Tenured professors don't quit very often. He must have had a good reason, or they let him go."

"Why are you so interested?" asked Jason.

"Oh, it's nothing. I'm just scrounging around for a new topic."

"Why don't you come to the concert?"

"No thanks. I'm going to study. I'm tired anyway."

Danny sat back down on the sofa and drank his beer.

"Okay, I've got another question. Why do you think they built that road to nowhere on the upper campus?"

"I don't know. It looks like it was built to make it faster for the President to get to his house."

"You're probably right." Danny quaffed down the rest of his beer.

"I have a suggestion," said Jason. "Have another cold one, brother. Life is short. Why ask why?"

"Yeah," said Danny, "Why not? I'll take another one."

Jason went to the refrigerator for a couple more beers. As he was returning with their beers, Jason put Van Morrison's Greatest Hits on the stereo. In an instant, Jason was singing along with the first selection:

Hey, Where did we go…?

Days when the rain came

Laughin' an a-runnin'

Playin' a new game………

Jason launched into a dizzying, swirling dance with himself, yelling,

BROWN-EYED GIRL!

YOU, MY BROWN-EYED GIRL!!!

In one furious pirouette, Jason spun completely around, jumped up in the air, and landed on top of Danny on the couch.

"Hey, get your silly ass off of me!"

"Why, you're no brown-eyed girl! You're a brown-eyed muthafucker!"

"Yeah," said Danny, poking Jason in the ribs, "You're not so hot yourself."

Jason, slumped back into the couch to catch his breath. After a few seconds of heavy breathing, he reached down and retrieved the envelope that Billy Sample had given Danny.

"What's this?" Jason asked.

"Oh, I don't know," said Danny, "Somebody left it for me at the paper. I haven't opened it."

"Why don't you see what's in it?"

"Okay, but it's probably a letter from a disgruntled reader."

Danny picked up the package and opened it. Inside there was a cassette tape. What is it?" asked Jason.

"It's a tape, but it's not labeled."

"Is it some kind of sales pitch?" asked Jason.

"Nothing's written anywhere—just a tape."

"Well, play the damn thing. Maybe it's from a gorgeous babe who secretly loves you."

"Yeah, right."

Danny went over to the stereo and put the tape in the machine. Momentarily, a deep-throated, distorted male voice commenced to speak:

….and it came to pass that it was a very ill time to be sick in. If someone complained of a solitary ailment, people immediately assumed they had contracted the plague. I remember in the early days of the dire pestilence faces were strangely altered and condemned. I detected malevolent transfigurations in a succession of prominent archaic structures; the entire community being wrought with a terrible sickness. The old gray portentous academic monuments appeared more sinister and imposing than usual, like medieval fortresses built to fend off invading foreigners. Chambers of horrors. Ominous black clouds hovered over the campus casting gloom and darkness on every living thing. Indeed, the Prince of Darkness was biding his time, lying in wait for anyone with vile blood, coursing veins, and affliction.

"Faint anemic odors were everywhere and sorrow and sadness should have sat upon every face; yet strangely not all looked deeply concerned, even though it was obvious that the campus was in the middle of a profound and ungodly plague…

Danny stopped the tape.

"What the hell is this?" asked Jason.

"Beats me," said Danny, "It's some kind of gibberish."

"No shit. Sounds like there's a lunatic out there."

"What do you think?"

"Let's hear the rest of it. Maybe there will be an explanation at the end. Maybe it's those guys in Rankin Hall goofing around. It's not going to blow up or anything is it?"

"I think it would have blown up by now."

Danny pushed the play button on the deck and once again the voice continued his eerie monologue:

"…..and I know not when I first noticed the beginning of the alarming scourge. I remember two years ago in the autumn of our time a blazing star appeared in the sky. Who was there to see the star? Studies had yet to begin, and foolishly, I decided to risk traveling beyond the confines of the campus. As my journey progressed, I was appalled at my discovery: for the world seemed unusually transformed from earlier times, as if Armageddon itself was clearly imminent.

"As I wondered throughout the countryside, I looked and gazed upon a multitude of strange and prophetic sights and sounds: prehistoric wino beggars huddled in soiled newspapers, freezing in the bowels of filthy city sewers; wild-haired wicked old crones dancing in the spidery graveyards, cursing the moon and worshipping the ancient Aztec gods; ragged orphan children with smudgy faces begging for crumbs in the homeless gypsy park; gorgeous young nymphs in brightly colored bonnets and bows promenading in the sunny poppy fields of love and addiction; drunken circus clowns marching recklessly down the main street with big red noses and floppy feet; loveless flophouse couples fornicating on dirty urine-stained mattresses; lonely old pocked-marked, gaped-toothed prostitutes peeking out of their dusty drawn window shades; crackhead city clockers selling bottles of despair to cloudy pipeheads; suffering carpenter's wives wrapped in brown paper bags; rum-soaked sailors staggering home from distant typhoon seas; phony psycho-babble gurus talking incessantly from every corner of the hungry hemisphere; hard body young men with earrings, tattoos and grim determination wagering guns and money with the devil himself; and finally, after thee, there came a-following, far beyond out in the hinterlands, beyond all civilization, the Prince of Darkness was laughing hysterically, forecasting ruin and damnation for all.

A few misguided persons in these depressed times believed they saw apparitions in the air, and I must say many heard voices that never spoke and saw signs that never appeared; but the imagination of the people gradually turned wayward and possessed. Locked in like criminals, they beheld things that were nothing but air. But then again, some of the people did see routine horrible things like black, horse-driven hearses and coffins carrying the rotting dead to be buried, heaping fetid corpses on fallen red angels, entombed in white clothing. Indeed, the grayness of the time seemed to produce an omnipresent dense smog in which the college students floated about aimlessly, as if they had lost all sense of direction.

Behold they lived, but never breathed, in the exile and the void—"

The tape suddenly ended and Danny turned off the tape deck. Neither of the young men spoke for a few seconds. Finally, Jason ended the momentary silence.

"There's a fuckin' nut out there."

"No, shit," said Danny. "Why would anybody send this to me?"

"Good question. How did you say you got it?"

"Billy gave it to me. It came to his office addressed to me. No return address, of course."

"Well, it's fuckin' spooky. Do you recognize the voice?"

"No, it was so muffled."

Jason went to the refrigerator, grabbed two more beers, and tossed one to Danny.

"That does it, said Danny, "I need to get out of this place. It's a fuckin' zoo, this proves it."

"It's a zoo, alright….and there's a real psycho in the cages. What are you going to do with it?"

"Nothing, I guess. I mean, what *can* you do with it?"

"I'd say throw it away."

"Nah, I'll keep it. Maybe it got sent to me by mistake, or maybe it's some-body's idea of a joke.. Who knows?…I'll let Billy hear it."

Jody was sitting in the union, totally wasted on beer and pot, waiting for her next victim, Carl Weldon. She was also checking out the bartender, whom she thought was hot-as-shit, but so far he was only paying average attention to her. She believed his name was Jim.

He's cute in a geeky sort of way, but he always wears the same ole dumb Wattford College sweatshirt. Maybe he's poor.

She glanced in the mirror behind him and noticed that her outfit looked astonishing. She was wearing a low-cut black mini-dress with a gold heart neck-lace, the tip of the heart pointing toward her cleavage, accentuating her breasts.

The Wonderbra is doing its job, making my boobs look big as shit. My black heels are showing off my well-toned legs. I'm glad I decided not to wear hose, wisely prefer-ring to show off my dynamite legs—fake-baked at the tanning salon, but who gives a shit?

She look more closely at Jim, the bartender and suddenly she was bored by how handsome he was She wished he had a scar on his face, or something. Or at least a zit. He looked strangely banal and characterless, like a department store mannequin. She desperately wanted a man who possessed the rugged good looks of Rhett Butler. It certainly wasn't Carl Weldon who looked more like a wimpy Ashley Wilkes.

Several students were beginning to drift in for a night of sloshing down draft beers and watching football on TV. Jody hated it when guys were glued to the stupid tube and ignore her. One time she took her clothes off in front of Billy Sturgall during a Monday night football game and he actually told her to get dressed because it was a close game and he had bet money on it.

A couple of fairly hot ZETE guys (I think I slept with one of them) are over by the pool table, checking me out, wondering if I'm available tonight. I looked in the mirror again, flipping my hair to one side, making my earrings more prominent. I looked at the door to see if anybody important was arriving. Sadly, a group of ordinary guys all wearing baseball caps on backwards lumbered in like thirsty cattle heading for the water trough, moving sluggishly like dull-witted Russian sots waiting in line for a loaf of bread. I wondered if Russian men would be attracted to me and I concluded that they would go crazy over my gorgeous red hair. Gradually, as the place began to fill up it started to resemble a kind of cheery playpen for precocious brats to throw their toys around. I can't believe this dork Carl Weldon is making me wait. He sure has some nerve. Maybe I haven't been waiting long. It's hard to tell time when you're stoned on pot. Maybe its only been a minute or two. For some unknown reason, Jim is ignoring me. Maybe I should strike up a conversation with him.

"Hey, Jim, can I ask you a question?"

He turned toward Jody, wiping a beer mug with a cloth.

"Sure, Jody. What is it?"

"There's this girl on campus who's bulimic, at least that's what everybody says..."

"You mean she eats and throws up?"

"Yeah, but something is really bothering me."

"What's that?"

"I don't know what she does with the vomit."

"What?"

"The vomit," she continued, "I wonder where she puts it."

Jim set the beer mug down and reached for another one under the bar.

"I don't know what you mean, Jody. Doesn't she throw up in the toilet or sink?"

"That's what gets me. There's no evidence or trace of vomit in the building. If she does it every day, you would smell it, right?"

"I guess so..."

"Well, there's the mystery. She's got to be doing something with the vomit."

Jody sat on her stool wiping her finger around the rim of the beer wondering where vomit girl would put her puke. Jim remained silent.

It's weird. I can't I get the mystery out of my mind. Jim left me and went down to the end of the bar to wait on some skinny cheesy freshman in a too-tight, look-at-my-tits tank top. Of course, he quickly tired of the cheesy freshman. He promptly came back and drew me another beer from the tap.

"Maybe you should follow her around," he said.

"You mean track her and see where she puts it?"

"Well," he said, "If you really want to know, that would be a way to find out."

"You know Jim, I think you're right. That's just what I'm going to do."

Jim left me again and started talking to the skanky tank top girl at the other end of the bar. I was about to leave and let Carl Weldon live for another day when he walked into the union. He saw me, smiled brightly, and came over to the bar.

"Hey, Jody. Sorry I'm late. We had a stupid dorm meeting."

"That's okay. I was just having a beer."

Carl ordered a beer and began talking about some inane problem in his dormitory. I had trouble following his story, but I think it was something about political correctness and some guys calling each other names. I've sure got a name for Carl Weldon: victim.

"Do you want to go to my room?"

"What?"

I really had trouble paying attention to Carl Weldon. I'm not sure why, but everything he said sounded distorted, like he was inside a bubble or something.

"I said, would you like to go to my room?"

"Sure. Do you have anything to drink."

"I've got some beer."

"Let's stop and pick up some vodka and cranberry juice, okay?"

"Sounds good to me."

Carl and I left for his crummy dorm room and I think he told me how good I looked, but I couldn't be sure because his voice sounded like he was speaking from the bottom of a well.

I now have two soon-to-be-dead guys named Carl listed in my record book. The other Carl was Carl Knouse, a computer nerd who was so geeky that he didn't mind when I lit a cigarette during our very boring sex. I even asked him to get me an ashtray and he stopped fucking me long enough to get the ashtray and continue his pathetic attempt to please me. The other Carl was somewhat better, but not much. We went back to his dumpy dorm room which was littered with biker magazines, beer cans, and Domino's pizza boxes. We fucked on a nasty brown couch full of dog hair. I found him strangely sexy for some reason. I don't know why, but I have this strong urge to fuck men who are inferior to me. Who knows when all this fucking for no reason, fucking for death, fucking for some lousy entertainment, or fucking for whatever began. I was an only child. Maybe it has something to do with me being spoiled—or molested. I can't be sure. My father should not have forced me into acting when I was seven years old. All those stupid children's plays like the Frog Princess and Jack in the Beanstalk. I must have been in a hundred dreadful plays for little children, all the while being molested by directors who were all dirty old men who wanted to have sex or get blows jobs from young girls. No wonder I'm a nut case. Every play I was ever in I associate with some weird sex act with an old perverted dude who liked to get his kicks off by feeling up little girls. I can just about remember them all. There was Peter Pan and I was playing Wendy. The nutcase director had me suspended in mid-air with a harness wire and he played Peter, also "flying" next to me. He made me give him a blowjob while we were swinging in mid-air. Believe me, that's not easy to do. I would put my lips around his cock, but it kept slipping out as we swung back and forth. I remember I played the part of Cinderella and another sick director dressed up like Cinderella and made me put on the Prince's costume. He kept trying to jam a slipper into his huge foot while he demanded a blowjob from the "Prince." Sometimes, it was downright funny. I mean, one director in Jack and the Beanstalk made me suck his "beanstalk" and kept yelling, "Give me some magic beans!!!" as I sucked on his penis. One director asked me when I was playing Pocahontas if I knew what Pocahontas meant. I didn't have a clue. He said it meant "she-who-likes-to-be-mischievous." Well, you can guess where that led to. He fucked me in a teepee on stage and kept yelling, "I'm the captain!!! I'm the captain!!!" while he plunged into me.

In the beginning I didn't know what the hell was going on. Nobody told me that all directors of children's play were sick, perverted psychopaths. I must have been about seven years old the first time and I just thought it was strange that someone wanted to see me with no clothes on. I knew it was not right, but I was strangely attracted to the thought of someone wanting to see me naked and touch me in different places. I guess it was the attention.

Later, I caught on and realized all about the "director's couch," so I started sleeping with directors on purpose around the age of fourteen. It was so easy, I don't see why every actress doesn't sleep her way to the top. For Christ's sake, all you have to do is suck his cock and presto!!!—you've got a part in a hot new show.

I remember auditioning for Puss in Boots and the director very lecherously asked me if I could play puss. I said, "sure" I can play a cat, and of course, he said, no, I mean play a pussy. Gee, this guy was hardly original, but I gave him a blow job while he was naked on a couch wearing only a pair of boots. I once made a list of the characters I fucked in costume. It's amazing how sick men are. They would all like to dress "in character" and fuck me. So, in my short, glamorous career I have slept with the Velveteen Rabbit, Captain Hook, Dopey (from Snow White), and a Hindu servant called Ram Dass. Mr. Ram Dass kept yelling for me to ram it up Ram Dass's ass,…whatever. I heard that one director made Judy Garland sing him "Somewhere Over the Rainbow" while she gave him a blow job. Now that's class. I figured if it was good enough for Judy Garland it was good enough for me. It sure beats not getting the part.

A week had passed since Danny Alderman's last Sound Bite and he was having trouble coming up with new ideas on his own. He went to the President's opening speech, but felt it was merely a "feel good" speech for the freshmen. The President did mention that it was the largest freshman class in ten years and Danny thought that he might be able to get some mileage out of that one. The Dean of the College circulated a list of six faculty colloquia for the upcoming year and Danny noticed the topics were curiously different from previous years. There was one lecture on creationism by a new professor in biology and another one on dismantling Affirmative Action Programs from one of the right-wing political science professors. He could not remember the topics being that conservative in the past and made a mental note to attend the sessions. He often thought about the girl in the student union and wondered if she had really gone and talked to Professor Mason, or just told him that to get rid of him. He wanted to ask her out, but was unsure about how to go about it. He periodically cursed himself for missing opportunities with women, blaming his lack of skills on his innate shyness. He envied Jason's ability to date many women and his easygoing casual attitude about life. Danny knew he took life too seriously and frequently lapsed into morbid, pessimistic thoughts without too much provocation. Danny also thought about the girl's suggestions for possible Sound Bites and concluded that she had some good ideas. Since he was not particularly motivated in any other direction, he decided to follow up on the Byrd disappearance. It was for this reason, he found himself currently standing on the steps of the Stratford Fine Arts Center, home of the theatre department at Wattford.

He walked down the stairs, entered a small reception area, proceeded through a narrow hallway, and came upon an empty theatre. The stage, elevated to his left, was in the process of being constructed. The partially erected set looked as if it might eventually be a living room of a grand Southern mansion.

"ANYBODY HERE?" Danny hollered.

No one answered.

He proceeded across the theatre and opened another door which lead into a long corridor. He passed several offices, but on one seemed to be around. He was about to give up when suddenly a figure appeared.

"May I help you?"

Danny turned and faced a large, rather imposing middle-aged woman dressed in a plain blue cotton dress. A pair of heavy black-rimmed reading glasses rested on the tip of her pointed nose, making her look like an old-time stuffy librarian. Danny recognized her as Professor Ellis and had heard that she was one of the few professors at Wattford who acted unnecessarily formal and condescending.

"Ahh…yes…My name is Danny Alderman."

"I am Dr. Ellis. What can I do for you?"

Danny immediately felt intimidated by the professor. But he decided to use the direct approach because he couldn't think of anything else to say.

"I was wondering what happened to professor Byrd."

Professor Ellis pursed her lips together as if she just bit into a fresh lemon. Reaching for her glasses, she moved them further down the tip of her nose, bent her head down, raised her eyes, and peered at Danny above her glasses.

"Professor Byrd doesn't teach here anymore." She said flatly.

"I know. That's why I'm here. I wanted to know why he didn't come back this year."

"I'm sorry," she said, "That's a faculty matter."

I don't understand," countered Danny, "Does that mean you won't tell me?"

"I do not see how that is any concern of yours."

Her whole tone and demeanor greatly annoyed Danny. This was, by far, the most officious person he had ever met in his life.

"Are you saying that students don't have a right to know why a faculty member leaves after twenty years?"

"He was here nineteen years," she corrected…."And yes, that is what I am saying."

"Was he fired?"

Danny knew he was pushing the matter, but at this point he didn't care. He also knew he was in for the quick reprimand.

"Perhaps, you did not hear me," she intoned dramatically, "I said that is a faculty matter."

Danny knew he was facing a brick wall and decided to withdraw. He wasn't going to get very far with Professor Ellis.

"All right. I am sorry to have bothered you. I was just wondering why he didn't come back. It's no big deal. I'm looking for a topic for my column."

"Column?"

"I'm the one who does Sound Bites."

Professor Ellis appeared more relaxed, as if relieved to change the subject.

"I've seen that one," she said, "It's very good."

"Thank you."

"I am sorry I can't help you. Perhaps you can write a column about our next play."

"What is it?"

"Cat on a Hot Tin Roof."

"Oh, yes," said Danny. Tennessee Williams. That's a great play."

Danny turned to leave, feeling disappointed with his efforts. As he meandered slowly down the corridor, he noticed a bulletin board littered with numerous posters, notices, cartoons, and brochures for graduate schools in theatre. Danny stopped and stared at an application for Columbia University. Professor Ellis followed in Danny's footsteps, directly behind him. Danny's eyes wandered over to the names and phone numbers of the actors in the current play. He knew he should be leaving the building, but he could not help loitering for just a moment. He wanted to ask Professor Ellis more questions, but he didn't know what to say. Finally, he broke the silence.

"Mendacity," he said.

Professor Ellis moved closer to the bulletin board and looked at the notices, as if the word was printed on the board somewhere.

"I beg you pardon?" asked Professor Ellis.

"Mendacity," Danny repeated, "That's what Big Danny keeps saying in the play. 'There's a powerful smell of mendacity in the room.'"

"Yes, of course," said Professor Ellis.

"Well, I'm sorry to have bothered you. Good bye, Professor Ellis."

"Nice to have met you."

Constance walked into the apartment, glanced forlornly into the mirror, and flipped her medium length, brown hair back over her shoulder. She looked around for her roommates, but no one was in sight. The television, as usual, was droning on without anyone listening. Constance resented the constant bombardment of her senses by the television, but she long ago gave up trying to keep Amy from keeping the television blaring incessantly day and night. She noticed that the boob tube was currently showing a Three Stooges Filmathon. Perfect, she thought, "That's us, the Three Stooges of Wattford."

It had been a week since Constance had passed out in the couch. Since that day, she began experiencing strange sensations. She couldn't get that sickly, sweet smell out of her mind and she was still having dizzy spells. She absently wondered if her roommates could possibly have something to do with it. Maybe it was just a normal reaction to this particular college at this time in history.

Constance spotted a book on the couch, apparently left there by Amy. It was *Sublime Women/Slime Men* and Constance remembered that Amy had told her she believes it is a lot better than *Smart Women/Foolish Choices*. Constance concluded that Amy was so devoid of self-awareness that she probably did not see the irony of her reading a book about "smart women" while continually watching mindless drivel like the Three Stooges on television.

Meanwhile, Jody was deep into her rehearsals and even more into herself. As a result of her new part in the play, she had adopted a phony Southern accent, coupled with an unending, silly posturing that made Constance feel even more nauseated. Constance watched with curious disdain as Jody gushed up to random guys on campus, grabbing them by the neck, kissing them wildly on the lips, while singing in a loud voice, "Kiss, me, I'm a princess!" Constance realized that Jody could not live without an adoring audience whether on stage or off, and that's what made it so hard to live with her. The only audience that really wanted anything to do with Jody were single guys on campus, and they were not after her for her acting talent. This kind of self-absorption brought out the worst in Constance and she could not help being insincere and vindictive. Once, Jody came into Constance's room with pictures of herself taken for a portfolio. Jody spread the pictures out on the bed and asked Constance to pick out the best ones. Constance, in spite of herself, picked the ones that made Jody's face look fat.

Constance couldn't imagine anybody taking Amy out for any other reason than sleeping with her. What was she going to say? Are you a slimebag or co-dependent? What did you think of the Rickie Lake show called "Men Who Cheat With Their Secretaries." Do you think Heather Locklear saved Melrose Place from cancellation?" Amy was a communications major who never read a newspaper or news magazine, viewed the evening news or watched CNN. Her idea of "communications" was calling her girlfriend on the phone.

Jody, on the other hand, was equally as difficult to figure out. Lately, she has been going out with practically every fraternity guy on campus. Constance was aware that most reasonable women gave up the fraternity scene after their sophomore year, but Jody seemed oblivious of this fact. She never tired of the fraternity scene and seemed as unstoppable as a runaway train. The other night Constance noticed that Jody came in from a date with her sweater inside out, looking extremely disheveled. She almost felt sorry for her as Jody remarked that she took it off in Bob Hargrove's apartment because she was suffocating from the heating system. Then Jody, in an instant, struck back and accused Constance of using her soap. Constance countered with an accusation that Jody used her razor the night before. And so it went throughout the semester. The three girls created a modern theatre of the absurd in their apartment, endlessly carping and nitpicking about the most trivial issues. Each of them, at various times, considered going to the Dean of Student's office and requesting a roommate change. It never happened either because they knew it could be worse with other girls, or they would remember something nice that they did for each other. After Constance passed out in the chair, Jody went out and bought Constance a Diet coke and Amy cooked dinner for her that night. For a couple of days, the girls treated each other kindly and with respect, but soon reverted back to their old ways. It was as if they were in an atmosphere that flourished on the negative energy generated by detecting the minor flaws of those around you. Constance could not see why they could not be decent to each other all the time, but the day-to day living wore her down and she could not escape the terrible feelings of emptiness within her. Constance, unlike most of her peers, was not obsessed with improving her self-esteem. Most of the time she felt a chronic disgust with herself and felt no particular desire to change that fact. She endured self-loathing as naturally as she endured the intense competition for male attention and the culture of self-adornment. At this point in her life, Constance believed that there was no pattern to her life, as if she was caught bouncing in a random sequence of numbers, like those lottery ping pong balls, floating aimlessly in space before being sucked into a vacuum cylinder. Her only refuge was the relationship with Tom Wilson, the English professor. She went over to his house several nights a week, spending quiet moments by the fireplace reading poetry, sipping wine and eventually retiring to the bedroom. Constance was not in love with Tom Wilson, but cared about him deeply. She knew that she did not have the capacity to love someone. She was too cynical and jaded to give that much of herself. Sometimes she wished she could return to the sweet, innocent years of her youth, to a time before she knew about boys and sex, but that era was long ago and now she wondered if she would ever feel any true, deep emotional feelings about anyone. She remembered how different Jody was in her freshman year. By today's standards, Jody was a picture of innocence. She was a sweet girl who was in love with her high school boyfriend, went to parties, did not sleep with anyone else, and came home afterwards. Something happened to Jody to change all that. Constance thought it had something to do with a play Jody was in her sophomore year. She played a trampy girl who gets raging drunk and climbs into a coffin and badgers the dead man for being unfaithful. As far as Constance was concerned, Jody had not been the same since that performance.

Constance looked into the mirror again and this time noticed another unwelcome blemish on her left cheek. Damn, she thought, another crisis. She plopped on the couch and turned up the volume on the Three Stooges. Why fight it, she thought. One of the Three Stooges was in the process of hitting another one over the head with a hammer.

Suddenly, Jody emerged from her bedroom, looking tired and dragged out, eating a cookie and drinking a Diet Coke. Constance immediately thought she would like to hit *her* with a hammer.

"What's for dinner?" Jody asked.

"I think it's some kind of chicken casserole," said Constance.

"Nasty," said Jody, "Let's go out."

"Where?"

"I don't know…" Jody muttered…"How about Spanky's?"

"Alright," Constance said, "Should we wait for Amy?"

"Hell no," Jody declared, "I'm tired of her."

Without warning, a beeper on Jody's watch started blaring loudly.

"It's time to take my medicine," Jody announced.

"Why do you have to take that medicine all the time?" Constance asked.

"I told you before. It's for my kidney ailment."

"What's wrong with your kidneys?"

"I don't know," Jody wailed, "Some infection. Don't bug me."

"Are you going to shower?" Constance asked.

"Of course, aren't you?"

"No, Maybe later. Go shower. I'm going to watch TV."

Constance grabbed the remote control and rapidly flipped the channels before settling on a rerun of the old Andy Griffith show. It was about Andy and Barney going on a double date with two women from Mt. Pilot. They went to a movie, then afterwards over to the soda shop for hamburgers and cokes. The show was so unbelievably corny that Constance was mesmerized by its content. Hamburgers and Cokes? Jesus, these were grownups, for chrissakes. Where was the booze? Drugs? Sex? Rock 'n Roll? How could they cope with the boredom? Constance tried to remember the last time she went to a party without drinking alcohol. She concluded it was around seventh grade.

By the time the show was over, Jody had finished her shower and came out of her room in record time. She was dressed in a long-sleeved maroon silk blouse and black leather min-skirt. Constance decided to stick with her typical ensemble: a pair of Levi's and a Wattford College sweatshirt.

"That was fast," said Constance.

"I'm starved. Let's go."

"What about Amy?"

"Leave her a note. She can catch up with us later."

Constance and Jody entered the restaurant and sat down in an antique wooden booth, facing one another. Unfortunately for Constance, there was a mirror behind her. Instantly, Jody began checking out her hair, lipstick, makeup, and just about every other detail of her appearance.

"I hope we get a hot waiter," Jody said to the mirror.

Momentarily, a young good-looking waiter arrived to take their order. As if sprung to life by a directorial cue, Jody quickly perked up and assumed her theatrical posing, quickly lighting a cigarette, flashing her eager eyes in his direction.

"Can I help you?" he asked.

"Yes, dah…..ling," Jody moaned seductively, "I'll take a hamburger and a Coke."

Constance ordered a cheeseburger, French fries, and a lite-beer. The two women sat in silence for a few minutes. Constance did not really want to talk about boys or theatre, but she knew much to her dismay that Jody would not want to talk about anything else. Jody was incapable of enduring a conversation that was not about her in some way. Constance finally caved in and relented to the inevitable direction of the conversation.

"How are rehearsals going?" Constance asked.

"Okay, but Bobby Crawford can't act. He's a dick anyway. We have to hold up rehearsals waiting for him to get his lines right. I don't know how he got the part. He's too short for a leading man."

As Jody was talking, Danny Alderman entered the restaurant by himself.

"There's Danny Alderman," Constance said.

Jody looked furtively in Danny's direction, then back to the mirror.

"He needs a haircut," Jody said to the mirror.

"I like longer hair," Constance said.

"Isn't he, like…24 years old or something?"

"I think he's older," said Constance. "Maybe he was in the army or something."

"Do you know anything about him? asked Jody.

"No, why should I?" Constance responded.

Danny momentarily looked around the room then ventured toward the booth where Constance and Jody were sitting.

"Hi, Constance, how's it going?"

"Great," said Constance, "Do you know Jody?"

"Oh, yes…Hi."

Jody barely looked up.

"Hi," she said flatly.

"What's new with Sound Bites?" Constance asked.

"Nothing much," said Danny, "I'm looking for a new topic. Got any ideas?"

"Not really," said Constance, "I thought what-you-did-over-the-summer worked pretty well."

"It was okay," said Danny, "but I need a little something with substance for October."

"On this campus?" Jody interjected.

"I'm afraid so," said Danny.

"Would you like to join us?" asked Constance.

"Sure."

Danny sat down next to Constance. Jody barely acknowledged him, focusing instead on the mirror in back of Constance and Danny.

Danny glanced at Jody, who was looking at Jody, putting on more red lipstick.

"Aren't you a theatre major?" Danny asked.

Jody once again sprang to life, like a super-charged Barbie doll who only talks when her name is mentioned.

"Yes, I am. Have you seen me?"

"No," he said, apologetically, "but I heard you're really good."

Jody warmed up to the moment with that comment, tossing the left side of her hair toward the ceiling, smiling seductively in Danny's direction.

"Thanks," Jody purred, begging for more. "We've got a really good department."

"What do you know about professor Byrd?" Danny asked.

"What about him?" Jody asked.

"Well," Danny continued, "He's not back this year. I thought you might have heard something."

"Like what?" Jody asked, staring into her Coke.

"I don't know. He left after 19 years, with tenure. It's kind of strange, don't you think?"

"I don't know anything about it," said Jody.

"You were there all year," Danny persisted, "Didn't you hear anything?"

"I told you no. Christ, Professor Byrd was the worst director in the hemisphere. Good riddance to the guy! He couldn't direct his way out of a wet paper bag. He was dumb as shit."

"I was just wondering, that's all," said Danny.

Jody's unpredictable behavior caught everybody off guard for a moment. Constance was astounded that Jody didn't flirt with Danny like she did every guy on campus. Jody returned to the mirror and her usual primping techniques while Danny stared into space just above Jody's mirror image. It was Constance who broke the silence.

"Danny, do you know Professor Wilson?"

"Sure," said Danny, "I had him for Romantic Poets."

"Well," Constance continued, "He's having his annual poetry party in a few weeks. He says it puts people in the mood for Halloween. I'm playing hostess. Would you like to come?"

"Sure," I'd love to. Do I have to read anything?"

"Not if you don't want to."

"Maybe I'll pick something out," said Danny. "Can it be anything?"

"Of course. We've had people read everything from Ezra Pound to Paul Simon."

"Thanks," said Danny, then added, "Can I bring somebody?"

"Sure, bring whomever you want."

Constance thought for a second that Danny might have a girl in mind and she was going to ask him if he was dating anyone, but decided she did not know him well enough.

The waiter arrived with the hamburgers and took Danny's order. Danny began talking about his political theory class and mentioned the current fighting in Bosnia. Jody and Constance did their best to keep up with the conversation, but they were both completely disinterested in national politics. Jody's mind wandered back and forth between the mirror and Danny's observations on President Clinton's chances to maintain his current high standings in the polls. Constance listened to Danny, but she was more interested in him as a person. She knew she would like to date Danny if she was not involved with Tom Wilson. She felt Danny did not have the silly-boy characteristics of most of the guys on campus. He was not a phony fraternity type who disrespected women and lied to them all the time. Constance felt men came in two quantities of masculinity: too much or not enough. Either they were the macho lounge lizards with gold chains around their necks or wimpy little wusses that you could push around. Danny was different. Constance thought Danny was strong and sure of himself and her mind drifted to thoughts of how sad and lonesome his eyes were and how she would like to just cuddle up to him like a teddy bear…

"…but he might have trouble if the budget problems continue and the Bosnia truce doesn't flare up…"

Constance bolted back from her daydream just in time to catch the last part of Danny's comment.

"Oh…I don't think the Bosnia thing will be a problem, do you?"

"I think it might be," Danny said seriously, "Those people have been fighting against each other for centuries."

"There's Amy!" Jody suddenly shouted.

Amy Toeffler glided into Spanky's as if she were a diva attending the opening night of a Broadway play. She was decked out in a green stretch spandex mini-dress with spaghetti straps, hip-belted leggings, glass shoulder duster earrings, and enough make-up to cover the wrinkles on an old prune.

"Hi, guys!" Amy gushed, as if she were a cheerleader exhorting the spectators at a local high school football game.

"Hi!" Everyone screamed at once. Even Danny seemed caught up in the giddiness of the situation and uncharacteristically raised his voice beyond its normal level of enthusiasm.

"GUESS WHAT?" Amy belted.

"What?" everyone responded in unison.

"I JOINED THE SASSY CLUB!!!"

There was a brief moment of silence. Danny, in particular, looked totally bewildered.

"Is that a club on campus?" Danny asked.

Constance couldn't help but feel sorry for Danny Alderman. He probably thought it was a legitimate club on campus formed to help foster kids or raise money for entertainment.

"No, Danny," Constance said, trying to keep her sarcasm in check. "The Sassy Club is the name of a club in a magazine.

"Sassy is a magazine?' asked Danny.

"Yes," Constance continued, "It's a magazine like Cosmopolitan, only for younger people, actually, high school students."

"No, it isn't," blurted Amy, "It's for high school and college students. It's a neat magazine and I'm glad I joined."

"What do they do in the club?" Danny asked.

Constance felt sorry for Danny. He probably hasn't been in such a mindless conversation in ages.

"You don't do anything," Constance asserted, "All they do is send you a bunch of junk, like a questionnaire to find out who you think is the sassiest boy in America, and they send you the magazine which has articles like, 'I was a Sassy makeover,' or contains vital information like Christian Slater's nickname is Thumper."

"THAT'S NOT TRUE!!!" screamed Amy, "They have serious articles on the Middle East and air pollution—and lots of things! You're just jealous!"

"Oh, sure," replied Constance, this time not withholding her sarcasm, "I'm jealous because you joined a club that takes everybody who sends them twenty five bucks! Boy, talk about exclusive!"

Amy slumped in the booth, folded her arms, with a profound look of disgust. Jody, who was thoroughly nonplussed with this scene because she had heard conversations similar to this countless of times, wondered absently if the waiter had a girl friend or was available. Danny stared uncomprehendingly into space, apparently unable to understand how these two women could possibly get into an argument over such a trivial subject. Constance was suddenly aware how she had ruined everyone's positive mood. She had hurt Amy's feelings and now she felt everyone at the table thought she was a bitch for putting down Amy's excitement over her membership. God, I hate girls, Constance thought to herself. But she knew she had to apologize because she had to live with this girl for seven more months.

"I'm sorry, Amy," said Constance, "I was just PMS-ing. Let's forget the whole thing."

Then the conversation shifted to the three girls talking about how cheesy the freshmen were and Amy said that Loretta Bunson was a very loud pee-er and Constance laughed and said, "How do you know?" And Amy said she hears her all the time in the bathroom and her pee is much louder than the rest of the girls. Then Jody laughed real loud and said they should record it and play it at the next apartment meeting. Jody, who was becoming increasingly manic, said she was in the cafeteria earlier this week and she saw one of the retarded as shit freshmen with gross tangled, mousy brown hair poking her small grimy fingers through the plastic wrap into the middle of a cheeseburger, making mooing sounds as she did it. Mooing sounds??? The other two girls screamed and they all started making real loud mooing sounds like they were drunken cows in a field. "MOO! MOO! MOO!" They bellowed. "GIMME A CHEESEBURGER!!!" And they began jumping up and down in their seats acting like hyperactive cows on Ritalin. Amy, laughing hysterically, began telling the girls about the latest edition of *Sassy* which had pictures of the very hot guys from Beverly Hills 90210 posing in their underwear. Jody immediately said something gross about skid marks and everybody yelled, "YUCK!!!" Then Constance laughed beyond control and said, "WOW, CAN I BECOME A MEMBER OF THE CLUB???" Then Jody screamed once more and hollered, "LOOK, THERE'S THE VOMIT GIRL!!!" And, sure enough, the thin blonde girl came into Spanky's and sat down at the bar. The girls made several disgusting comments about her and then Jody asked, "What does she do with the vomit?" and Constance said, "Why do you always ask that question?" Jody responded, "I don't know" and they all started to laugh hilariously once more and they ordered another pitcher of beer and they all started flirting with the hot waiter, and made more fun of the vomit girl, the freshmen, and all the funny articles in *Sassy*, then ordered more beers and at one point Jody asked where Danny Alderman was and they all looked around but they figured he must have left because they couldn't see him anywhere.

It was late September and the majestic ranges of the Blue Ridge Mountains faded in a chill purple mist and the western sky burned with ragged bands of red and orange, streaked with high wispy cirrus clouds. Emily Patterson felt a slight chill overtake her as she looked out toward the mountains, so achingly beautiful in the late afternoon sunlight, marveling at regal beauty of autumn approaching in the Shenandoah valley. Beyond several ivy-covered red-brick administration buildings, she could see fields of tender grass, growing softly, like delicate hair streaking the land. Fat dairy cows grazed lazily across the wide pastures and rich acres of bucolic land. Small wood-frame houses and rock-walled farms dotted the pastoral landscape, interspersed with patches of woodland breaking up the verdant rolling hills. The tranquil country scenery and wooded dales with their finely groomed flowerbeds and sprays of dogwood made Emily feel vibrantly alive in the throes of Mother Nature showing off the best she had to offer.

As she crossed the south end of quad, heading for Dr. Mason's office, Emily had several things on her mind and they all pertained to Danny Alderman in one way or another. She had not forgotten the conversation with him; nor had she forgotten how she felt about seeing him again. In truth, she had nurtured a mild crush on him since they first met her sophomore year. But for the last four years until recently, she had maintained a steady, if somewhat stormy relationship with her high school boy friend. He was currently attending military school ten miles from Wattford, and in Emily's eyes, he had become too conservative and dedicated to a life in the military. They had gradually drifted apart and finally broke up over the summer. She wanted to see Danny again, but was not sure how to go about it. Danny was different. That was the conclusion she came up with. She didn't even know for sure what that meant, but there was something about him that made him stand out from the rest of the guys she knew at Wattford. Maybe it was the fact that he was more mature, but at the same time, he did not take himself too seriously. She knew that he was a couple years older than most seniors and she did not know where he spent those extra years. In fact, unlike most of the guys on campus, he did not seem to want to talk about himself very much. She knew he transferred here two years ago, but that was about it. She reasoned that perhaps he did not go to college right out of high school, so maybe he had to work and save money for college. Danny was hard for her to categorize; to put a label on. I guess he's an independent, she thought, whatever that means. He certainly did not think like everyone else; he focused on people and things happening outside himself; yet he appeared to be troubled by personal problems. It's just like me, she thought, to fall for a cute guy with problems. God, she moaned to herself, I'm probably just an infatuated fool who's in for a rude awakening. He's probably just some crazy psycho who has his grandmother locked up in the attic.

Just as she was chuckling to herself with the image of Danny Alderman, she arrived at Carlson Hall, home of the infamous Dr. Mason. She walked up the marble stairs to the entrance, entered the lobby, and spotted a glass-enclosed directory on the wall which indicated that Dr. David Mason's office was located on the third floor, office 315. Forsaking the elevator for the stairs, Emily trotted briskly up to the third floor, down the hall, and quickly found room 315. The door was slightly ajar, so she cautiously entered without knocking.

"DAMN IT, MG! THAT'S IMPOSSIBLE AND YOU KNOW IT!"

"Professor Mason?"

"HE'S JUST A CRAZY INDIAN! WHAT DOES HE KNOW?"

Professor Mason was not paying attention to the young lady who had just entered his office. He was currently sitting on a chair with a Ouija board resting on his lap, his fingers placed on a piece of plastic, moving randomly along the outer edges of the board. Emily stared at the disheveled professor who was dressed in ragged brown corduroy pants, a red plaid shirt, complimented by a green and orange striped tie loosely hanging from his collar. His long, curly brown hair was a mess of tangles and knots shooting off in all directions. He looked like Einstein's younger, even more badly dressed, brother.

"OF COURSE HE DIED AT LITTLE BIG HORN!"

"Dr. Mason?" Emily quietly repeated.

Professor Mason finally looked up from the Ouija board as if in a trance. He stared at Emily, then looked at the board, then back at Emily.

"I don't believe it…" he said calmly. "I just don't believe it."

"I beg your pardon…"

"Oh, I'm sorry. I was just talking to MG and he said something really outrageous."

"MG?"

"Yes, he's an Indian who died in 1892. Now he claims that George Armstrong Custer survived the battle of the Little Big Horn and lived with an Indian tribe for 20 years. He's completely lost it."

"I'm afraid I don't understand."

"Well, it's the Ouija board. I'm in touch with several spirits. MG is just one of them. Don't you believe in the spiritual world?"

"Yes…but I didn't know you could contact spirits with a Ouija board."

"Oh, yes. It's quite common. Would you like to get in touch with someone?"

"No..no thanks. I came here for another reason."

"You look familiar. Are you in one of my classes?"

"No, I'm Emily Patterson. I met you at the Junior Dad's reception last year. We talked about faculty salaries."

"Of course! I remember! What do you want to know?"

"Well, you told me then that the faculty had not received a raise in three years. I am working with Danny Alderman who does Sound Bites. We're looking for a topic for the next issue of Broadside. Do you mind if I ask you a few questions?"

"No, of course not. Let me see…First of all, you're not entirely correct. The faculty did receive raises, but only three percent, barely a cost of living raise, considering inflation."

"Is that okay?"

"In a word, no. Our comparable colleges are getting eight and nine percent, and we're already way behind them overall."

"What is the faculty going to do about it?"

"Nothing."

"Why not?"

"Because our faculty is a bunch of spineless, cowardly, ass-kissing, do-nothing hypocrites."

"You mean they just let the administration take advantage of them?"

"Precisely. They don't even have the balls to be called *Lumpenproletariat*, pardon my language."

"No problem."

Professor Mason stood up and placed the Ouija board on his office desk. His demeanor changed dramatically from the wild-haired man screaming at a board game. He seemed to transform before Emily's eyes into a thoughtful, intense, dedicated intellectual. This was, in fact, what he was. He took off his thick, black-rimmed glasses, placed them on a book shelf, and reached for a cup of coffee brewing in the corner.

"Coffee?"

"No thanks."

"Emily this is a very peculiar institution, much like slavery, "Dr. Mason began. "It used to be a good school, possibly even great. But that was at least ten years ago. We have declined in many ways. Students are weaker, less civil, less concerned with ideas and more concerned with treating the diploma like a union card for a job. The endowment has not increased like it should have, which is the administration's fault, and then the administration cries poor every year when it comes to raises. Jesus, they raise money for every hare-brained scheme that comes down the pike, but nothing to support the faculty, or the library for that matter."

"What kind of hare-brained schemes?"

"The Master Plan, for one thing. Haven't you heard of it?"

"Not really."

"Well," said Professor Mason, "It is a massive, ill-conceived architectural plan designed to shift everything to the upper campus. The only trouble is, nobody wants to go to the upper campus because it's an up hill two-mile walk from anything else on campus."

"Is that why they built the road to the upper campus?"

"You got it. The only place it goes is the President's house. I think it is a forty thousand dollar driveway. But what are you going to do about it? Neither the faculty, or a newspaper can change an architectural plan carved in granite. Is that a mixed metaphor?"

Not waiting for an answer, Professor Mason took a sip of his coffee and walked over to his sturdy mahogany bookcase which had hundreds of books jammed into the dusty shelves in every conceivable angle.

"Worse still...." continued Professor Mason. "...the faculty has changed. We used to get fiery, spirited types who would confront the administration when they took advantage of us. Now all we have are faculty members who resemble administration more than independent rebels. They're cowardly. That's the only word for it."

Professor Mason, paused, took another a sip of his coffee, and looked at Emily.

"Not a pretty picture, is it?"

"I had no idea," said Emily. "It sounds depressing."

"It is."

"I sensed low energy and apathy among the students," said Emily, "But I guess I didn't think it was that bad."

"Most of our students don't care about books or ideas. It's sad to say, but the truth."

"Do you mind if I use my notes here to write a piece for the newspaper?"

"Sure," agreed Dr. Mason, "But to be honest Emily, I think it's a losing battle. Maybe I'm just jaded, but there doesn't seem to be any hope for this college."

"I see…Well, I won't take up any more of your time."

"Sure."

"Is there anything else?"

"No, I guess not. Well maybe one thing. It's not only that the new faculty are meek and mousy, they're also more conservative."

"You mean politically?"

"Yes, certainly politically. They're hiring right-wing buffoons if you ask me. My new colleague in political science is just to the right of Attila the Hun. He thinks the Emancipation Proclamation was a bad, liberal idea. Oh yes, and there's that crazy new creationist in the psychology department who doesn't believe in evolution! Can you believe it? I'm surrounded by peanut brains! I need my spiritual connections!"

"Thank you for your help, Dr. Mason. You've been very helpful."

"Don't mention it. Just remember, Don't let the bastards get a leg up!"

"I'll remember."

Constance walked into the room, glanced into the mirror, and noticed the brisk autumnal wind was drying out her smooth youthful skin. She had a momentary fright when she saw a nasty red splotch the size of a nickel on her left cheekbone, right next to a freckle that she really despised. But she was relieved when she discovered that it was only a wind burn. Constance was worried that perhaps her skin was not as youthful as it should be and wondered how old you had to be before considering a facelift. The television was on, but nobody was watching it. Currently, a rerun of *Get Smart* was playing to no one in particular and Constance thought it was ironic because she could not think of any of her friends who were getting smarter.

For Constance, who was now chronically dissatisfied with college life, the days spent inside her apartment lingered on interminably. She was losing motivation to study. She was not involved in any of her courses except short story with Professor Sloan. She had to admit that Tom was right about Dr. Sloan. He was unorthodox, but she felt her writing was improving. She had completed three short stories about her childhood in Seattle and was generally pleased with the results. In spite of her cynicism and continuing protestations that the relationship with Tom Wilson was only a matter of convenience, Constance found herself becoming more attached to the older professor. They were seeing each other on a more regular basis, and much to her surprise, Constance had ceased to date any other men, nor did she care to meet anyone else. Constance did not trust her own feelings; she was so used to making fun of men and relationships that she feared letting her true feelings surface. She knew the other girls would laugh at her and think she was crazy for becoming attracted to someone so much older. She wondered if perhaps she was outgrowing the college scene and ready to enter a more mature phase of her life. Her dizzy spells had ceased, but she now saw them as an omen, or warning, although she had no idea what she should be warned against.

Amy, meanwhile, continued to read her co-dependency books, borrow Constance's clothes, cheat on her boyfriend, and work out to the new *Buns of Steel* video. Constance felt Amy was stuck in college life and would never be able to adjust to adulthood. She would inevitably marry Chipper, get pregnant, have a couple of kids, gain weight, and become dependent on a male for the rest of her life. All the books in the world could not save Amy from a life of dependency on a man because she never developed the skills necessary to make it without one.

Constance was beginning to worry about Jody. She was still dating regularly, but spending more time by herself in her room. Jody admitted the other day that she might have mono because she feels tired all the time. Constance thought that the play *Cat on a Hot Tin Roof* might have worn her out because it was such a demanding role. Well, thought Constance, at least she doesn't go around imitating Maggie, the Cat anymore. Jody mentioned the other day that she was going to audition for the lead in *Gentlemen Prefer Blondes* in the spring and hoped that she would not go prancing around the apartment acting and singing like Marilyn Monroe.

Constance sat down on the couch and began leafing through a copy of *Cosmopolitan* magazine. Her roving eyes landed on an article called, *"Love, What's In It For You?"* Without her usual hyper energy and dramatic flair, Jody emerged from her bedroom, looking dragged out and lethargic.

"Christ, you look like shit."

"I feel like shit. Do you have any soup?"

"Yeah," said Constance, "You can eat the chicken noodle. Where's Amy?"

"Working out. What are you doing?"

"Nothing…reading *Cosmo.*"

"Oh."

Jody retreated to the kitchen to make the soup and Constance returned to her article. She figured out that the main point was that there was nothing for you. In a few minutes, Jody returned with a bowl of soup in her hands and sat down beside Constance. She looked pale and sickly. Constance thought that maybe she really did have mono. She was losing weight and her complexion was bleached out.

"Jody," said Constance, "Maybe you should go to the doctor. You haven't been feeling well in a long time." Constance felt sorry for Jody in spite of her general dislike of her She was beginning to miss the old, enthusiastic Jody who demanded everyone's attention.

"I'm going to the doctor on Monday," Jody finally responded, "What are you doing tonight?"

"I think I'll go to the union and just hang out. There's a folk singer playing."

"Cool."

"Do you want to go?"

"No. I'm going to save my energy for the weekend."

Amy burst into the room as if shot out of a cannon looking like an MTV video queen wrapped in black spandex, sweating profusely, wiping herself vigorously with a towel.

"WOW, WHAT A WORK OUT!! IT'S A GREAT STEP ROUTINE!! YOU GUYS OUGHT TO TRY!!"

Neither of the others said anything. Both were pretty far removed from performing an aerobic exercise. Jody could barely eat and Constance had long since given up trying to be a size six.

"Amy," said Constance, "Let's go to the union. There's a folk singer playing. I hear he does some James Taylor."

"Really? I love James Taylor. Let's go!"

Constance waited another hour for Amy to get dressed, but eventually the two made their way to the union.

The union was fairly crowded for a Wednesday night. There were the usual number of guys playing pool and video games, and two groups of female students were sitting and talking in the booths which lined the perimeter of the Wattford

College recreational center. Constance spotted the folksinger right away and thought he looked like a throwback to the sixties, like a scruffy young Bob Dylan in jeans and leather jacket, clutching an acoustic guitar with a harmonica strapped around his neck. She could hear a wistful, melodious version of "Sounds of Silence" emanating from the stage. Good choice, she thought, as she heard a refrain in the background: *The words of the prophets are written on the subway walls…and tenement halls.."*

Amy looked stunning as usual, decked out in a cute Anne Taylor black crop jacket with golden toned buttons, over a white wide-strap camisole dress. Constance was wearing a pair of Guess jeans and an over-sized Arrow men's dress shirt. The attention of every male in the room quickly shifted to Amy who, by her presence, demanded eye contact and lustful glances. Christ, thought Constance, she dresses like this to get a lousy beer in the union?

"Let's get a beer…uh…Amy?"

Constance was trying to get Amy's attention, but she was competing with every guy in the room.

"Who's the guy playing the pinball machine next to Danny Alderman and Jason Sparrow?" Amy asked.

"Jesus, Amy" Constance said, "Do you want to get a beer?"

"Sure." said Amy, without making eye contact, "Do you know his name? Is he a senior?"

"Amy," said Constance, on the brink of homicide, "I don't know who the fuck he is. Do you want to sit down, or what?"

"Sure."

The two women went over to a table across from the video games and pinball machines so Amy could get a better look at one of the guys playing the pinball machine. Constance was immediately sorry for having come to the union with Amy. She was sure that they would be hassled by a couple of geeks interesting in sleeping with Amy and pretending to listen to her ideas about co-dependency. Much to Constance's surprise, Danny Alderman and Jason Sparrow, came over and sat down next to them. She wondered which of them was more interested in Amy.

"Hey," said Jason.

"Hey," the girls responded.

"Mind if we sit down?" Jason asked.

"No, not at all," said Constance, encouragingly, "What have you two been up to?"

"Nothing," said Danny, "Just hanging out."

A brief moment of silence followed. It was Constance who spoke first.

"Hey, what's going on? Is it a dull time or year, or what?"

"It's so dull, Jason has been studying.".

"Wow," exclaimed Constance, "I didn't think things were *that* bad!"

The waiter arrived and Danny ordered a pitcher of Budweiser for the table.

"So," said Jason to Amy, "I haven't seen you in a while. What have you been up to?"

"Oh," responded Amy, "I'm great."

Constance, who knew these guys would not stay in a boring conversation for long no matter how evident Amy's cleavage, tried to elevate the level of discussion.

"What's up with Sound Bites?" Constance asked.

Danny leaned toward Constance. "Well, I thought the last one was okay, but I'm looking for more serious stuff now.

"Like what?" Constance asked.

"Well, I'm trying to find Professor Byrd for one thing."

"Maybe you should ask Jody's uncle about him."

"Jody's uncle?"

"He's on the board of trustees. His name is Dr. Chambers."

"I had no idea," said Danny, "Do you think the board could have something to do with it?"

"I don't know," said Constance, "I really don't know what they do."

"That's a possibility. I'll check it out."

"Well," said Jason, "This is all very interesting, but it's not as important as who is the best pool player in the Western hemisphere, which is me by the way. Who wants to be humiliated on the pool table?"

To everyone's surprise, Amy took him up on the challenge,

"I'll play!!" yelled Amy. "I used to play in our rec room with my father, but I haven't played in a long time."

"Hey, no problem," said Jason. "Just don't get any ideas about beating me."

Jason and Amy left the table to shoot billiards. Constance and Danny remained at the table, drinking their beers, watching Jason and Amy from a distance. A few minutes later, Emily Patterson entered the union. Danny's eyes instantly lighted up when he saw her enter the room. He motioned from a distance for her to come and sit with them. As Emily approached, Danny stood up and offered Emily a seat next to him.

"Hi," said Danny. "How about a beer."

"Sure," said Emily, sitting down in the booth. "Hi Constance."

"Hey."

"So what's going on?" asked Emily.

"I don't know," said Constance, "It's a slow time of the year."

"I talked to Professor Mason the other day and he totally agreed. This campus is on the skids."

"You talked to Professor Mason?" Danny asked, intrigued.

"I told you I would, didn't I?"

Emily told Danny and Constance what happened at the meeting with Professor Mason. She didn't leave out any of the details, including Professor Mason's contact with MG, the American Indian. Danny listened intently, not only because he was concerned as a reporter, but he was becoming more attracted to Emily and the way she handled herself, especially her dedication to finding a good topic for the next Sound Bite. Constance was also interested in Emily's encounter with Professor Mason. The energy Emily displayed was contagious and Constance felt she was around an important person who was serious about life and social issues, not her self-absorbed, immature roommates. When Emily was through, it was Constance who made the first comment.

"I knew this place was screwed up. I just didn't know how much."

"That's great," said Danny, "We'll run the piece next issue. I think doing a Sound Bite about his contacts with spirits would be terrific. Why don't you go for interview number two, Miss Patterson."

"You haven't read my first piece yet."

"Hey, I trust you. Besides, Billy Sample can edit any changes. But I'm sure it's gonna be alright."

"Okay," said Emily, "I'll talk to him again. He's really an interesting person. It seems we've got two issues—faculty salaries and hiring right-wing professors. I don't think we can do anything about changing the so-called Master Plan."

"Three issues," said Danny. "I went to Dr. Ellis' office to find out why Professor Byrd left and she was not exactly loaded with answers. I'm not sure hiring conservative professors is an issue. I mean, that could be just a coincidence. Besides, Professor Mason is very far to the left, so anybody would be to the right of him."

"I think it's still weird," said Constance. "This college was always a place for eccentric, oddball teachers. Believe me, Dr. Wilson has told me about the some of the cuckoos on the faculty. These new guys look like they came out of the military, or something."

"So, said Emily," Danny asked, "When are your going to get the crazy Professor Mason to tell you about his spirits?"

"I'll think I'll call him tomorrow, or maybe early next week."

"Terrific. Meanwhile, I'm going to follow up on the Byrd disappearance. I need to talk to more people about that."

"You know," said Constance, "I bet Dr. Wilson has some good ideas for Sound Bites. I'll ask him."

"Hey," exclaimed Danny, "Maybe we're on a roll! We'll have so many burning issues we won't know what to do with ourselves!"

"This is awesome," declared Constance, who was excited about something significant happening on campus for the first time in her academic career.

"Hey, what's up?" asked Jason, who had just returned from shooting pool with Amy.

"Oh, we're solving all the world's problems," said Emily.

"Sounds like you're having a pretty good time doing it."

"Actually we are," added Constance, laughing and tipping her beer into the air. "Let's drink to the team of Alderman and Patterson!"

Danny and Emily were immediately self-conscious about being linked together as a team, but reveled in the spirit of the moment by hoisting their beers into the air, joining Constance in a rare and remarkable display of camaraderie among the students at Wattford College.

"Let's go out on the town!" cried Amy. "There's a band playing at Trax!"

"Sounds good to me," exclaimed Jason.

"Come on! Let's rock this town.!" screamed Amy.

"I could use a night out," said Constance.

Danny looked at Emily to gauge her reaction to the suggestion. He was hoping she would say no and they could spend some time together. Emily was non-committal.

"I think I'll just hang out here," said Danny, "I've got a long day tomorrow."

"Me too," responded Emily. "You guys go ahead."

"Hey," said Jason, "Do you think you two can behave yourselves all alone?"

"Well," said Danny jokingly, "You can pay me to be good or I'll be good for nothing."

"Yeah, good for nothing is more like it," cried Jason. "Come on everybody, let's partake in a tour of the downtown bars. Let's do an old-fashioned pub crawl!"

Jason and the two other girls stormed out of the union, leaving Danny and Emily alone at the table.

Danny motion to Jim at the counter to send over two more beers.

"So, here comes the first standard question: what year are you in?"

"A senior."

"How come I haven't seen you around?"

"I don't know," Emily said casually, "I'm not really a party person. I spend a lot of my time reading, and working out. I'm kind of a health nut."

"You do aerobics?

"Yes, and just about everything else, jogging, swimming, tennis. It keeps me sane. It keeps me down to earth."

"Are you from around here?"

"I'm from a little town about fifty miles from here called Scotsville. I come from a fairly normal background. My family's not even dysfunctional. I mean, they're still married…Do you think he plays Dylan?"

Emily alluded to the folksinger who was currently singing *The Wreck of the Edmund Fitzgerald* by Gordon Lightfoot. "I think I'll ask him."

Emily stood up and walked over to the singer. He watched her cross the room and wondered why he hadn't noticed how good-looking she was when they met two years ago. She didn't wear a lot of make-up, yet she had a natural, seductive quality about her. She was blessed with large, round deep brown eyes, high cheek bones, full-hearted lips, and shiny, silk-like, raven-black hair that cascaded down to the small of her back in long, flowing waves. She was about five feet eight inches tall, medium built, and looked terrific in the perfectly fitting blue jeans and a bulky red turtle neck sweater that she was wearing tonight.

Emily sat by the singer and waited until he finished the Gordon Lightfoot song. She said something to him, then returned to the table. Presently, the mournful, plaintive sounds of *"Lay Lady Lay"* came drifting from the stage.

"Do you like Bob Dylan?" Danny asked.

"Yes. He's my favorite right now."

"Do you think he can really sing?"

"Of course," she said, "Don't you?"

"Actually, I do. But I think we're in the minority. Everyone else thinks he sounds like a chicken with his head caught in barbed wire."

Danny thought Emily would find his remark amusing, but instead, she stared at him intensely, as if searching for the window of his soul.

"Hardly anybody sings a Bob Dylan song better than Bob Dylan," she said emphatically.

"I agree with you, but I don't know why. He has such a rough voice."

"I think that's the point," she continued, "You really shouldn't have a pure, perfect voice if your going to sing about tough times. He sings hard hitting songs for hard-hit people."

"You're right. He's more of a blues singer. Okay, one more basic question: what's your major?"

"Philosophy."

"Uh, oh. A deep thinker," Danny said, with mock suspicion. "Do you know the meaning of life?"

"Sure."

Emily hesitated for a moment. Danny thought she was going to quote the Bible, or a philosopher, like Albert Camus. Instead she looked at Danny, grinned mischievously and proclaimed:

"Don't look back, something may be gaining on you."

"Oh, I see. Philosophy according to Satchel Paige."

"He was also a great pitcher."

"Baseball fan, too?"

"My dad used to take me to see the Indians play when we lived in Cleveland."

"I've never met a Cleveland Indian fan before."

"There aren't many who will admit it in public. Until this year, they hadn't been in a World Series since 1954, the year Willie Mays made that great catch."

"Off Vic Wertz."

"My dad was there that day with my grandfather. I come from a long line of suffering Cleveland Indians fans."

"You have my deepest sympathy. Maybe they'll win the series this year."

"Let's hope so, but I think Atlanta's pitching may be too tough."

A few more students were beginning to file into the union, crowding around the folk singer who had just launched into *"It Ain't Me Babe."*

"Listen, Emily. I missed dinner tonight. Would you like to go downtown and grab a pizza, or something?"

"I'd love to."

Two days after his impromptu date with Emily, Danny had an important appointment downtown. But beforehand he decided to stop by the Broadside office and see Billy Sample. He wanted to give him an update on his ideas for the next Sound Bite. As he entered the office, Billy, as usual, was peering at his computer with a discourage look on his face.

"Hey, man, you don't look too happy. What's up?"

"I'm not," said Billy. "There is no way you can work for the *Wattford Broadside* and be happy. They are two mutually exclusive experiences."

"What are you working on?" Danny asked.

"I'm on the internet, getting information about Watergate."

"Watergate?"

"I figure I'll do a piece on Nixon next semester. He was complicated."

"Yeah," said Danny, "A complicated crook."

"True enough. By the way, you have another plain manila envelop."

"You mean, like the last one?"

"I don't know, but it looks the same, and no return address."

"Well, I hope it's not as strange as the last one."

"No kidding. Let's have a listen."

Billy inserted the tape in his tape player and within seconds the same eerie voice that they had heard earlier bellowed from cassette player:

"...and I was told that the plague was raging elsewhere, but I lost track of events in other parts of the countryside. One trip outside the campus was enough for me. Perhaps, there are pockets of sincerity where exile and separation are not the dominant order of the day. I try not to be concerned with the entire progress of the disease. Indeed, it is too much too comprehend...

...In the beginning, certain signs in the heavens foretold of drought, famine, and pestilence. But lo, they were mistaken, for there was no drought in any season. We had several great rains. There was no famine. As far as I know, the cafeteria never ran out of food. In fact, the students thought more about food than anything spiritual. And indeed, food and talk of food dominated the course of their lives.

Some of them took to looking for royalty to guide them, but like I say, they were out of their wits already. Many persons were fraught by discourses, filled with terror and spoke nothing but dismal things. And they brought the people together with a kind of horror; they sent them away in fear, prophesizing evil tidings, terrifying the populace with the apprehension of being utterly destroyed; not guiding them, at least not enough to cry to heaven for mercy.

One mischief always follows another...

"These terrors and apprehensions of the people led them into a thousand weak, foolish things, such as running about to fortune tellers, preachers on empty boxes, astrologers, and mind entertainers. This modern folly made the campus swarm with a wicked generation of pretenders to magic; to black art, as they called it.

With what blind and ridiculous stuff these oracles of the devil pleased and satisfied the people I really know not; but it is certain that innumerable attendants crowded about the false prophets of the sorrowful streets and back alleyways, hoping for a final shot at frightful redemption.

Life was very absurd. If a grave fellow in a velvet jacket and black coat was seen in the streets, the students would follow him and ask a lot of questions This plague...this terrible plague must be a sign of the end of time. For the minds of the students were agitated with many other details, and a kind of sadness and horror at these things sat upon their countenances and everyone began to think of their graves, not of mirth and oranges.

...and some took to Jesus and looked to Him as the merciful savior for pardon, imploring His compassion on them in such a time of their distress, and developed a quite contrary extreme in the common student, who ignorant and stupid in their reflections, as they were brutishly wicked and thoughtless before, were now led by their fright to extremes of folly. As I have said, they ran to conjurers and witches and all sorts of deceivers who were in the media all the time. The woeful deceivers fed their fears and kept them alarmed and awake on purpose so as to delude them and pick their pockets.

I can still see them merrily guzzling frothy beers in rathskellers and local pubs, anxiously checking their mail in the post office, getting on line, watching countless movies on their television machines, weighing in on dietary fads, munching on peculiar things like Smartfood Kentucky Popcorn and Funions onion-flavored rings, and all the while I could see them deteriorate, faint, and suffocate. I see them running after quacks, and drug dispensers for medicines, potions, and preservatives, as they were called. But they not only wasted their money, they poisoned themselves, and the poison prepared their bodies for the plague, instead of purifying the body and soul.

Indeed, everyone thought they could find a universal remedy for they plague, but they were looking in the wrong direction. They looked inward and saw only emptiness and ennui. And as they looked out among their classmates, their hearts sank with a heaviness and foreboding numbness, for they also had the plague and could be of little help. They were looking inward also. In spite of all this weary despondency, the students still possessed a morbid fate in the future. It was as if they were denying all the chaos and consternation. They took to engaging in foolish and quite stupid actions to avoid the exile and separation of the plague. Many pretended they had true friends. Some even thought they were civil, decorous, and au fait.

I must record these things as objectively as possible...

My spirit was drained in the ghoul-infested darkness. It seemed as if every sound was a moan or scream. Are you a moaner or a screamer?......I heard these soft words echoing from beyond the lonesome chambers. I wandered listlessly down the clammy passages of the dismal campus hearing crazy, rabid wolves baying at the moon, eerie animal noises from subterranean caves; hungry, squealing flea-infested rats from London town in tenebrous alleys, and I witnessed malodorous, smoke-filled bodegas where students hunched together, sweating and pissing their life away. Eternal cries of human pain filled my ears and I looked for relief. I wonder when this plague will end and how many more lives will be wiped out. 'Tis a sorry tale indeed.........

I do not understand these puerile agitations and strange indifference to one's fellowman.

It seems the night before a dead cart stopped at Brewster Hall and a cocky freshman from Des Moines had been brought down to the door dead, and the buriers or bearers, as they were called, put him into the cart, strapped only in an Alabama University flag, and carried him away. I Could hear the buriers calling out in the distance after they passed a Four Star pizza truck: "Bring out your dead!!!" But I could not hear anyone answer; nor were there any bodies deposited on the doorstep.

How these college students and everyone else found the insufficiency of those things, and how many of them were carried away in the dead carts and thrown into the common grave and Black Ditch of every church, with these hellish charms and trumpery hanging around their heads and skulls and cross bones imprinted on worn out clothes of every variety, remains to be seen—.

The tape ended. Billy clicked off the tape machine.

"Well, that makes about as much sense as the last one," Billy said.

"Maybe less, said Danny. "I mean, what's the point?"

"I don't know Danny. It beats me. Sounds like an Old Testament preacher forecasting the end of the world."

"You're right. It's very apocalyptic."

"What's that stuff about the plague?" Billy asked.

"Well, he's saying there's a plague on a campus. I guess ours, but that's ridiculous."

"Yeah," said Billy, "But he's also pretty tough on our students. What did he say? Something about how insensitive they are, only looking out for themselves."

"I know," said Danny, "He sounds like a preacher moralizing about people not caring about one another."

Billy paused for a moment, then went over to the coffee pot.

"Do you think he's really been on campus?" Billy asked. "Maybe he's never been here. He never mentioned Wattford by name."

"That's true," Danny said, "But it could also be a student prank. Maybe it's part of a fraternity initiation. I wouldn't put it past the Greeks."

"Do you think a student could be that creative? I mean, the language is so different. Like you said, something out of the Old Testament."

"I don't know," said Danny, "The voice is muddled, but it definitely sounds like an older man."

"I don't get it." said Billy. "Why is this guy sending it to you?"

"It sounds like we're being alerted to an impending crisis, or plague. But it's too grotesque to be real. I mean, dead carts? Come on, the guy's nuts!"

"Maybe it's all symbolic," said Billy, "Maybe it's a spiritual plague. He does say that the students are empty and bored."

"Well, who the fuck could argue with that?" exclaimed Danny.

"What are you going to do?"

"I guess there's nothing to do. Are we being harassed?"

"I don't think so. He's not threatening anyone."

"Well, said Danny, "Let's just forget it."

"Yeah…until the next one."

Danny was five minutes late for his appointment downtown. He walked into the James D. Harris Correctional Center just after ten o'clock in the morning.

"Good morning, Mrs. Pietrowski," Danny said cheerfully.

"Good morning Danny, have a seat. Mr. Jones will be with you in a moment."

Danny took a seat in the reception area. Within minutes, Selden R. Jones, probation officer for Crozet county, peaked his head out from the door marked "Administrative Personnel Only."

"Come on in Danny"

He entered and took a seat. Mr. Jones was behind his desk, facing him.

"So, how's it going?" asked Mr. Jones.

"Fine. I had a good month."

"Keeping clean?"

"Of course," said Danny. "Don't you trust me?"

"Trust has nothing to do with it. It's my job to keep you straight, and out of jail.."

"I'm not going back. Don't worry."

"Danny, I don't spend my time worrying about parolees. I hope you make it, but believe it or not, I have a life, and my own worries."

"Yeah, well…I'm not going back."

"Have you heard from Frankie?"

"No, but Joey Deluca says he's in Florida. I think he's into golf now. Works in a pro shop down there."

"I hope he stays down there, for your sake."

"You think I can't deal with that situation?"

"You let other people influence you too much, especially Frankie."

"That's in the past. It's over."

"If you say so."

"What? You don't think I can handle Frankie coming back into town?"

"All I know is that you two together are bad news."

"He's a get-high freak."

"What?"

"A get-high freak. Every time you see him you want to get high."

"That's what I mean," said Mr. Jones.

"I wonder why I get so messed up around him?"

"I don't know. I'm not a fuckin' psychiatrist. My job is to keep you out of jail. And if you screw up, send you back. It's all up to you."

"Cocaine doesn't interest me any more. It's a drag. The last year…it just made me nervous and irritable."

"That's a common response. Don't feel like the Lone Ranger."

"Who?"

"Never mind. It's before your time."

"Is anything before your time?" asked Danny.

"Careful. Remember, I have some control over your future."

"I'm not doing white any more—never."

"I wouldn't even be around it if I were you."

"No shit."

"One more thing. I want you to do me a favor."

"What?"

"I want you to talk to some kids for me."

"What kids?"

"Some high school kids."

"About what?"

"I want you to talk to them about going straight and keeping out of trouble."

"Who me? Are you kidding?"

"No, I'm not kidding. These kids are cocky and stupid and are headed for the same place you went to."

"Gimme a break. I'm no do-gooder counselor."

"Look, fuckhead. I don't give a shit what you think about yourself. You're one false step away from a fifteen year stretch and I'm strongly suggesting that you talk to these kids and tell them what the fuck is going on out there. It probably won't do any good because they're hardheads who think they'll never get busted, but I want you to try."

"Why me?"

"Are you fuckin' dense? You've been through the whole thing—dealing—busted—jail—this fuckin' office—!

"Okay—okay. Just don't get so worked up. You'll have a heart attack."

"Hey, it's guys like you who give out all the heart attacks in the world."

"Thanks."

"Be at Palmyra High School at three o'clock on Wednesday. Go see Mr. Shea. He's the guidance counselor. He'll set you up with the kids. Now beat it."

"Good bye, Mr. Jones. Have a nice day!"

"Yeah, sure."

HALLOWEEN WEEK: OCTOBER 23-31

A late afternoon red sun rode low in the skies and the green mountains were crystal clear in the horizon as Emily walked once again to the office of Professor Mason. This was her favorite time of the year in the Shenandoah Valley, when the air was brisk and clean, and the smell of burning leaves filled the air. The forests of white pine, hemlock and hawthorn were bursting with a full spectrum of color, in addition to reds from maples and dogwoods, yellows from hickory, and orange from sassafras. To compliment the picture perfect scene, spruce, fir, and pine provided the green backdrop. In the distance, across the meadows, she saw among the quiet oak glades the sparkling sight of yellow wildflowers and red and purple berries. She spotted a young white-tail deer languidly browsing on some tender plants, as a majestic hawk circled high overhead. A rush of billowy clouds streamed across the sky darkening the trees below with their floating shadows. A dog bayed faintly from a isolated farm house, his howl spent and broken by an upsurge of the wind. Emily took in all of this natural beauty, wondering how she could ever leave such a lovely environment. Her mood gradually became more melancholy as she reminded herself that this was her last year of school and was not sure about the future. Her four years of college had provided her with a convenient postponement of the real issue at hand; namely, what was she going to do with her life? Her father told her that the two biggest decisions of your life was who you were going to marry and what you were going to do for a living. Emily was confused on both counts. She had picked philosophy as major because she thought it might answer all the big questions: *What is the meaning of life? What is ethical? Are there moral absolutes?* After four years of studying, she had to admit that she had no idea why she was put on this earth. She certainly did not know the answers to the big questions. She did not regret her choice, but it was clear that the most important answers, or questions for that matter, lay ahead in the uncharted future. Perhaps, she thought, at least one of the graduate schools she applied to would accept her, thus delaying entering the work force for another few years. In truth, she did not feel like "entering the work force" as it was usually defined. She wanted to avoid a bureaucratic job in an office or cubicle, chained to a computer all day, having to follow regimented rules and mortgaging up her life with financial debt. She considered herself a bohemian at heart, with a serious distrust of the materialism and utilitarian spirit of the middle class. She remembered when they asked the writer French Stendhal what happens to people who do not become artists, he simply replied, "Nothing." Emily thought about that statement and concluded that she wanted to create something besides a good job, something more creative and spiritual. It was as if normal jobs did not offer enough life for her. She had an all-consuming passion to shake things up and refused to accept the narrow pursuits of employment taken seriously by just about everyone she knew. She wanted deep down to make herself a work of art, like painting, music, or literature. Maybe she could write a great novel about the illusion of free will, or ignite a new, flamboyant spark in the American character. She reasoned that there must still be some unknown discoveries, some unknown truths to be formulated. She wanted to invent new variations on themes, try different combinations of ideas, sounds, poetry, and logic; to plumb the depths of her consciousness and seek out the muse of the inner self to guide her. She told her adviser in Philosophy that she wanted to be an "exuberant anarchist"—breaking all rules on a thrilling ride through life. But at the same time, Emily knew that she was no die-hard hedonist, willing to surrender reason and control to a life of constant anarchy and debauchery. She was aware of the Dionysian/Apollonian split from her reading of Nietzsche, but did not find complete deregularization of the senses very appealing. She had far less experience with drugs than most of the students at Wattford, only smoking some marijuana in high school. She thought of drugs as an artificial paradise, and told everyone she "preferred the real world, crummy as it is." Emily was basically a shy, reserved person who did not enjoy being around boisterous people. She preferred meeting individuals one-on-one to hanging out at a party with a bunch of people. Emily was also the kind of person who would not mind putting all her energies into a relationship. Others would speak about committing yourself to one person as the sickness of co-dependency, but Emily wanted to find a life partner to form a whole greater than the sums of its parts. She reasoned that you could only truly love someone by sacrificing a large measure of your own self toward pleasing the other person. She was beginning to become very attached to Danny Alderman, more attached to him than anyone in a long time. The night they went out for pizza was the best time she had had in quite a while. Unlike much of the time she had spent with the opposite sex, the time with Danny was relaxed, and so natural that it almost threw her. She was expecting those old feelings of tension when you first date someone, and was genuinely shocked at how relaxed she was around him. She reflected on the few weeks they have spent together since that first date; the time he called her the next day and asked if she wanted to go horseback riding along the trails of the Skyline Drive; the night he rented the movie *When Harry Met Sally* and how she broke up laughing at Meg Ryan's infamous "fake orgasm" scene in the restaurant; the long leisurely walk they took around Gypsy Hill park, feeding the ducks and rolling down the grassy hill toward the baseball field like two kids at play; the game of strenuous tennis they played on Saturday morning when the sun was just rising above the mountains; his subsequent embarrassment when she beat him by one set; the quiet time spent studying and reading together at night; and most especially, the time spent making love, either at his apartment or hers. Danny was a tender, compassionate lover and they had consummated that part of the relationship as effortlessly the proverbial walk in the park. They had already vowed to be exclusive in the relationship and were not going to date anyone else. The relationship was definitely moving forward, but neither Emily nor Danny knew exactly where it was going. All they knew was that they were having a great time together, and for the moment, that was enough for both of them.

Her long daydream had consumed her thoughts, and time vanished before her eyes. Before she knew it Emily was standing in front of Dr. Mason's office for the second time. This time the door was not ajar, so she knocked gently.

"Come in!"

Emily walked into Dr. Mason's office and saw him at his desk reading the campus newspaper.

"Hello, Dr. Mason," Emily said.

"Hello. Nice to see you again." Dr. Mason did not taken his eyes off the newspaper. "Have you seen this issue of the Broadside?"

"Yes."

"Did you happen see the interview with Professor Ellis?"

"No, I glanced at it, but I didn't read the whole thing."

"It's very interesting, maybe even disturbing."

"I don't know what you mean."

"Well, Professor Ellis is in charge of the theatre since Professor Byrd left."

"I know."

"Well, the plays for this year were chosen last year, and announced. Byrd was going to direct the play *"The Lesser Evil."* But they—Ellis—dropped this play and inserted another one in its place."

"Is that unusual?"

"Well, I could see replacing Byrd's choice with another one. The new guy in theatre, Harry Coursen, supposedly made the new choice."

"What's the new play?"

"Faintly Heard Sorrow."

"I never heard of it."

"Well, I have. Do you know what *"The Lesser Evil"* is about?"

"No."

"It's the story of a young teenager who gets pregnant and doesn't tell her parents. She is anguished by this, but doesn't think her parents will understand. So, she goes through an abortion, but comes out of it okay, and eventually she develops a good relationship with her parents, but they never find out. So, now *"Lesser"* is out, but guess what?"

"What?"

"Faintly Heard Sorrow is a virulent, strident attack on abortion rights. It's not a play. It's pure propaganda. It was written by a member of the Christian Right who advocates bombing abortion doctors. The play ends with a girl committing suicide following an abortion.

"Do you think it was done on purpose, for ideological reasons?"

"I don't know, but it sure looks fishy, doesn't it?"

"Kind of."

"Let's get on with our interview. What do you want to know?"

"Well, I want to know about the Ouija board, and your contact with spirits."

"I must tell you right off that ninety percent of this spiritual stuff is bullshit—pardon my French. But there is a serious five to ten percent worth looking into. It's like a lot of parapsychology stuff, ESP, astrology, out of body experiences, *déjà vu*. You have to be careful that you don't take it too seriously. I believe in the spiritual world and I think we can communicate with spirits who have gone over to the other side.

"Why did you pick the Ouija board?"

"It started in college. I walked into a professor's office and he was sitting with another professor, playing this silly game. I thought they were nuts. I laughed and made fun of them. Then they asked me to ask a question, so I asked their contact the name of my uncle who had just died. I knew there was no way they could know this. Well, the monitor spelled out the name Smythe, and my uncle's name was Smith. That caught my attention.

"And now you talk to an Indian?"

"Yes, right now I am in touch with MG, an American Indian who died a hundred years ago. We talk on a regular basis through the Ouija board. Would you like to see how it work?"

"You mean talk to him?"

"Sure. He's always home."

"Do I need to participate?"

"Sure, we'll do it together." Professor Mason got up from his desk and walked over to a small table where the Ouija board was resting. "Here sit down!"

Emily sat in one of the wooden straight-back chairs facing Dr. Mason. She looked at the Ouija board. It was just like a regular game board, but with a series of words, letters and numbers in no particular order that she could discern.

"How do we start?" asked Emily.

"We sit apart from each other like this, then we put our fingers on this monitor. MG will guide us to the letters which usually spell something out, although sometimes he's cranky and doesn't make sense."

Dr. Mason and Emily placed their fingers on the outer edge of the monitor which was a small board with legs that traveled over the larger board with numbers and letters.

"Okay, MG are you there?"

The monitor moved to the word "yes" on the side of the board.

"Alright, Emily. Ask MG a question."

"Like what?"

"I don't know, anything. Ask him what you would ask the Psychic Network, something personal that you want to know about."

"Okay. Who am I currently going out with?"

Their fingers slowly moved to the letter "D," then "A," then "N," and finally to "I".

"Wow, that's pretty close."

Emily thought that perhaps Dr. Mason had intentionally or unintentionally guided her toward those letters because he may have guessed they were dating. She decided to ask MG something that Dr. Mason did not know.

"Okay, what is Danny's birthday?"

The monitor moved inexorably to an "M," an "A," then an "I," then to the number 13.

"Is that right?" asked Dr. Mason.

Emily was stunned. "Danny's birthday is May 14th. That was pretty damn close."

"Okay, one more question."

"Alright, where are Danny and I going to eat dinner tonight?"

The monitor went to "D," "A," "N," "S," "C," "O," "K," "P," "R," "O," "B."

"Gee, that doesn't make sense. It sure isn't a restaurant in town. The right answer was The Pullman. Is that "coke?" Maybe he thinks Danny will order a coke at the restaurant. Maybe it's "cook" like at a restaurant. That last part looks like "probe." Maybe he's referring to one of Danny's Sound Bites. Probe of coke? Probe of the cook?"

"MG isn't always on the ball. Maybe he's tired."

"Well," said Emily, "This was fun. At least he knew Danny and was close to his birthday. Thank you for the experience Dr. Mason. This will make a great article for the paper. It should come out after Christmas break."

"Don't mention it…I wish MG could have been more accurate."

"Good Bye."

"Good Bye, Emily."

Constance walked into the apartment, glanced in the mirror, and noticed that her eyes looked tired and droopy. She made a quick mental note to avoid black eyeliner from now on. Tonight, she thought, I'm going for a softer, more demure look. I will use a taupe pencil or eye shadow to give a more subtle definition to my baby blues, actually, hazel, but close enough.

The television was blaring, but no one was watching it. Constance knew that Jody would be arriving any minute because it was almost 4:30 and Jody watched *The Brady Bunch* religiously everyday. Constance thought that it was ironic that Jody always talked about how dumb Amy was, yet she watched *The Brady Bunch* and *Gilligan's Island* all the time.

Constance decided to go into Amy's room and see what she was doing. She opened the door and saw her lying on the bed reading *Seventeen* magazine.

"Hey, what are you doing,"

"Reading a good article."

"Oh, yeah? What's it about?"

"Well," began Amy, "It's called '*Six Reasons You Don't Want To Be Popular.*'"

Constance, in spite of herself, audibly groaned and rolled her eyes toward the ceiling. Never, she figured, in her wildest dreams could she have imagined college to be like this.

"Oh, really?" Constance remarked, feigning interest. "Like what?" Like what's a bad thing about being popular?"

"Well," said Amy, "People have great expectations for you…like there's a lot of pressure to be in the coolest group all the time."

"Yeah…I guess so…" Constance mumbled.

Constance's spirits took a noticeable nosedive and she slumped back into her chair and stared at the *Seventeen* magazine. Why would Amy have to know about being popular? She was popular and got dates because she was cute and has a great body. Period. Girls who look good are popular no matter how brain dead they are. If Amy wasn't attractive, she'd have a hard time getting a lonely freshman to take her out. Besides, isn't trying to be popular a high school thing?

"Do you want to work out with me?" Amy asked.

"When?"

"How about right now? I have the *Buns of Steel* video. It's awesome."

"No thanks. I'm tired. Where's Jody?"

"In the theatre. They open in two days. Are you going to the play?"

"Sure," Constance said. She really only went to Jody's performances to see if see would screw up her lines and embarrass herself. Unfortunately, Constance thought, Jody was a total professional on stage, but a total amateur as a human being.

"Hey, guys!"

As if on a director's cue, Jody bounded into the room like Tinkerbell wired on amphetamine.

"That Harry Coursen is stupid as shit!" Jody screamed.

"Who?" Amy and Constance asked at the same time.

"Professor Coursen!" Jody squealed. "He's the new faculty member in the department—and he sucks!"

"Why?" Constance asked, although she did not care anything about what happened in her narcissistic capital of world. Constance felt theatre people always gave the impression that standing up in front of people reciting memorized lines was a big deal.

"He's a dick!" Jody continued, "He said my accent was phony! He thinks I'm laying it on too thick. He's a wannabe from nowhere!"

Whenever Jody got into one of these moods, the other two girls had learned about how to deal with the situation. They had learned the best way to avoid Jody unleashing her unpleasantness on them for a long period of time. First, they totally agreed with her point of view. If they disagreed with her assessment of the situation it would only add fuel to the fire and prolong her rantings. Secondly, they gave her several compliments to sooth her fragile ego. Jody could not withstand a negative comment about her acting, even if it was true or meant to improve her as an actress. After every audition in which she did not get high marks, she would blame the judges and write nasty letters about how unprofessional they were. Constance thought Jody's accent was totally unconvincing, but she was not about to tell her that to her face.

"Oh, Jody," Constance said sympathetically, "Don't worry about that asshole. What does he know? Where did he come from?"

"Some stupid as shit college in Ohio. I don't know where they dug him up. I'd rather have Professor Byrd back in the department."

"Don't worry," Amy interjected, "We know you're a great actress. I've heard your accent and I think it's terrific."

Amy may not be the brightest girl in the world, but she too had learned how to deal with Jody's neurotic outbursts. Amy and Jody got along pretty well together because they never spoke about anything serious to each other and they did not compete for acting parts or for men.

"Amy's right," Constance said, "You sound great. Don't listen to that creep."

Jody calmed down, walked slowly to the mirror and looked at herself. She was not displeased. Flipping her hair back in her usual fashion, she commenced to delivery her exaggerated Southern belle delivery:

"Big Daaaa..ddy, don't you think there's a paaa...er....ful smell of mennn...dasss...i...ty in this room."

The other two girls stared at Jody, unsure of what to say. They both felt it was an awful, but didn't dare tell Jody to tone down her overacting.

"Hey! It's time for *The Brady Bunch!*" yelled Constance.

"Omygod, you're right!," exclaimed Jody, "Let's watch it!"

Jody ran to the television and switched the channel to *The Brady Bunch*. Amy decided to begin her afternoon workout, maniacally cheerleading through another series of jumping jacks while lip-syncing to the music of the *Monkees*. Jesus, Constance thought, a perfect group for Amy, mindless, cheerful and adolescent. Constance quickly grew weary of watching a perfect body working out and sweating in yellow stretch pants and was torn between going to her room or watching *The Brady Bunch*. At this moment she did not feel like being alone, so she opted for television with Jody. She sat down next to Jody and the two women remained silent for a few minutes before Constance broke the silence.

"Are you going to go to the poetry reading Friday night? It should be fun."

"I guess so," said Jody, without taking her eyes off the screen. "What should I wear?"

"I don't know," said Constance, immediately falling into another minor depression.

"I've got an outfit that looks kinda hip," said Jody. "You know, the painter's smock dress, ruffle shirt, and beret."

"Sounds fine."

"What are you wearing?" Jody asked.

"I don't know. I haven't thought about it."

"What's the matter with you?" Jody asked.

"Nothing. I'm just tired."

Constance's mood took a severe downward spiral and she was beginning to feel nauseated again. She felt a dizziness overcome her and smelled the same sweet smell begin to consume the room. She floated back into her chair, feeling light-headed and confused. She looked at Jody, but all she saw was a sloth hanging upside down from the branch of a tree. Christ, I'm hallucinating, she thought. Why is the room swirling around? Who the fuck is Jody? She doesn't seem real. I mean, who is she?

She's a slug, that's it. She's a slug in real life. But when we go out, she miraculously transforms herself into a vivacious, charming beauty queen, laughing and joking with everyone, as if she never had a depressed moment in her life. She berates the hell out of everyone behind their backs, then kisses their ass in public. She's even nice to the snobby Texas girls next door, and *nobody's* nice to them.

The two women continued to follow the trials and tribulations of *The Brady Bunch*. They found out that Marcia was eventually allowed to go to her pajama party after all. Then they proceeded to *Happy Days* wherein Ritchie wrecked Mr. Cunningham's car and he had to enlist Fonzie's help to save the day. Constance slowly came out of her dizziness. The monotony of the television made her feel more comfortable. Why was television so irritating and soothing at the same time? She listened to the music of *Happy Days* and gradually felt more at ease. Jody stood up and went into the kitchen to get a Diet Pepsi. When she came back she was more upbeat and seemed somewhat alive.

"What's for dinner?" Jody asked.

"Some kind of Mexican deal, tacos and stuff," Constance responded.

"Are you going to go?" Jody asked, slumping back down on the couch.

"Yes, I don't have the money to go out."

"Me neither," said Jody, "My father hasn't sent me any money."

"Why should he? You're suing him for chrissakes."

"He owes it to me. He promised he would send me some."

Jody was, in fact, one of the few college students in America who were suing their father. As part of a divorce agreement, he promised to send her to college, but he did not say where he would send her. Jody applied to the most expensive schools in the state, and now her father was having trouble paying the tuition at Wattford. Jody became enormously upset when he asked her to transfer to a less expensive school.

"When are you going to shower?" Jody asked. "Before dinner?"

"No, I'm going to wait until I get back. I think I'll wear my baby cord overalls with a turtle neck and boots. What do you think?"

"That's a cute outfit," said Jody. "Wear the brown boots and hoop earrings. You'll look awesome."

Constance was aware that Jody was being nice to her. On occasion Constance actually felt sorry for Jody. She was such a small person trying to make it in the big world of theatre. Sometimes, she could be so nice and caring when she wasn't trying to impress people with her personality. Jody could be very charming in a quiet way, and there were times when she was very sympathetic and warm. There were even occasions when she would let down her guard and reveal to her room-mates that she felt insecure and that no one loved her. She revealed to Constance that her mother and step-father told her that she could not stay at home after graduation. They made it clear that she was not welcome to live in the house any longer. The other two girls' parents wanted their daughters to go out on their own, but only Jody's parents put the matter so bluntly. Perhaps, this explained in some way Jody's supreme lack of concern or empathy for other people. Constance often said that she was the most thoughtless person she ever knew. Jody did not necessarily intentionally hurt other people; she simply did what she felt like doing and could not understand how people could be upset with her actions.

The television show *A Current Affair* was ending and the evening news began. Jody could not sit through a news program.

"Let's go," said Jody.

"Alright," said Constance, "I'll get Amy."

Constance went into Amy's room just as she was getting out of the shower.

"Hey, look at this!" Amy exclaimed, reaching for a book on top of her dresser. "I got it from the bookstore. It's called, '*Honoring the Self: Personal Integrity and the Heroic Potentials of the Modern Woman.*' Look's good, huh?'"

"Yeah, let me see it when you're done with it."

If there was anyone in the world who did not need to focus on her self any more it was Amy. Honoring the self? Amy must be kidding. Constance couldn't think of anything else that Amy *did* focus on. She was currently in the process of putting on her "sixties make-up kit" which included black eyeliner, frosty pink lipstick, matte face powder, mascara, and shimmering blue eye shadow.

"I'm ready!" screamed Amy.

"Great," said Constance, "Let's get out of here."

There was something very peculiar about the girls' dining hall behavior. Constance, Jody, and Amy usually went together, almost never alone, and they always joined the same group of girls to avoid all the people they dislike. These included: Deadheads, computer geeks, dumb jocks, Texas debutantes, unattractive lesbians, cyber-punks, freshmen, and anybody generally considered "uncool." They always sat at the same table in the West End of the cafeteria, where they could easily see other students enter. As people came in, all the girls make disparaging remarks about them—what they're wearing, who they were sleeping with, how stupid they were, and so on. They were hyper at the table, displaying the phony fervor of individuals insecure with a moment of silence—moments that might reveal the emptiness of their lives. Rather than fill up their own lives with meaning, they ridiculed and criticized those around them At the moment, Jody was holding court, complaining that there were no decent looking guys on campus with interesting personalities. No one disagreed with her.

"Men…" Jody remarked with a pretence of professional authority, "…have an unusual talent for making a bore out of everything they touch."

Constance laughed at the remark. She felt it was probably not something Jody made up, but she seemed to have gotten away with it.

As Jody spoke, an attractive senior on campus, Will Gilbert, entered the dining hall.

"How about Will?" Amy asked no one in particular.

"Omygod, he's hot!" squealed Courtney Ginsburg, who, according to the bathroom wall, liked it up the butt.

"Does he have a girl friend?" asked Patty Clover who spiked her tongue so she could give better oral sex.

"Omygod, he looks awesome in tight jeans! What an ass!" observed Mimi Fountain who was currently questioning her sexuality.

"He's a trash dick," said Jody. I'd never go out with him. You might catch something."

"Hey, Jody," Constance said, "I thought you hooked up with him last year?"
"Are you crazy?"
"It's okay. We'd all sleep with him if we got the chance."
"Well, I didn't," said Jody.
"There's the vomit girl!" Amy yelled.

The thin, statuesque blonde girl entered the cafeteria alone. Constance wondered if she had any friends. She had never seen her eating with anyone. Constance felt sorry for the girl and wanted to go up to her and offer some help. But before she could pursue the thought, the girl was hit with a new barrage of invectives.

"God, I can't imagine throwing up on purpose," said Amy, who did it plenty of times in high school.

"Me neither," said Miriam Potts, who was more than sixty pounds overweight.

"She's a fuckin' sicko," said Grace Pallavancini who washed her hands twenty times a day.

"God, what a fuckin' loser," said Deirdre Bourroughs who just undergone her third abortion.

"I've been following her," Jody said.

"What?' Constance asked.

"I've been following her," Jody repeated.

"Why?" almost everyone asked.

"Because I want to know what she does with the vomit. Jim Cresson, the guy who works in the union, gave me the idea."

Constance could no longer control her hurt and anger.

"JESUS CHRIST!" She screamed, "YOU'RE AS SICK AS SHE IS! WHY WOULD YOU DO A THING LIKE THAT?"

"Come on," Constance," Jody said "I just want to make sure she is not a health risk. We don't want our building to smell like vomit, do we?"

Constance knew it was impossible to convince Jody that she ever did anything wrong. Jody calmly told the group that it was important to know such things because the vomit could be anywhere and it was unhealthy not to know the whereabouts of old vomit. That killed everyone's appetite, except for Miriam Potts, who kept eating her spaghetti.

Constance sank back into her chair and stared out the window as her thoughts for some unknown reason drifted to the actress Grace Kelly. She had watched the movie *Rear Window* with Tom Wilson a few nights ago and she was impressed how classy and cultured she was. She could not think of any of her girl friends who had the breeding, style and pleasing personality of Grace Kelly. God, she thought, today's women are gross.

"Omygod look at that haircut."

"Her hair is green."

"That is the most hideous haircut in America."

"It's sickly green."

"She looks like a mutant green pineapple."

"Is she dressed up for Halloween already?"

"I hate her."

"She's a bitch."

"She never showers."

"Gross."

"She's hasn't changed her sheets all year."

"I think she's a lesbo."

"She dates townies."

"Didn't Byron Utley go out with her?"

"That wusse?"

"Utley's a penis."

"He fucked her?"

"He'll fuck anything."

"He's a good kisser."

"Who?"

"Utley."

"NOT!!!"

"I kissed him sophomore year."

"He slobbered all over me."

"Yeah, but you slept with him anyway."

"So?"

"Look who's talking. That's the first time your legs have been together all year."

"Fuck you."

"NOT!!!"

"Not, what?"

"Omygod, there's Danny Alderman."

"Omygod, he's hot."

"He's a dick. He's stupid as shit."

"I think he's cute."

"You would."

"What's that supposed to mean?"

"Why are you being such a bitch?"

"I'm tired of talking about me."

"Why don't you talk about me."

"I really want to know what we're talking about."

"Nothing. Forget it."

"I'm tired."

"Of what?"

"I don't know…life."

"There's a fly on my hamburger."

"I want something."

"What?"

"I don't know. I always want something."

"Maybe I want this fly off my fuckin' hamburger."

"Who's fuckin' your hamburger?"

"Jason Sparrow."

"Why not? He's screwed everything else around here."

"Hey, lay off Jason, okay?"

"What are your wearing for Halloween?"

"I'm going as a condom"

"A used one?"

"I heard Dorothy Newberry ate one by mistake."

"A used condom?"

"No way!"

"When's Halloween?"

"Saturday, stupid."

"Are you going to the poetry reading?"

"What's that got to do with Halloween?"

"What the fuck do you wear to a poetry reading?"

You could read Poe."

"Who's poor?"

"You know, quothe, the raven…"

"A rave?"

"Quothe the raven, whatever…"

"Let's go back and watch Entertainment Tonight."

"Wait!—How do you accidentally eat a used condom?"

Danny and Emily arrived together at Tom Wilson's house at eight o'clock. Constance greeted them at the door.

"Would you like a beer or some wine?"

"Sure," said Danny.

"The spirits are in the kitchen. Tom bought a keg and there's red and white wine. California I think."

Constance led the couple through a large foyer furnished with a French antique love seat; an elaborate crystal chandelier hung from the ceiling and several authentic seventieth century oil paintings graced the walls. The house evoked a comfortable Victorian atmosphere, decorated to complement the colonial style of the house. The antique furniture, hand-carved wooden banisters, deep burgundy drapes, and Persian Oriental rugs all combined to deliver an excellent showcase for an evening of poetry and culture.

To the left, there was a large, expansive room where a group of students huddled around a huge marble fireplace. Adjacent to it, several students were gathered around a grand piano listening to one of the guests playing a jazzy, melodic rendition of "Smoke Gets in You Eyes." Danny and Emily waved to a couple of people they knew and proceeded to the kitchen in back of the house. Professor Wilson was pouring himself a beer as they entered.

"Hi folks," said Wilson.

"Hi, Dr. Wilson," said Danny, "I'm Danny Alderman, and this is Emily Patterson."

"Pleased to meet you."

Dr. Wilson stared at Danny for a second, then recognized him.

"Weren't you in Romantic Poets last year?"

"Yes, I was. I'm afraid I didn't do very well in your course."

"What did you get?"

"Well, I got a B, but I could have done better."

"Hey that's good. I don't give out many As. Are you two going to read anything tonight?"

"Well, I'm going to read something by Rimbaud and Emily brought one of her own poems, but she's acting like she might get cold feet."

"Nonsense! We'll have no slackers around here. You must read your poem! I insist! I'll never invite you back if you don't!"

Emily smiled at Dr. Wilson.

"Well, in that case, I guess I'll have to read my masterpiece."

"That's the spirit!" Now make yourself at home, grab a drink, and let the drunken poetry reading commence at 9 o'clock—sharp!"

Dr. Wilson left to join the group at the piano. Danny and Emily poured themselves a beer and leaned back on the kitchen counter.

"He seems very nice." said Emily.

"The last of a dying breed."

"What do you mean?"

"I don't know. I guess he's the last of the drunken poets who loves to seduce younger women."

"He's a ladies man?"

"He's certainly got the reputation. I think he's having an affair with Constance Stewart."

"He's very charming," said Emily. "I can see why women are attracted to him."

The couple walked through a narrow hallway and ran into Roy Henson, a senior literature major.

"Danny! Hey man. How you doin?'"

"Great. Roy, this is Emily Patterson. Emily, meet Roy Henson—the next Ernest Hemingway!"

"Hi Earnest," said Emily, "Glad to meet you."

"Hey, don't call me that just yet. Wait until the public recognizes my genius!"

"That may take a while," said Danny.

"Okay, so in the meantime, you can call me Roy, the Greatest Unpublished Novelist in America?"

"How about just Roy?" said Emily.

"Okay. Let's toast to bad behavior!"

The three students raised their glasses and clanked them together.

"To bad behavior!"

"Bad behavior!"

"So, dude, what's happening with Sound Bites?" asked Roy after gulping his drink down with one swallow. "You still on the press beat?"

"Yeah, I'm still pounding the beat. But there isn't much to pound these days."

"What? No hot issues on the sleepy campus of Wattford College?"

"There isn't much that I know of."

"Have you heard of anything?" asked Emily.

"Not really. It's pretty dead…Okay, there is one thing."

"What's that?" asked Emily.

"Did you hear they are taking the condoms out of the dormitories?"

"No," said Emily.

"Yeah, man. I went to get one last weekend and the machine had disappeared. It was weird. This is serious! Someone is messing with my sex life, such as it is!"

"Did they take them out of every dormitory?" Emily asked.

"They sure did! I know because I ran around all night looking for one. I finally borrowed one from Howard Becker. He's had the same one in his wallet for three years!"

Danny made a mental note to check out the story.

"Hey, poets!" cried Dr. Wilson, "It's time for the show to begin!"

Danny and Emily went into the living room with the rest of the guests. Dr. Wilson was standing at a podium in front of a large poster which read, "Carpe Diem," a reference to the movie *Dead Poets Society.*

"Good evening ladies and gentlemen, drunken poets, cons, ex-cons, drifters, grifters, rounders, scoundrels, debutantes, deadheads and deadbeats. Welcome, all ye who enter to the fourth annual Drunken Poetry Reading! Of course, you don't have to be drunk to read your poem, but judging from those of last year, it will help to be a little tipsy to listen to them! Just kidding, folks. We had a wonderful group of poetry lovers read some outstanding poems last year and I'm sure this year will be equally superb. Now let's begin. Here's the hat! Pick a number! Any number! Don't be shy!"

Danny looked at Emily. She seemed apprehensive and a bit bashful.

"Well, poetess, Danny said, "Now's your big chance. Are you sure that your last name is not Dickinson?"

Emily laughed.

"Oh, I'm sure of that!"

Danny reached in and drew number eight.

"Well, at least I'm not number one," he said.

Several students and professors began picking numbers. Emily hesitated for a few seconds, then reluctantly took out number twelve.

The first reader was Dorothy Manchester, a senior drama major, who read a depressing poem by Anne Sexton about a daughter's relationship with her mother. The other readers were eclectic in their choices. One student read a funny limerick, another read an original poem about a disastrous bus trip to Florida. Jack Kelly, a junior English major, sang a drunken Irish folk ballad, falling off the stage in mock drunkenness when it was over. When it was Danny's turn he read a poem called "The Drunken Boat" by Rimbaud. Then Emily's turn came and she advanced to the podium. She gripped the lectern and spoke in a quiet unassuming voice:

"I would like to read a poem I wrote two years ago after going through a difficult time in my life. I won't bore you with the details, but I was on the verge of giving up, and I always considered myself a strong person. I remember what my grandfather told me before he passed away. He said, 'Do not ask for an easy life; ask to be a strong person. I have tried to follow his advice, but at this time, I was really down in the dumps. So, now that I've thoroughly depressed you. Here goes:

Can I lie next to you, when I'm frail, thin and pale

In danger of giving up

 Are you with me now?

Or a wistful dream formed here to protect me from myself?

When my aching heart yearns for a love lost

 Will you remember me?

When your watery eyes close to forget how lonesome…

   The past that never ceases to rust or fade

Like black and white photos from birthdays torn asunder

Curled up, surrendering to a life with desperate hands

   Reaching for each other

…Like fingers moving down the wanton vine

Is this our last reward for the pain we've known?

   How many years were tossed aside?

No more apologies for the shortcomings of the toppled timepiece

   …Or the lives we're living suspended in the frozen hourglass

In the end I only need

To be………

   Old with you.

The audience was silent for a moment, then Emily stepped down from the podium. She approached Danny, who smiled and clapped his hands softly together.

"Hey, you really are Emily Dickinson!" said Danny.

Danny and Emily stayed at the party for a couple more hours, drinking beer, telling stories, and dancing to some raucous rock 'n roll played on the piano by Horatio Allen, one of the music teachers at Wattford.

At one point, Danny saw Tom Wilson leaning against the fireplace talking to Constance. Danny thought this would be a good time to ask him if he knew anything about what was happening on campus.

"Great party," said Danny.

"This is the best year yet. I really liked Emily's poem. She should take more English courses."

"I'm afraid she's got the philosophy bug."

"She could do worse."

"Dr. Wilson, can I ask you a question?"

"Sure."

"Do you know what happened to Professor Byrd? He didn't come back this year."

"Yes, I heard that. He's in our division, but we were not informed about the decision. I don't know if he quit or was let go."

"Wouldn't it be unusual for a tenured faculty member to just up and leave?"

"Well, it used to happen all the time, but because of today's job market, more instructors are staying put. Theatre jobs are particularly hard to find."

"Do you know where he is?" asked Danny.

"I have no idea. You might ask Professor Ellis."

"I tried that," said Danny. "She was not exactly forthcoming."

"As the head of the department now, she would know, if anybody. Of course, Dean Parsons would have been the one to fire him and appoint a search committee for his replacement."

"Maybe I'll talk to him."

"Why do you want to know all this?" Dr. Wilson asked.

"Oh," said Danny, "I work for the Broadside. It's a story I'm trying to check out."

"Well, I wish I could help you, but I just don't know what happened to him."

"Thanks," said Danny. "I guess we'll be leaving soon and thanks again for a great time."

Ton Wilson and Constance were driving along country club road on their way to Cannonville's fourteenth annual awards ceremony for Big Brothers and Big Sisters of America. Wilson was being granted an award for being "Big Brother of the Year." He became involved in the organization after his divorce four years ago and, in addition to spending time with his little brother Joey, he served as a member of the board of directors. Constance was pleased that he asked her to come along. They usually tried to keep their relationship a secret, but Wilson told her that it was time to ignore public opinion and "come out of the closet."

The couple continued their slow cruise down the winding road. To the right, they saw an Olympic-size swimming pool, tennis courts, a driving range, and a small pond with several ducks waddling slowly through the still water. To the left, beyond a row of high sycamore trees, they could see the lush, well-manicured fairways and greens of the golf course.

"Do you play golf?" Constance asked.

"Yes, but I'm afraid not too well."

"Can you break a hundred?"

"On a good day."

"Isn't golf a bit bourgeois for an English teacher?"

Wilson smiled ruefully. "Contrary to what people think, you do not have to be a Republican to play golf."

"You just have to have money."

"That's true."

As Wilson turned into the parking lot, Constance saw an attractive middle-aged couple getting out of an expensive luxury automobile.

"Who is that?" she asked.

"That's Ellsworth Chambers and his wife Dolores. He's on the board of trustees at Wattford. She's a big wheel with Big Brothers."

"Jody Hershberger is their niece."

"I didn't know that."

"She's always talking about him like he's a God, or something."

"She's pretty special too. She practically started this organization all by herself."

Wilson and Constance got out of the car and walked toward the club house. They entered the building just as Dr. and Mrs. Chambers arrived.

"Good evening, Dr. Chambers—Mrs. Chambers," said Wilson.

"Hello, Tom," said Chambers. "How are you this evening?"

"Fine. I'd like you to meet Constance Stewart."

"How do you do Constance. This is my wife, Dolores."

"Pleased to meet you."

The four guests entered the main ball room of the luxurious country club and looked for their name tags on the tables. Chambers and his wife were seated at a large table in the front, while Wilson and Constance found their table three rows back. They were joined at the table by two elderly ladies and a young, fashionably dressed couple. Following introductions, Wilson asked one of the ladies if she was a member of the organization.

"No, she replied, "I'm here to see Dolores get her Life-Time Achievement award."

"She's quite a woman," said Wilson.

A waiter arrived and the guests ordered drinks. The young couple, Brad and Erin Oppermann, were both participating in the program for the first time.

"I think it's great that you volunteer your time to help these kids," said Constance.

"We get so much pleasure from helping out," said Erin.

"I don't see how you find the time, "said Constance. "I'm so busy with school…"

"We find the time," said Brad. "It only takes one night a week and some week-ends."

Following dinner, the master of ceremonies, a big fat man in an ill-fitted tux, read out the names of all the participants in the program and thanked them for their contributions. He announced that the Big Brother of the year was Tom Wilson and asked him to come up and say a few words. Wilson approached the podium and greeted the audience.

"I just want to say that my participation in this organization has been one of the great highlights of my life, and has brought more joy to me than I could have ever imagined. I think my little brother Joey should really receive this award because without him I would be an incomplete person. Joey has made my life so much more rewarding. I know this is how all of you feel who help out in the organization. It is really the adults who win in this situation. The kids are lucky to have us, but we are lucky to have them too. I want to thank all of you who are a part of Big Brothers and Big Sisters for this award, and let's never let the kids down."

Wilson returned to his table. The master of ceremonies announced that, for the first time, they were giving a Life-Time Achievement award to Dolores Chambers for her "uncompromising hard work and dedication to the welfare of young people throughout the region."

Mrs. Chambers stood up and walked toward the podium. She was elegantly dressed in a long, sleek black evening gown, high heels, and a string of pearls around her neck with matching earrings. Her long, straight gray hair was stylishly twisted up over her shoulders, with tiny ringlets falling on the sides. Mrs. Chambers stood very erect with perfect posture and chose her words carefully and deliberately.

"I want to thank everyone connected with this terrific organization for the award bestowed on me tonight. And especially, I want to thank my dear husband, Ellsworth, for his unwavering support over these past fifteen years wonderful years with Big Brothers and Big Sisters. My real reward is seeing the happy faces of these children as they become involved with all of you. I want to thank you for taking the time to spend quality time with kids who didn't get many of the breaks we got in life. I can only hope that we have at least fifteen more years of service to our community, and many more happy faces on our children. Thank you."

As they left the country club following the ceremony, Wilson and Constance ran into Ellsworth and Dolores Chambers once again.

"Congratulations, Mrs. Chambers," said Wilson.

"Thank you, Tom. Congratulations are in order for you too."

"Thanks."

Wilson was about to turn toward his car when he suddenly thought of a question for Dr. Chambers.

"Oh, by the way, Dr. Chambers, do you know anything about Professor Byrd not coming back?"

Dr. Chambers, who was about twenty feet away, turned toward Wilson.

"Professor Byrd?"

"He's not back."

"I didn't know that. Did he retire?"

"I don't think so. He was a few years away."

"Well, perhaps I can find out from Dean Parsons. He would know."

"Thank you."

Later that evening in Wilson's apartment, Constance was sipping a glass of California merlot while sitting in her bed reading *Heart of Darkness*. Wilson finished grading papers in the den, turned out the lights downstairs, and came up to the bedroom.

"How's the book?" asked Wilson.

"I like it."

"Did you know that the film *Apocalypse Now* was based on that book?"

"I heard that, but I haven't seen the movie."

"We'll have to rent it. It's good."

Wilson went over to the table, poured himself a glass of wine, and slipped into bed next to Constance.

"Here's looking at you, kid."

"Cheers," said Constance, setting her book down.

"You have the look of someone with something on her mind."

"Oh, I'm not thinking big thoughts. I'm worried a bit about my roommate situation."

"What about it?"

"I don't know....There's something wrong with them. I can't put my finger on it."

"You mean there is something wrong with their personalities?"

"Yes, I guess you could say that, although Jody has been looking very pale lately. I think she might have mono. Is that contagious?"

"Yes."

"I passed out a few weeks ago. I wonder if Jody had something to do with it."

"You said it was their personalities."

"I just feel I'm a different person around them. I don't like who I am around them."

"You think it's their fault?"

"No, not really. It's mine. I get caught up in this college crap and I can't seem to function very well."

"What do you mean?"

"Those people tonight were real—that couple, and those little old ladies, and the rest of the volunteers."

"Of course they were real."

"I'm sorry. I'm not making any sense. How about pouring me another glass."

Wilson reached for the bottle. "You mean the people at the ceremony were more sincere?"

"Yes. My roommates just think about themselves all the time."

"That's pretty common in college," said Wilson, pouring Constance more wine.

"Is it common to act like the people you're living with? Isn't that kind of lame?"

I went through a period where I copied anybody I thought was cooler than I was."

"Who'd you copy?"

"I walked around like James Dean for about two years, then I went through my wild Beatnik stage. We're influenced by who we live with, what movies we see, our parents, lots of things."

"Weren't you afraid of losing your real self?"

"I think we are who we pretend to be. If you act like your roommates, then that's who you are."

"That's scary."

"So is me trying to be James Dean."

"Well, I think they're having a negative impact on me."

"You have a negative impact on me."

"What do you mean?"

Wilson reached over, took the glass of wine from Constance's hand, rolled on top of her, and kissed her on the lips.

"You know what everybody says, don't you?"

"What?"

"I'm a man of Constance sorrow."

Amy Toeffler was sitting in mass media class leafing through the latest edition of *Cosmopolitan*, wondering if she had time to go shopping for a new spandex outfit before her daily aerobic workout. The professor was droning on about new forms of communication and she occasionally caught a few words like, "computer chip technology…Silicon Valley…Internet of the future…" Her eyes glazed over and her mind went numb over any mention of technological terms. Despite her choices of reading material and disinterest in her studies, Amy was not among the worst students at Wattford. She always attended class, took careful notes when she had to, did her homework, and kept up with the reading. Her problem was an inability to focus on abstract concepts and she had a short attention span. She often felt a combination of restlessness and boredom, especially in class. She had trouble sitting still for any long periods of time.

The professor finished his lecture. Amy gathered her books and magazines, and got up to leave. As she was walking out of class, one of the guys from the class approached her.

"You're Amy Toeffler, right?"

"Yes."

"I'm Stuart Pennington."

"Hi."

"Can I talk to you for a minute?"

"I guess so…"

"How about going to the union for something to drink?"

"I don't know…I was going shopping…"

"Hey, that can wait. Let's go."

"Okay."

The two students walked in silence for a few minutes before arriving at the union. They found a table and sat down. Stuart ordered two Cokes.

"What do you think of mass media?" Stuart asked.

"It's okay. Is that why you asked me here?"

"Sort of. I noticed you're always carrying magazines like *Cosmopolitan* and *Seventeen.*"

"I like the articles, but I still don't see what that has to do with anything…"

"What do you think of them?"

"They're okay. I think they help people deal with problems and relationships. I like the ads and gossip about the stars…"

"I think they're pretty vacuous."

"Vacuous?"

"Empty…you know, kind of mindless."

"Funny you should say that. My roommate gave me hell for joining the Sassy Club."

"That's even worse."

"Did you ask me here to insult me?"

"No, I think you—and everybody else—should be reading better material."

"What's wrong with these magazines?"

"Why don't you tell me?"

Amy had once again been asked to defend her taste in magazines and it was beginning to raise doubts in her own mind. She had canceled her *Sassy* subscription after Constance's put-down of her, although she did not reveal this to her roommates. Amy thought it odd that this guy was questioning her reading so soon after the incident in Spanky's.

"I canceled my *Sassy* subscription."

"Why?"

"My roommates thought it was stupid, and for high school students."

"They're right."

"Boy, you're no fun at all."

"Did you hear the lecture today?"

"I didn't pay much attention."

"Did you hear Dr. Jackson talk about the Internet?"

"What's that?"

"It's a new way of communicating…computers connecting with each other."

"For what?"

"It's called the information highway and people will be able to create all kinds of things, like businesses, sending messages to each other, collecting data, listening to music, all kinds of things."

"Is that what he was talking about?"

"Yes."

"I still don't know what this has to do with me."

"You're a communications major, aren't you?"

"Yes."

"Well, so am I. We should get into this. It's the future."

"What do you mean 'get into?' It's too complicated for me."

"No, it isn't. Don't worry about all the tech stuff. I need your help."

"My help?"

"Yes, I want to create a magazine that exists in cyber-space—the Internet. You can help me create something much better than *Cosmo* or *Seventeen*."

"But I like those magazines…"

"Do you?"

Amy had not been challenged like this for some time. She was used to people putting her down for reading her books on personal growth and popular magazines, but she always thought they were wrong, or jealous of her for some reason. Stuart was taking her seriously and she was thrown by his respect for her opinions. She also figured that this might be his way of hitting on her, although he was just a skinny guy with glasses whom she figured did not date much.

"…Well…do you?"

I know they're shallow, but they're also entertaining. You think I can help you start a magazine? I don't know anything about that. What would I do?"

"I want to start a magazine for college women, an interactive magazine that they can read and exchange ideas over the Internet. I bet you know a lot about how college women think and what kind of magazine they would find appealing."

"So, what would I do? I still don't get it."

"First, we have to create a web-site."

"A what?"

"Listen, let me take care of that. I just want you to write down some of the things you'd like to put in a magazine where all the readers would have instant access to each other."

"Okay, but I don't think I'm really good at this sort of thing."

I am fading more quickly than I thought, but that's okay. It's so bad I can't wait for death. It will be a burden lifted from my doomed soul. I will never have to look in a mirror again. I will never be embarrassed by my declining physical appearance. I have developed an ugly purple lesion on the lower part of my left leg. I have to make sure I keep my leg covered or it would be a dead give-away. I am so tired all the time and I have a chronic sore throat and mild flu conditions. As far as I know, no one suspects me, but it is just a matter of time. I have decided to end my life soon anyway. I just can't make up my mind about how to do it. Perhaps, I will slit my wrists or drown myself.

So far I have slept with at least 23 boys and I hope they all get this insidious virus. Not one of them said they loved me, except Jason, of course, who is madly in love with me. If it wasn't for Jason's love, I'd really go crazy. I don't care about those other losers. They're stupid as shit. In the beginning, I was so angry. I couldn't believe it. I tore my room apart. I screamed furiously. I railed against God. I spit and cursed Him—and my fate. I was supposed to be a beautiful, famous actress, admired by thousands of fans, but no, God hates me. He gave me this terrible disease because He is jealous of my good looks. I wonder what color HIS hair is? I know He's jealous of my beautiful red hair. That's why he got the Byrd-Dick to infect me. God's eyes do not glitter on stage like mine. He doesn't possess the sensuous red lips and slender, delicate figure that I do. What a terrible person God is—condemning me for looking better than Him. Why did he create such a beautiful creature if he was going to get so jealous?

Lately, though, I'm not so tortured by my fate. In fact, I see this an opportunity to play another role. I think it's a good part. I have begun thinking like an infected person and trying to learn the appropriate body language. I practice walking like a leper in front of the mirror.

It's kinda strange, but I have the feeling that I am being transformed into something ugly. I'm not really sure about this, but I think I may be metamorphosing into a rat. My ears are growing more pointy and I twitch my nose like one. I crave cheese all the time. I crave cheese more than attention. Whiskers are growing out of my nose and my whole face is beginning to look skinny and rat-like.

So, I mean check this out. I spotted the thinner-than-me bulimic chick coming back from McDonald's carrying a bag of food and a milkshake. She was walking from the parking lot toward our apartment. I quickly drove around the block and hid behind a bush, waiting for her. She strolled up the steps, eating a big, fat greasy hamburger and sucking on a straw. I expected her to go up to her room, or maybe throw up in the bathroom, but to my surprise, she turned left and headed down the stairs to the basement. *What the hell was in the basement? Anyway, I stealthily sneaked down the stairs in back of her, making sure she didn't see me. She walked along a narrow, filthy corridor until she came to the storage bins where we keep our extra furniture, broken stereo equipment, and shit like that. Nobody ever comes down here. It's like a morgue. It's dirty as shit. She finished eating the hamburger and drinking the milkshake. Then she sat down in the middle of the filthy floor and seemed to be in a trance for about two minutes. I mean, God, what a psycho. I'm beginning to think nothing will happen because, well, I guess she comes down here to get away from the bitches in our apartment. You know, like who could blame her? I'd rather be sitting on a dirty, filthy basement floor than talking to Doreen Lonberg, the prissy bitch from Louisiana who's father owns half of Baton Rouge. (But she still won't buy her own shampoo). Then all of a sudden, I'm transported back to the actions of the blonde bulimic because she quickly puts her finger down her throat, gags, and throws up everything into the Styrofoam container. I mean, gross me out! Streams of totally gut-wrenching, smelly heinous, fuckin' puke!! It started to stink like shit, but after a moment, it stopped because the vomit was sealed in a container. Now what was she going to do? She went further back into the bowels of this cave-like cellar and opened a large chicken wire cage filled with cardboard boxes and old luggage. I couldn't see what she was doing, so I went back up the stairs and waited until she left. I hid behind the bushes again for about three minutes and, sure enough, she emerged from the tomb and goes up the stairs to her room. I was a little baffled. Like, what's with this chick? I head back down the stairs, not knowing what to expect. I'm beginning to doubt I really saw this weirdo in the first place. I arrived at the chicken wire cage and loosened the latch. It's funky and dusty in here. I can't see too well, so I pull out my bic lighter and look around. At first, I don't notice anything unusual, but after my eyes adjust, I spot an amazing, in fact, unbelievable, thing. There are HUNDREDS of McDonald's bags piled in the corner. I mean, HUNDREDS!! I think I'm going to throw up. I finally get the nerve to open one of these packages. They are very carefully stapled together and Christ almighty, I can't believe it, but sure enough, there is the distinct foul (really foul) smell of vomit emanating from the bag I just opened. This is the grossest moment of my life. I ran out of there and hurried back to my apartment and I think, omygod, I think I'm going to be sick, so I ran into the bathroom and began to spill my guts all over the toilet. I saw the little yellow and red specks of the remains of a bacon, lettuce, and tomato sandwich I had for lunch. I wiped my mouth with a gross, cheap brown paper towel that tastes gross as shit, then I made my way back into my room. I went into the refrigerator to get a coke because I thought it would calm my stomach, and ten minutes later I was not feeling too bad. Then I think, hey, I might have lost some weight by throwing up and I went over to the scale and I do believe I lost a pound somewhere between yes-*

terday and today. Maybe this girl is on to something. She does look great. Everyone is jealous of her figure, including me. So, that's how she does it. How thoroughly gross, but hey, it's effective. If I wasn't so far gone physically, I'd consider doing it myself.

I've never played the part of a bulimic.

SCHOOL DAYS, AUTUMNAL NIGHTS: NOVEMBER 10-30

The last couple of weeks of the semester for Danny Alderman were a series of dead ends, false leads, and uncooperative behavior from school administrators. He was getting frustrated trying to get reliable information about Dr. Byrd. He talked to a couple of theatre majors and several other professors, but nobody seemed to know what happened to him. He thought Harry Coursen, the new instructor who replaced Byrd, might be helpful, but when he went to see him, he brushed him off, stating it was none of his business. Danny discovered that he did not have any relatives except for his mother who lived outside of Charlottesville. He tracked her down, but she told Danny that he was an "impudent twit" who should mind his own business. Danny felt that was his new role in life, getting older people to tell him to mind his own business. He also called the police to see if he was listed as a missing person, but he was not officially missing. Byrd seemed to have vanished from the face of the earth. As a last ditch effort, he decided to drive by Professor Byrd's old neighborhood. He figured there might be somebody around who could tell him what happened to him. Dr. Byrd had lived down by the railroad tracks in the historic wharf district of the town. Danny located his apartment complex which was renovated from an old abandoned flour mill called the White Star Apartments. Walking along a bumpy cobblestone driveway leading to the apartments, he noticed several gift shops, restaurants, and antique stores that were once part of the old train station. He hesitated a second before entering the complex. He did not feel like randomly knocking on someone's door. He looked at the names below the intercom system and did not recognize anyone. *What was I doing here? I feel like an idiot. Who do I think I am, some kind of great detective?*

He left the complex and walked along the railroad tracks. He passed by a recently refurbished red caboose operating as a fancy Italian restaurant. He could see the faces of well-dressed men and women enjoying their dinner. He passed by a few more shops before arriving back at the complex. He saw a large, sweaty puffy-faced man in denim overalls emerging from the cellar of one of the apartments, probably the maintenance man.

"Excuse me, sir."

The obese man eyed him suspiciously.

"Yes?"

"Do you work here? I mean, all the time?"

The big man relaxed a bit, setting his tool box on the ground. He looked hot and tired.

"I'm the super. Do you have a problem?"

"Well, I was wondering if you could tell me about professor Byrd. He used to live here."

The man seemed to take forever before answering. He looked up from the ground, his eyes drifting toward the sky.

"Oh yes. I remember him. Strange bird, if you'll pardon the pun."

"What do you mean?"

"I don't know...who are you?"

"I'm Danny Alderman, a student at Wattford."

"Well, he left about a year ago, I think."

"Why did you say he was strange?"

"I don't know...He kept strange company."

The superintendent looked even more cautious and evasive. He scrutinized Danny once again.

"Maybe I shouldn't be telling you this, but you look okay. He had a lot of gentlemen friends who came and went all hours of the night."

"Gentlemen friends?"

"You know...male friends."

"Oh, I see," said Danny. "Well, that's okay. A man's entitled to have some friends, right?"

"Not that many."

"Do you know where he went?"

"I have no idea, probably San Francisco."

"Do you know the names of any of his friends?"

"Sorry. I have no idea. Like I said, he was a strange one."

"Thanks. You've been a big help."

"Don't mention it."

Danny called Emily as soon as he got home from talking with the super and arranged to meet her in front of the union.

"Let's go for a walk," he said.

As they walked along a country road in back of the tennis courts, the sky seemed to darken in a matter of minutes as ominous gray clouds raced across the sky. The temperature was dropping rapidly; winter was coming on fast. They walked down the winding road, passing a small pond where several mallards, scarcely disturbed, waddled up from the clear water and regarded them gravely.

The air was filled with the silent beauty of dropping leaves before being interrupted by a swirl of black birds screaming in the trees; a cacophony of shrill voices, anxious for their flight southward. An old woman, in a field spotted with random cows and a herding sheepdog, stared curiously at them with shaded eyes.

"I don't understand," said Emily. "I never heard anything about Professor Byrd being gay. Do you think that was why he was fired?"

"It's a possibility, but not very likely. There are several known homosexuals on campus and I never heard of any of them being harassed or threatened. Besides, I think the school could get into legal trouble."

The couple passed a cemetery dotted with elaborate marble mausoleums; finely-carved granite headstones; simple worn, faded tombstones, and generous assortments of flowers gracing the final resting places. A few cows grazed openly in a distant field, and beyond a fenced-in farmhouse they could see the warm yellow blur of town lights in the distance. They walked a few more moments in silence, each letting the quiet of the evening consume them. Suddenly, Danny stopped them.

"I think Professor Byrd has AIDS."

"To tell you the truth," said Emily, "I was thinking the same thing. Why else would there be such secrecy concerning his leaving? Why all the cover-ups and denials?"

"Well, it makes about as much sense as anything," said Danny. "Maybe somebody got rid of him because of AIDS"

"Or he quit for health reasons. We don't know how sick he was."

"Right. Hell, we don't even know if he *was* sick."

"Wait a minute!" exclaimed Emily, "This is ridiculous. We're jumping to conclusions. After all, most homosexuals don't have AIDS."

"You're right. But it sure would go a long way in explaining his curious disappearance and the stonewalling by the administration."

"I don't know…There could be another explanation."

"Like what?"

"Maybe he has some other illness, or maybe we're making a big deal out of nothing."

"Maybe you're right," said Danny. Let's think about this some more. We do agree that it is a possibility, right?"

"Sure,"

"Well, let's assume we're right, just for hypothetical reasons. What's our first move?"

"Well, it doesn't sound like too hard of a story to track down. We could either find Byrd, or someone sympathetic in the administration. We need someone on the inside who is willing to talk."

"Hey." said Danny, "Do you know Jody Hershberger?"

"Yes."

"Well, her uncle is on the board of trustees. Constance Stewart told me a while ago. We were talking about Professor Byrd being fired and she said to talk to Jody's uncle. I didn't think it was important at the time, but it might be a lead."

"That sounds like a good idea."

"I couldn't hurt. Maybe he knows other things that are going on, like faculty salaries....or why the hell they took the condoms out of the dormitories."

"Do you know Jody Hershberger very well?"

"Not really," said Emily. "I've just been around her a couple times."

"Why don't you call her and see if you can get her uncle's number?"

"Sounds good," said Emily.

By this time the couple had circled the winding road in back of the school and arrived back at Emily's apartment, which was the downstairs of a impressive older home just off campus.

"Let's sit out here for a while," suggested Emily. "It's a beautiful evening."

The young couple sat together on a swing chair, rocking gently, on the porch, quietly gazing out into the blackness of the Virginia autumn night.

Amy left her meeting with Stuart Pennington with mixed emotions. She thought that the magazine was probably just a ruse to get her to go out with him. On the other hand, he did not ask her out, but the next class he asked her if she had put any of her thoughts on paper. Amy was not used to putting her opinions on paper because no one outside of teachers had ever asked her to do such a thing. She told Stuart that she had not gotten around to writing down any ideas. She decided to get Jody's opinion before committing to anything. She knocked on her door.

"Come in."

"Hey, how's it going?"

"Okay. I have a test in plays and performance tomorrow."

"Got a minute?"

"Sure."

Amy told Jody about her conversation with Stuart.

"I know him," she said. "He's a computer geek. He hasn't asked you out?"

"No. I think he might be serious about this magazine stuff."

"Hard to believe, really."

"You think I should work with him?"

"It's kind of vague," said Jody. "What kind of magazine does he have in mind?"

"I'm not sure, but I think he wants one with more substance, especially about male, female relationships. And I think he wants to deal with more important social issues."

"That sounds boring."

"Maybe I should just forget it."

"This Internet might be something. You never know."

"I asked Professor Jackson about it."

"What did he say?"

"He thinks it's going to be big, really big."

"It wouldn't hurt to write some things down. Do you have any ideas?"

"I was thinking of a magazine that would offer services over the Internet for college students, like where to get cheaper books, CDs, movie reviews, match-making, stuff like that."

"I don't know if that would work. Do you think the Internet is going to be that popular?"

"It could be. Stuart certainly thinks so."

"I say go for it. What does Chipper think?"

"I haven't mentioned it to him. I'm sure he will think it's ridiculous."

"Chipper thinks?"

"About sports."

"Right," said Jody. "Hey, what's happening with Constance and Professor Wilson?"

"I think they're getting more serious."

"Is she out of her mind, or what? Can't he get into trouble?"

"I don't think there is a rule against dating professors, as long as they are not in your class."

Jody closed her textbook and reached for a cigarette. "He'll wind up dumping her."

"You think so?"

"Sure. He's a man, isn't he?"

"Why are you so down on men?"

"I don't trust them. They're all liars."

"Not all of them."

"Name one who isn't."

"Okay, but everybody lies a little bit."

"Not like men."

"I think Chipper's cheating on me."

"Why?"

"He told me he was studying the other night, and when I called his apartment he wasn't home."

"He could have been anywhere."

"I know, but I just have this feeling..."

"But Amy, you've been out with other guys..."

"I know."

"Maybe both of you should just admit it and start dating other people."

"I think you're right. Hey, I'm gonna work out. Wanna come?"

"No thanks. I'm tired."

Ellsworth R. (Chuck) Chambers III, chairman of the board of trustees at Wattford College, was not having a good day. It started with his alcoholic wife pouring orange juice into his bowl of cheerios at breakfast. Then he hurried out the door on his way to work, only to find the battery in his car was dead. This forced him to be late for the meeting with the Advisory Committee on Academic Affairs. And now, he had to deal with Sarah Cotter, Dean of Students, and in his eyes, one of the most incompetent administrators in the long, distinguished annals of higher education He reached for the phone and soon was connected to the Dean.

"Listen, Sarah, said Dr. Chambers, glaring solemnly about him with an air of brutish earnestness, "I've been thinking about this male visitation policy in the female dormitories and I'm deeply concerned. I thought we had an agreement on this..."

"I'm sorry, Dr. Chambers, but Academic Council approved the new policy. I only have one vote."

"Damn it, Sarah! Don't give me that 'one vote' crap! You're the Dean of Students, for crying out loud. You should be protecting these girls! You're going to have a hundred hot-blooded young punks spending the night—every night!"

"Well, I'm sorry," said Dean Cotter, "but there was nothing I could do about it. I tried to argue for stricter visitation privileges, but they wouldn't listen."

"Overturn it."

"Dr. Chambers. I can't—"

"Listen, Sarah, do I have to remind you that your contract is a *one year* appointment?"

"No…I…"

"Just get the policy changed…understand?"

"I'll see what I can do."

Chuck Chambers settled back into his chair, stretched his arms, and reached for one of his expensive Panamanian cigars. He refused to smoke Cuban cigars because of the Cuban Missile Crisis in 1962. He hated Communism everywhere. A bigger-than-life man of prodigious appetites, he wore Armani suits that never seemed to fit him and had the always-wrinkled look of someone who slept in his clothes. Chambers complemented his suit with a Texas longhorn string tie and a pair of brown leather cowboy boots. This, despite the fact that he had only been to Texas once for a business meeting in 1979. A lazy plume of smoke swirled toward the ceiling and Chuck Chambers, as he was wont to do, began ruminating to himself about the current condition of the college.

It was clear that Sarah Cotter would have to be replaced. She was obviously an incompetent administrator with no backbone or leadership abilities. I hate people with without leadership abilities. That's another problem with today's society. Nobody has any backbone, no gumption. We're creating a nation of spineless wimps and faggots. Sometimes I wonder where the leaders of tomorrow will come from. Certainly not from these kids. These kids….these soft, namby-pambies have no drive or determination. They're spoiled, unwilling to take on the hard challenges of the future. It's going to take a great deal of time and patience, but I think I can succeed. It just takes a little knowledge and discipline and good old fashion hard work and virtues. It was good enough for my generation, and by God, it's damn well good enough for this generation. It takes morality. The kind of morality that made this country great. Christ-almighty, where would we be today without our Christian heritage? In the stone age! We'd be like animals in cages—a beast to our fellow man! Thank goodness, there's still time left. I don't believe all this crap about 'it's too late to turn things around.' Hell's bells! We beat the stuffings out of those damn krauts when nobody thought we had a chance. It just took a little good old fashioned American know-how and get up and go—and we got up and went!!!

"This college used to be great institution when I went here. We had respect and discipline. Hell, we had required courses: history, logic, and philosophy. Now, the curriculum is watered down with feminist crap, de-constructionist horse shit, Afro-centric history, and Experiential learning. Hell, before long, they'll be giving credit for taking a good crap! I've got to change things around before its too late. Fortunately, I've got Parsons to make a decent agenda for the faculty colloquia. That new guy in Political

Science is going to work out fine. That's a start. We've still got some faculty who have traditional values. Imagine not teaching creationism in college. It's sacrilegious!

It's time to clean house. All I want is to get back to the basics of life before our whole society goes into the dumper. Just when I manage to get the condoms out of the dormitories, that old bag Cotter causes a setback by letting this liberal visitation policy get passed…"

The phone in Chuck Chambers' office rang, interrupting his thoughts.

"Yes, Muriel."

"Emily Patterson is here. She's a student."

"Oh, send her in."

Chuck Chambers wondered what this student could possibly want with him. It was unusual for one to make an appointment with him. They usually went to Dean Parsons to complain about classes and social life. The only thing that he knew was that Sarah had informed him that this student wanted to talk about a couple of issues on campus. Sarah opened the door to admit a strikingly beautiful girl with long black hair, dressed smartly in a tailored navy dress, carrying a brief-case. Chuck Chambers was impressed, but also felt on the defensive.

She looks, serious, he thought, like a feminist.

"Hello, Dr. Chambers. I'm Emily Patterson."

"Nice to meet you. Sit down, please. What can I do for you?"

"Well, Emily began, "I came here because there are a couple of things happening on campus that we are concerned about."

"We?"

"Oh, I guess I should explain. Danny Alderman works for Broadside and he asked me to follow up on a couple of stories for the paper."

"I see. This concerns a campus issue?"

"Well, two of them, really."

"What are they?"

"Okay, do you know why they took the condom machines out of the dormitories?"

Chuck Chambers felt an instant pain in his mind, like he was struck by an arrow to the brain. However, he did not flinch; nor did he think Emily noticed any change in his demeanor.

How could this young women understand this dangerous and liberal idea of trying to encourage premarital sex right in front of our noses. I hate the idea of young couples ruining their lives by having sex before marriage. It's immoral. It's an insult to all of us who really care about Wattford College.

"Frankly, Emily, I did not even know they were there in the first place. As you know, I'm on the Board of Trustees, and normally Board members are not even on campus. We meet twice a year to conduct college business. But President Cronin asked me to spend some time on campus this year to help him out with some administrative problems. Normally, that is not a matter that would concern the board of trustees."

"Do you know who would be responsible for such an action?"

"Well, Emily, I am assuming that would be policy set forth by the Dean of Students office—Mrs. Cotter."

"We've talked to her and she said it was an administrative decision."

"That's pretty vague."

"That's what we thought. It seemed we were getting the run-around."

I felt like telling this feminist twit she hasn't seen anything yet. She wasn't getting anything out of me, that's for sure. Who did this bossy young thing think she was, Barbara Walters? I hate Barbara Walters.

"I understand," said Chambers, "Listen, I'm glad you came to see me I think it is inappropriate to change something like this without consulting the students."

"I think that's what the majority of the students think."

Yeah, well, the majority of the students think with their sex organs and I am going to put a stop to all this rampant Sodom and Gomorrah.

"Of course, I'll look into this matter right away. I will report back you. Now what was the second item?"

"Well…" Emily hesitated…"I'm not sure about this one."

"What do you mean?"

"We do not have any hard evidence, but we think professor Byrd may have been fired because he has AIDS."

"That's outrageous! How could such a thing happen in this day in age?"

"Dr. Chambers I'm not—we're—not exactly sure, so I don't want to make any accusations, but we have been getting the run-around whenever we try to find out any information."

"Who is the professor?"

"Professor Byrd…in theatre."

"He's not back?"

"Didn't you know that?"

"Oh, yes, now let me see….there was something about a new faculty member in theatre at the last executive staff meeting, but to tell you the truth, I don't pay much attention to those things. I don't remember any mention of…who did you say?"

"Professor Byrd."

Chambers leaned back in his chair, reached for a used, unlit cigar and lit it.

"Oh, I'm sorry! Do you mind if I smoke?"

"No, not at all. I like the smell of cigars."

"Now where were we?" Chambers asked. "Oh, yes, Professor Byrd. Why don't you just ask the professor? He lives in town, doesn't he?"

"Yes, in fact, Danny Alderman went to his apartment down by the wharf district and the superintendent said he left awhile ago and no one seems to know his whereabouts."

Honey, how could you possibly care about that queer son-of-a-bitch? That faggot probably slept with a hundred men. How disgusting! How could you care about that worthless queer son-of-a-bitch? Jesus, just thinking about two hairy guys doing God-knows-what between the sheets makes me sick.

"Emily," said Dr. Chambers, "My contributions on the board are mostly on the finance committee."

"I see."

"Now listen," Dr. Chambers said. "I really don't think you have anything to worry about. I'm sure there is a logical explanation. Let me see what I can find out. By the way…have you talked to anyone else?"

"I have talked to Dean Parsons and several faculty members and Danny talked to Professor Ellis in the theatre department."

"And what did you find out?"

"Not much. The Dean said he quit for personal reasons and the rest of the faculty knew nothing about it. I tried to talk to the search committee who hired professor Coursen, but no one would talk to me. Professor Ellis said it was a faculty matter."

"What makes you think he died of AIDS?"

"Well, that's where we may be out of bounds. I feel awful making this assumption, but we do know that Professor Byrd was gay."

He was, honey, a regular three dollar bill.

"…and I know it's terrible to think that he automatically has AIDS, but he left after 19 years and that's pretty unusual, especially for a tenured professor.

Yeah, he left, alright. Right after I had him fired by that numbskull Parsons. He was a sick pup and should rightfully be punished for his wrongdoing. By God, it's not natural and you should know it. God wanted man and woman together. He made Adam and Eve—not Adam and Steve."

"I can see why you might not have gotten straight answers. Maybe they're just trying to protect Professor Byrd's privacy."

"I know. That's why I feel so bad. Maybe Professor Byrd doesn't want a couple nosy students poking into his life, but I really don't understand why no one will even tell us where he lives. It just seems too hush-hush…"

"Why did you come to me?"

"Oh yes! I almost forgot! I called your niece, Jody, and she told us how to get in touch with you. We thought that, well…you might be easier to approach…we were not sure where to turn."

"Listen," said Dr. Chambers, "You certainly did the right thing, and you definitely came to the right person. I'm going to get to the bottom of this, mark my words! They won't give ole Chuck Chambers the run-around, you can believe that!"

"What should we do?"

Well, sweetie why don't you go back to your liberal feminist friends who promote fairies and fruitcakes, and jump in the lake.

"This may take some time. I have to be careful not to tread on any toes. We live in a political world, don't we?"

This poor girl doesn't know the half of it. This is all politics. It's my politics that will transform this college. It is also politics, sweetheart, that keeps me from revealing my plan to you.

"When should I get back with you on this," Emily asked.

"I will call you. Just leave your number with Muriel and I'll get in touch with you as soon as I can."

"Thank you, Dr. Chambers, you've been big help."

"Don't mention it. Besides, I haven't done anything yet. Wait until I do something, then you can thank me. Okay?"

"Goodbye, Dr. Chambers.

"Goodbye, Emily…and thanks for contacting me."

Later that day, Chambers drove home with the thoughts of the meeting with Emily still on his mind. He was not sure what to do, but as he pulled in the driveway, he was beginning to formulate a plan to deal with the recent intrusion on his grand scheme for Wattford College. Upon entering the front door of his estate on the banks of the Sherando river, Chambers went to the phone in his den.

"Hello, Jody. This is uncle Chuck."

"Oh, hi. How are you doing?"

"I'm fine, Jody. How are things going?"

"Great!"

"That's terrific. I've called you several times but I haven't been able to catch you. Is everything okay?"

"Oh, yes! I've just been busy with my courses, that's all."

"Jody, I was wondering if you would come to dinner Tuesday night. Dolores and I would love to have you."

"Sounds good to me. I'm certainly tired of this campus food."

"I bet you could use a good meal. How about seven o'clock?"

"Terrific! I can't wait to see you. I've missed you!"

"I've missed you too, Jody. Well, it's settled then. See you on Tuesday."

"Goodbye, uncle Chuck."

"Goodbye Jody."

Chuck Chambers hung up the phone, went over to his leather easy chair, plopped down, and lit another cigar.

Maybe Jody can fill me in on this campus nonsense. I'm not sure what to do about this professor Byrd business. I need to contact Dean Parsons and tell him what the hell is going on. This Patterson girl could be trouble. There's no way she can find out I fired him unless Parsons—or Ellis—spills the beans. They'll keep their mouths shut, if they know what's good for them. Maybe I shouldn't do anything. The semester is almost over. They may drop the whole thing over Christmas break. Then again, this Emily feminist does not strike me as someone who would give up very easily.

"Dolores! Is my dinner ready yet?"

"In a minute!"

In a minute, my ass. That old cow takes forever to get my dinner.

"Well, hurry up, will ya? You know it's my bridge night."

I also wonder if that Alderman boy will be any trouble. It sounded as if they'd formed a damn pact, or something. Maybe I can close down the campus newspaper. Tell them it's a necessary budget cut. I wonder if I can get them thrown out of school. I'll have the registrar pull their grades, although they don't seem like the type to be in academic trouble. Maybe I can get them thrown out of school on a trumped up charge, like possession of drugs. Parsons could handle that for me.

"Dolores!!"

Damnit, that old rummy needs a boot up her ass. She's probably out there right now slugging her tenth highball and taking God knows how many pills.

"Okay, it's about ready."

He crushed his cigar out in the ashtray, arose from his easy chair, and lumbered into the dining room. His wife Dolores was basting a turkey with one hand and clutching a highball with the other.

"Be careful you don't spill the drink on the bird. You might get him drunk."

"Very funny."

My God, she's beginning to take on that sad, matronly look that clings unforgiving to aging women alcoholics. Her complexion (what's left of it) has begun to look pasty and sallow, like a dried up prune. Her eyes have become sunken, with a dark purple ring around them. Sometimes I want to count the wrinkles in her flabby arms and when she bends over her ass seems to dominate the room, like an old sow that's been placed in a pen that's too small for her. Some day she might not be able to make it through the door. She might get stuck in the kitchen forever. So be it. God, if only Big Brothers knew that their best Big Sister was a big time drunk.

"It's almost ready."

I wonder how I can get rid of this rummy. My goodness, what a liability. It's a good thing for her that I don't believe in divorce, or she would have been shown the door a long time ago. Perhaps she will die soon. The bottle might take its toll. One can only hope…

Dolores was busy getting the table ready for dinner. She carefully lifted the turkey from the oven and placed it on the table, along with a bowl of mashed potatoes, and portions of green beans, cranberry sauce, and candied yams.

Jesus, she must think it's Thanksgiving. That was last week. She's so drunk, she probably thinks it's Thanksgiving all over again.

Dolores sat down at the far end of the dining room table as each of them commenced their daily routine of staring blankly into their food without comment.

"I invited Jody over for dinner,"

"Oh, that's nice, dear."

"Does everything have to be nice? Couldn't you use a different word once in a while, like marvelous, pleasant, wonderful, or terrific?"

"Is something wrong dear?"

"No, Dolores. Everything is just perfect. It couldn't be nicer, now could it?"

I think I will set up an appointment with Parsons after the break. I have to get to Parsons before those snooping students begin asking a lot of questions. They've already gone too far. It just takes a couple of bad apples and pointy-headed liberals to wreck a good college. Maybe they will try to contact Byrd. He should be dead fairly soon, so it shouldn't make any difference.

"How's your turkey, dear?"

"Fine, Dolores, just fine."

Sometimes I feel like the whole world has forsaken me. It's as if things are falling apart all around me. Why can't we just go back to the simple times—the good times when family, church, and country meant something. I loved the fifties. It was the best generation in the history of the world. America was on top of the mountain. Nobody made better products. Hell, we used to call those crappy products from Japan— Gyp-anese! Now every other car is a Japmobile. Kids don't even go to church anymore and they have no respect for their country. I went to a baseball game the other week and half the kids didn't even take off their caps during the national anthem. Of course, some of the players had earrings in their ears. Can you imagine Joe DiMaggio with an earring in his ear? For God's sake, give me a break. If only women would just stay in the home and take care of their children. Why on earth do they want to do men's work? Is that such a bad life? Now we have dykes in the workplace, homosexuals in the army, and AIDS freaks carrying deadly diseases throughout the country. And people call me crazy for wanting to put an end to this nonsense. It's an abomination….a damn abomination, what's happening to this country.

"How's you turkey, dear?"

"Dolores, for God's sake, you already asked me that."

"Oh."

If only this professor Byrd hadn't gotten AIDS. I should have known some fag-loving liberal student would start snooping around trying to cause trouble. What was I supposed to do? Let a degenerate teach our kids? I should be given a medal for firing him. Instead, I had to cover it up and bribe that spineless Parsons and make Ellis the head of the department. I need to nip this investigation in the bud…

"Would you like some dessert, dear?"

"No, Dolores, I'm late for bridge."

"Oh."

"Dolores?"

"Yes."

"Don't wait up."

Three nights later, Jody Hershberger arrived at her uncle's house for dinner. She was looking forward to seeing her aunt and uncle again and taking a break from school and her roommates. Chambers greeted her at the door and lead her into the study to relax before dinner.

"Jody," said Dr. Chambers, "You look absolutely terrific. I know you got that beautiful red hair from our side of the family, right?"

"Thank you, uncle Chuck. I guess it did. My father's family all have dark hair."

"Have you heard from your parents lately?"

"Not really. I talked to my mother on Thanksgiving day. She and Hal were vacationing in the Bahamas. I haven't heard from my father since September."

I'm so glad to be in the company of my niece. I love Jody more than anything else in the world. She is such a sweet and beautiful child. I continually dote on her as if, well, as if she was my real daughter. I wish Dolores and I could have had children, but she ruined our chances. I swear I will never forgive her for that. I need someone to love in this world and Jody is all I have. I have certainly done a lot more for Jody than her parents. Eileen tried to be a good mother, but Jody and my sister never got along. Her father is a no-count worthless bum who travels around the country selling bogus real estate.

"Jody, I'm glad you could come over tonight. I've missed you."

"I've missed you too. I would have come over sooner, but I've been busy in the theatre department."

"Dolores should be getting dinner ready soon. You must be famished."

"Oh, not really. I've been trying to keep my weight down. You know how directors all look for thin actresses."

"You're a wonderful actress, Jody. I loved you in *Cat on a Hot Tin Roof.*"

"I had a great time with it."

"Are you going to be in a play this spring?"

"Yes, I'm trying out for the lead in *Gentlemen Prefer Blondes.*"

"Oh, that's a great show. I saw the movie with Jane Russell and Marilyn Monroe."

"I'm auditioning for the Monroe part. Of course, I'll have to dye my hair."

"I hope you get it. You'd be perfect. By the way, is anything interesting happening on campus?"

"You mean entertainment?"

"No, I was thinking of controversial issues, like teachers leaving, or changes in school policy."

"I can't think of anything. I think all the teachers are back, except for Professor Byrd in our department."

"Oh, Professor Byrd. Well, he's having a grand old time."

"He is?"

"Oh, yes, he left to take an ocean cruise. I remember him telling us in executive staff. He's a history buff and he went on a long cruise to Europe and eventually around the Mediterranean retracing the voyage of Ulysses. I believe he will eventually settle in Greece."

"Gee," said Jody, "He never mentioned that to anyone. He's not coming back?"

"I doubt it."

I'm sure Jody will spread the word that Byrd is traveling around the continent. I'm sure she'll tell her friends and that should take care of any nasty rumors—providing Parsons gets rid of those annoying twits, Patterson and Alderman.

"Come and get it!" Dolores exclaimed from the kitchen. "Soup's on!"

"Well, Jody, I guess it's time to eat....You'll be sure to tell them if they ask, won't you?"

"I'm sorry, uncle Chuck. What do you mean?"

"Professor Byrd. If anybody asks about him I'm sure you'll tell them about his trip, okay?"

"Of course."

Danny Alderman eased his 1989 Volkswagen Jetta into the last remaining parking spot near the courthouse circle of Cannonville. It was a gorgeous autumn day. Danny took in the diversity of activity of a small Southern town when the weather is terrific and people are out and about. He could see townspeople out window shopping near the downtown mall, peering into the string of charming shops featuring arts and crafts, antiques, art work, jewelry, books, fine china, and women's clothes; a young teenage couple leisurely strolling in the park near the courthouse; old weathered farmers in bib-overalls pitching horseshoes across from the Little League field; a middle-aged couple eating barbecued chicken from the open grill of the Crawford Brothers' barbecue stand; several daring boys weaving their bicycles carelessly around pedestrians on the sidewalk; and an old man outside his antique store tinkering with the internal mechanisms of a German-made Grandfather clock. Unlike many of the towns and cities in the country, Cannonville had not abandoned its past for the financial appeal of urban sprawl and grotesque fast-food franchises; but rather embraced its past and preserved the unique heritage and history of the city and its dwellings. Danny, however, did not have time to enjoy the scenery. He had his monthly appointment with Mr. Jones, and he was not the kind of person you kept waiting. He quickly headed for the third floor of the courthouse building, got clearance from the secretary, and made his way into the office of his probation officer. As usual Mr. Jones sat implacable and business-like behind his large oak desk.

"So, tell me, how was Thanksgiving break?"

"It went really well. I went to my girl friend's parent's house for Thanksgiving dinner. I was a nervous wreck, but I think they like me. I didn't drop a turkey leg on my lap or anything. We went to her old high school to watch the homecoming football game. I found out my girl friend was a homecoming queen in high school. Her younger brother plays on the team. I had forgotten how much fun you could have at a football game.

"What's your girl friend's name?"

"Emily. I am now in a relationship, believe it or not. She's awesome. I think she's the best thing to happen to me in a long time."

"Does she know about your past?"

"Are you kidding? No."

"Well, don't you think she'll find out eventually?"

"What do you want me to tell her? Hey, Emily! Guess what? I got my first two years of college in the joint after being busted with a half kilo of the finest Colombian cocaine you ever saw."

"Stop being a sarcastic asshole. You have to face reality. She will find out and it's best she hears it from you."

"Come on. I can't do that. You think she's going to keep dating a former coke head with a felony conviction?"

"You said former, didn't you?"

"So what. I still did it. I don't have any excuses."

"You don't need any. Just tell her the truth. You fucked up. You're not the first kid to make a mistake. If she really cares, she'll see you've changed."

"It's too risky. I don't want to blow this one. She's the first girl I ever felt serious about. I don't have a good track record with women, either."

"So, you're growing up. Hey, it happens to the best of us."

"Are you saying that *you*—Mr. Perfect—has made some mistakes?"

"What do you think? That's how we become probation officers. We screw up, then try to help other people avoid our mistakes."

"Like what?"

"Like that's none of your business."

"Okay, so the great Mr. Jones is not perfect. I'm not ready to tell Emily. We have a great thing going and I don't want to mess it up."

"It's up to you. I'm not your father or psychiatrist, but don't say I didn't warn you. By the way, what are you going to do over the Christmas break?"

"I don't know. Hang out."

"With who?"

"I think Emily and I are going to New York for New Year's."

"What about Frankie?"

"As far as I know he's in Florida. I don't think he'll come in the wintertime."

"Frankie Beauchamp is capable of anything."

"You've got a point there. Maybe he will show up."

"What are you going to do if he comes back into town?"

"I guess I'll avoid him."

"You guess?"

"Yeah, what do you want me to say?"

"I want you to definitely stay away from him. You two are like matches and dynamite."

"You still think I'm weak, don't you?"

"Yes, Danny, You'll always be weak, but that's okay. It's part of the recovery process, admitting you have a problem *and* a weakness."

"You know Frankie and I were in a bar one night, really fucked up, and ran into this girl, and Frankie started talking to her. After about ten drinks the girl leans over and says to him: 'I have a weakness for cocaine.' Frankie turned to her and said, 'That's okay, I have a weakness for people with weaknesses.' He got laid that night."

"So?"

"So, I think that's my problem too. It's not just cocaine, but I like people who are screwed up in one way or another. I have a bias against the mentally normal."

"Hang around with coke heads and you'll be right back where you were."

"I know. I've been doing okay."

"You got finals coming up, right?"

"Yeah. I have four of them—and it's not pretty. How would you like to take a final comparing Marx's theory of Dialectical Materialism with Machiavelli's *The Prince?*"

"No, thanks. I just want to make sure you stay out of trouble."

"You say that every time."

"I'll keep saying it, at least for three more years."

SPRING SEMESTER

WINTERTIME BLUES: JANUARY 17-31

Danny was sitting in the living room watching television with Jason. For the two students, it was a pretty bleak time of the year. The semester started late because the biggest blizzard in twenty five years blasted the entire east coast, dumping as much as twenty-five inches of snow in parts of Virginia. Classes at Wattford College did not resume until the middle of January, and when they did, the area was bombarded with unrelenting sleet, frozen rain, snow flurries, cold, gray blustery skies, and bone-chilling winds. Aside from the weather, the basketball team was on an eight game losing streak, the school was in the grip of a major flu epidemic, one of the water pipes froze up in Hazard Hall, a concert by the rock group *Everything But The Girl* had to be canceled because of the weather, and many of the seniors were in the grip of "senior-itis," a disease whereby one is inflicted with the desire to escape the confinements of college life while at the same time being afraid to graduate. Danny and Jason both had relatively mild cases of the disease.

Despite the fact that it was weeks away, more than half of the students' conversations were about what they were going to do during Spring Break. Most of the students were so bored and unmotivated by classes, and books in general, that shared thoughts of escape to Florida or the Caribbean took on an exaggerated importance that permeated nearly every social encounter. It was as if the daily monotony of their lives could only be relieved by thoughts of happy diversions on the balmy shores of a tropical paradise. Jason already knew he was going to Panama City, Florida to witness MTV's annual Spring Break fest, but he did not talk very much about it, especially in front of Danny who thought the whole notion of Spring Break was vastly overrated. Danny had nothing against fun, but he felt that his fellow students should enjoy their courses and the school year instead of waiting around for Spring Break. He was bemused by the fact that many seniors spent more time talking about and planning Spring Break than their future after graduation. For his part, Jason couldn't understand why Danny did not enjoy the usual college hi-jinks like guzzling beer, chasing bikini-clad college girls, drooling over wet T-shirt contests, jumping in the ocean, smoking pot, listening to loud rap music, and generally acting like a carefree college student freed from the wintertime rigors of books and classes. Danny and Emily were different; they both agreed they would go somewhere together over the break, but that was the extent of their plans.

In the current winter doldrums, the only consolation for Danny was the fact that he had a tremendous Christmas break. He went home and spent time with his parents, two brothers, and sister and visited with their respective wives, husbands and children. He was amazed at how much better he got along with his family now that he had settled down and was going to a "real college" instead of one provided by the prison. In truth, Danny had cast out many of the demons that plagued him when he was younger and under the influence of heavy drug use. He could tell that after a while his real personality was beginning to slip from him and he felt himself spiraling out of control. Now, as he looked back at all his drug-related behavior, he did not recognize the person who dealt thousands of dollars worth of cocaine, associated with a hard-core criminal element, carried a gun, and once considered hiring a body guard. These things were in the past, but they still haunted his memory, and he was determined never to go back to a life of crime and drugs.

He saw Emily regularly over the break and she spent Christmas night at his parent's house. They exchanged gifts. Danny bought Emily a gorgeous tennis bracelet laced with diamonds, and Emily bought Danny a CD player and five of his favorite CD's. His parents were crazy about Emily. Brother James said she "charmed the socks" off them. They also went to New York city to see the giant silver ball drop from Times Square on New Years' eve. Standing in Times Square at the stroke of midnight on December 31, 1995, Danny and Emily kissed passionately in front of thousands of people reveling in the night and swore their undying love for one another.

But now he was back at school for the final stretch before graduation. Things were going slowly for him at the moment. He still continued Sound Bites, but was unable to break through with anything substantial; nor was he able to get any further with the Byrd disappearance. Emily was a great help. In fact, she had taken over the job of trying to find Professor Byrd. They had pretty much decided to wait until Dr. Chambers contacted them, but so far he had not gotten in touch with either one of them. Danny was not convinced it was much of an issue. He was beginning to think Dr. Byrd simply resigned because of his illness and there was no terrible plot to get rid of him. It was Emily who was more tenacious; she felt certain that there might be something to it.

Things on the news front were so bad, Danny was considering asking women what they wanted their boyfriends to give them for St. Valentine's, and that was three weeks away. Danny also tried to run down a story about why the topics for faculty colloquia were so conservative, but Dean Parsons told him the professors choose whatever topic they wanted. When he asked him why only conservative faculty members were chosen, he was told that they were the only ones who volunteered.

Danny's relationship with Emily continued to improve, and they genuinely loved one another. They were officially a couple now, but not to the point of discussing marriage or engagement, or even what they were going to do after graduation. They were taking it slow, but the calendar was moving inexorably toward graduation and they both knew they had to make a serious decision about what they were going to do with their lives. For the moment, they decided not to decide.

Danny wanted many times to tell Emily about his past, but never got up the nerve. The timing never seemed quite right and he knew now that time was running out. He had fallen in love so quickly with Emily that he didn't want her to see any faults in him. The closest they ever got to talking about the future was when Danny said he thought that they should "definitely be together" after graduation. Emily told him she would like to live in a big city, but beyond that there was little discussion between them about the future.

As he was sitting on the sofa watching television on this cold January day, Danny was thinking about where he was going to wind up after graduation, and how he would go about including Emily in his plans. He wondered if it was this confusing for his parents. They were college sweethearts and they just got married after graduation, had four kids in seven years, and lived in a small town all their lives. Danny was thinking that his generation was more lost and non-committal; at least that described most of his friends.

"Hey, man! You awake?" Jason asked, breaking Danny out of his daydreaming. "You sure do drift off a lot. You sure you're not crazy?"

"Of course I'm crazy," said Danny, "I'm rooming with you—that should be proof enough."

"Are you seeing Emily tonight?" Jason asked.

"I'm going over to her apartment."

"I think I'll study a little, then maybe get a beer in the union."

"No date?" Danny asked. "You must be losing your touch, Romeo."

"I'm tired of these girls on campus. They bore me to death. You're lucky you got Emily. She's the only real girl on campus. Can she clone herself out?"

"I'll ask her."

Jason got up from the couch and went to the refrigerator to get a couple beers. He tossed one to Danny.

"How about Amy Toeffler?" Danny asked, snapping off the beer cap, "I thought you liked her."

"Not really," Jason responded, plopping himself back on the couch. "She's not the sharpest knife in the drawer, if you know what I mean. All she talks about are dumb TV shows. Besides, she likes some dork named Chipper. How could you take a girl seriously who dated someone named Chipper?"

"How about Jody Hershberger?'

"She's okay, but a little weird. Maybe it's because she's a theatre major. She also may be a little loose, even for me."

Jason grabbed the remote, apparently not satisfied with what he was watching. He quickly scanned the channels before settling on an old Paul Newman picture.

"Maybe I'll call her…"

"Who? Jody?"

"Yeah, she is cute."

"Go for it."

Sipping his newly opened beer with renewed energy, Jason turned to Danny.

"I'm going to ask her out. I mean, why not? What do I have to lose?"

Emily Patterson was sitting at a table in the union waiting for Danny. She was thinking about him and Professor Byrd. She understood why she thought about Danny so much: she was in love. But her continuing obsession with Byrd's disappearance was not so easily understood. She now cared more about the issue than Danny, and he was the reporter for Broadside. Perhaps, she felt more seriously about the issue of AIDS, or maybe she was just upset at not getting forthright answers from many of the faculty She was still on the story and this week she had found out new information that she was going to share with Danny tonight. Certainly, Danny and Professor Byrd both had an air of mystery about them. Emily loved Danny, but he was very close to the vest when talking about his family or his past. She thought this was very odd. Almost every guy she ever knew talked about his family, childhood, previous friends, and high school experiences. Danny was content to discuss almost any subject, but himself. She knew he was a little older, which was fine with her, except she couldn't help but feel he was hiding something from her. The irony was not lost on her that she felt people generally talked too much about themselves, and the one person she wanted to open up to her was the silent type. She thought that he would open up to her after they told each other they loved one another, but he remained closed-lipped. She decided not to push the issue.

She, too, was beginning to worry about what she was going to do after graduation. All she knew was that she was going to graduate with a philosophy degree, she loved Danny Alderman, and she wanted to continue the relationship. Beyond that, things were very hazy for her. She had applied to several graduate schools, including American University in Washington DC, Columbia University in New York City, and Boston University. She had yet to hear from any of them. At least graduate school would give her a goal, she thought, instead of just going home and doing nothing, or getting a job she did not particularly like.

"Hi!" greeted Danny suddenly.

"Well, hello!"

Danny bent down and gave Emily a vigorous hug and kiss.

"Were you waiting long?"

"No, I've only been here a few minutes."

"How's studying going?" Danny asked.

"I don't know," Emily responded, "I keep reading, but I don't know how much I am accomplishing. Right now the *Age of Reason* is giving me fits."

"Sounds reasonable to me. I never got past: 'I think, therefore I am.'"

"I wish all their ideas were that succinct."

"I've really slacked off," said Danny. "My energy level is pretty low. It must be this damn weather. What are you drinking?"

"A Coke."

"I think I'll get one myself."

Danny went up to the counter and momentarily returned with a Coke in his hand.

"So, what's been happening? Anything new on Byrd?"

"Yes, a couple things. I talked to a few more theatre majors and they all pretty much said the same thing. Professor Byrd was excited about the upcoming year and had planned to produce one play and direct two others."

"That doesn't sound like a man ready to quit."

"Right. One of the plays was a senior project for Clara Baldwin. She spent her whole junior year writing the play and Professor Byrd was going to be involved in the production, direction, and stage management. It's strange that he would back out of that commitment without telling her."

"Really."

"I also talked to Joyce McBride in French. She was rumored to have dated Byrd."

"Wait a minute!" exclaimed Danny, "Dated Byrd?"

"Apparently, Byrd is bi-sexual."

"No kidding. Did she tell you that?"

"No," said Emily, "I found out from Larry Burton."

"Larry Burton?"

"He works for the Dixie theatre collecting tickets. I asked him last Tuesday if he ever saw Byrd on a date with someone. He told me he saw him with Dr. McBride a couple years ago, holding hands, no less."

"What did McBride say?"

"She was no help," said Emily, "Actually, she was a real bitch."

"Why?"

"She called *me* a bitch."

"Really?"

"Yeah. She said I should mind my own business and asked me who I thought I was to be prying into other peoples' lives. That pissed me off, so I told her to kiss my ass, in French. Then she called me a bitch, in French."

"Wow, you girls can get nasty."

"Only when it is necessary for our survival."

"Has Chambers contacted you?"

"No, but I expect him to get in touch soon. It's been awhile."

"So, we're pretty much stagnating," said Danny.

"You mean on the Byrd situation—or us?"

"We may be doing a lot of things, but you and I are *not* stagnating. We're moving like Michael Jordan through a pressing defense.

"Is that a sports metaphor meaning that we're having a good time?"

"We're slam dunking, baby!"

"You watch too many sports."

Chambers needed to speak with Harold Parsons, the Dean of the College. At most colleges the Dean was in charge of academic affairs, but Wattford was no ordinary college and Chuck Chambers was no ordinary member of the Board of Trustees. Most members of the Board at small colleges were peripheral figures who made large-scale financial decisions, rarely getting involved in the running of the day-to-day operations of the college. But President Cronin and Dean Parsons had long since abdicated their powers to Chambers. The college was in deep financial straits and the President and Dean thought Chambers was their only hope for survival. He continually dangled the prospect of giant sums of money being donated to the school by him and his associates. The President and the Dean had somewhere along the way forgot that colleges were places where the free expression of ideas and professional integrity took precedence over everything, including the financial condition of the college.

"Muriel," said Dr. Chambers, "Send in Dean Parsons."

"Yes, sir. Right away."

I was hoping that I wouldn't have to do anything about these two snoopers on campus. You would have thought they'd just drop the whole damn thing. But no. That Emily piss-ant has been all over campus, sticking her nose into my business. She must have talked to 20 faculty members. People are beginning to ask questions. The last straw was putting a notice in the school paper. Imagine asking anyone on campus to contact her if they knew the whereabouts of Byrd. She should contact the Bureau of Missing Queers! I need to stop this infernal investigation of that nuisance Byrd. These meddling liberals could be a real pain in the ass and definitely pose a threat to my plans. Who did they think they were? Dan Rather and Connie Chung? I hate Dan Rather and Chinese people.

Chambers' thoughts were interrupted by his secretary Muriel Worthington who suddenly appeared at his office door.

"Dr. Chambers, Dean Parsons is here."

"Send him in."

Harold Parsons entered Dr. Chambers' office with all of the confidence of a rabbit approaching a lion's den. Parsons was a short, wiry, rapidly balding man in his late fifties who had been Dean of Wattford college for the past three years. He had been hand-picked by Chambers to succeed Dean Snizek who retired after serving the college for 20 years.

"You wanted to see me."

"Yes, Harold, please sit down."

Chambers leaned back in his usual blustery manner, expanded his chest, and reached for one of his expensive cigars. He gave the impression of a fat-cat mayor of a small town who ruled with an iron fist and intimidated everyone around him. He sighed deeply, lit his cigar, tossed a match into the ash tray and stared down at Parsons from his massive desk which he kept at a higher position than any of his visitors.

"You remember how we handled the Byrd incident?"

"Of course, I had to let him go."

"Let's be honest, Harold. You know why you fired him. This school needs my money and if it goes down the tubes, you'll be the first to go, believe me."

God, look at this pathetic creature. Harold Parsons is like most college deans who always hide moral cowardice and fear of authority with a phony air of professionalism, as if they were not above kissing ass and covering their butt in a time of crisis. No matter how contemptuously I treated Harold, he ignored my insults and proceeded to speak in bureaucratic horse shit. It's as if he knows my office is bugged. Nevertheless, I needed Parsons in my hip pocket, so I am going to control my disgust of him. Instead of denying that Byrd was fired because I threatened to withdraw my contribution to the college, Harold acted like I never mentioned it.

"Professor Byrd needed to be fired for obvious reasons," said Parsons.

Chambers was willing to put up with this charade. At least for the moment.

"Precisely," said Dr. Chambers, "You and I both know that kind of person doesn't fit into our plans for the school."

"Is Professor Byrd suing us?"

Another spineless Dean remark. Deans are always worried about being sued. It's a fear that must be implanted deep in their DNA.

"No, Harold," Dr. Chambers responded, "He wouldn't do that. He knows our payments to cover his medical expenses would stop and he's afraid his disease will become public knowledge. He's still hiding out."

"So, what's the problem?"

"Well, there are two students who are trying to find out why he didn't come back this year. One of them works for the campus newspaper and the other one is a feminist trouble maker."

"You mean the Patterson girl? I talked to her last year. Is she still snooping around?"

"Apparently, you didn't do enough for her to desist in this behavior."

"I told her he left for personal reasons."

"Well," said Dr. Chambers, "They aren't going away and I think we need to put a stop to this investigation."

"What do you suggest?"

Chambers was quickly losing his patience. He made a mental note to get rid of Parsons at the end of the year, no matter what happened.

"Damnit," Harold, you're the Dean. That's why I called you in here. Can't *you* think of something?"

"Is it the Alderman kid? What's his first name?"

"Daniel."

"Yes, I remember him. He's a good student and also a good reporter."

"Well," Chambers said flatly, "Get rid of them."

"I can't do that. They're not in academic trouble and as far as I know they have not committed a serious honor violation."

Lord above, how can I possibly be surrounded by such incompetent people? Parsons can grate on your nerves like a Ted Kennedy speech. Without me, this weasel piss-ant would be stocking shelves in the local supermarket.

"Listen, Harold, we both know I'm not going to fork out ten million dollars unless my programs are implemented."

"Of course, but I was planning on announcing the contribution at the next faculty meeting."

"Too bad. That will have to wait."

Harold Parsons rubbed his hands together, a habit he developed when he was in trouble and needed to think about something.

"This could be very difficult," Dean Parsons finally said. "I need to figure out how to do this without arousing suspicion."

"Tell you what, Harold. If you take care of these students, I'll sweeten the pie."

"What do you mean?"

"In addition to supplying funds for the new school of business, I'll build a new chapel."

"A new chapel?"

"Yes. Isn't that generous of me?"

"Why, yes. We could use a new facility."

"There's one catch though."

"What's that?"

"I'd like it named after me."

"I don't see any problem with that."

Chambers leaned forward in his chair, propping his elbows on the desk.

"Harold, you have been here three years. That's not very long. I assume you want to continue to serve the college. That means you have to help me achieve my goal of returning this college to greatness. I can do it with you or without you. It's your choice."

Jesus, is that all this spineless worm can do is wring his hands? Harold Parsons has the guts of a marshmallow. He must have gotten beat up a lot when he was a kid. He reminds me of one of those mamma's boys I used to pick on when I was a kid. In fact, right now I'd like to smack his face and take away his notepad like I used to take away the bikes of mamma's boys. Unfortunately, I need sycophants like him around; but on the other hand, his lack of intestinal fortitude appalls me. He looks like a petty criminal squirming in his seat, under interrogation with a 40-watt light bulb dangling over his head.

"Dr. Chambers, Parsons pleaded lamely, "I really don't see how I can prevent two students from following a news story."

"They can't follow a news story if they are not on campus."

"So, you want me to find some reason for their dismissal from the college?"

"I thought I made myself perfectly clear, Harold. The college doesn't want to lose a ten million dollar donation, does it?"

"No…but…"

"Oh, by the way, Harold. I want you to take over the task of outlawing male visitation."

"That's Sarah's responsibility."

"I fired Sarah Cotter this morning. You can form a search committee for her replacement next week. Thank you, Harold. I look forward to hearing from you."

"I'll see what I can do."

"Good day, Harold."

Two days after Parsons talked to Chambers, Parson's secretary placed a call to Emily Patterson asking her to come and see the Dean. Emily was surprised because she was expecting a call from Dr. Chambers. When she asked the secretary about the nature of the meeting she vaguely answered, "I think it concerns a faculty matter." Emily surmised that the Dean wanted to talk about the Byrd situation, but wondered why Chambers did not get in touch with her himself.

Emily went to see Dean Parsons the next day, feeling a little uneasy. She wished Danny was with her for support. She entered the Dean of the College section of the administration building and walked up to a receptionist, a neatly dressed student whom she recognized as Brittany Langdon, because they had both served on the Student Affairs Committee two years ago.

"Hi, Brittany! How are you?"

"I'm fine, Emily. I guess you're here to see the Dean. I'll let him know you're here."

Following a brief phone call, Brittany told Emily to go into the Dean's office. As she entered, Dean Parsons, immediately came up to her and shook her hand.

"Emily, It's so nice to see you again."

Emily was a bit surprised at the Dean's demeanor. He was much more reserved the last time they met. Emily sensed that perhaps it was a little *too* warm, the kind of suspicious salutation that you might get from a used car salesman.

"Have a seat, please."

Emily sat down in one of the high-back leather chairs directly in front of his large desk scattered with a vast array of formal-looking papers, folders, notepads, books, magazines, brochures, and a computer, printer, and fax machine.

"Emily," Dean Parsons began, "I want you to know that I really respect everything you have done for this college. Your record is quite impressive. I think you have served on more committees and performed more community service than any other student in recent years."

"Thank you," Emily replied, still wondering what she was doing here. Surely, she thought, he didn't call me in to compliment me for my extracurricular activities.

"I also want you to know that I think it is a fine thing that you are concerned with the status of Dr. Byrd. I know you may have thought we were giving you the run-around the last time you were here, but this is a very sensitive matter and I'm sure you understand that a faculty member's privacy is very important."

"Of course."

"And the administration would not want to do anything to jeopardize anyone's career, or reputation…."

"Yes."

"Well, what you have been doing, you and Danny, may not be in the interest…you know…the best interest of the college if you and Danny continue to pursue this story. I mean…it may not be the best for everyone, including Professor Byrd."

Emily now knew why Dean Parsons had called her in. He wanted to get her and Danny off the story. She decided she must have touched a nerve somewhere. Though she did not know where this conversation was going, she went with her gut instinct and took the offensive.

"Dean Parsons." She began respectfully, "Danny and I have no intention of hurting or embarrassing anyone in any way. I do not see why we haven't received any straight answers. We have not talked to that many people. We're not exactly conducting a large-scale investigation."

"Well," said Dean Parsons, "I was under the impression that you talked to a number of our professors including Professor Ellis—and I don't think she needs to be troubled by this business. She's trying to run a department."

"I still don't see why we can't get a simple answer. Why didn't Professor Byrd come back? And where is he? That's all we want to know. It's that simple."

Dean Parsons leaned forward, rested his elbows on the desk and put his hands together as if he was about to pray, rubbing them together earnestly as he spoke.

"It is *not* that simple, Emily. I wish it was. But you have to trust me. I want you and Danny to just drop this whole thing. Believe me, it will be the best thing for the college, and for you."

Emily was dumbfounded that the Dean was actually telling her to back off the story. She concluded that they must be on to something for sure.

"I don't understand," she countered, "Who or what could be hurt by finding out about Professor Byrd? Why the big mystery?"

Dean Parsons leaned even closer to Emily and began speaking in a low, hushed confidential voice, like they were being bugged and he didn't want anyone else to hear them.

"Emily," he said quietly, "I want to confide in you. I want you to listen to me and take my advice. Get off this case. It's not worth it."

"Dean Parsons," Emily said sternly, "We are not 'on a case.' We're just a couple of students who are interested in the whereabouts of Professor Byrd."

"I understand Emily. However, if you really care about your college career, you'll just work on graduating in May and everything will be fine."

"Well, I don't see how that is possible."

Dean Parsons sat back and relaxed, appearing to ponder his next move, like a poker player deciding whether or not to bluff.

"Let me just say that there are powerful people in this world Emily, people much more powerful than you or I, and some people would be very upset if your efforts continue.

"Who?"

"I'm not at liberty to divulge that information." Once again, let me say that it would be in yours, and Danny's interest to drop the whole matter."

"Excuse me, but I don't understand how this could be so serious. Why would any of these so-called powerful people be concerned with Dr. Byrd."

"It's more than Dr. Byrd, Emily."

"What?"

"I can't say."

She was getting more and more frustrated. She was also getting more confused and wished Danny was here for moral support.

"Dean Parsons, I want to take your advice, but I'm afraid you're asking me to do something against my principles."

"Not at all!" Dean Parsons exclaimed, "I don't want you to compromise any of your moral or reporting principles. I am just asking you to think about how your actions could hurt other people. It's that simple."

"Pardon me, Dean Parsons, but it's *not* that simple. You won't even tell me who I would hurt."

"I told you—important people—influential people. People who love the college, and the students."

It became obvious to Emily that Dean Parsons was not acting on his own behalf; that he was being instructed by some person, or persons, to put a stop to the inquiry into Byrd's disappearance. She knew she needed to be careful. She didn't want him to know that she was anxious to find out who these "powerful people" were. She decided to call his bluff and see what happened.

"Well, with all due respect," Dean Parsons, "Suppose we don't listen to you and continue this probe."

Dean Parsons' face seemed to lose a pound of air, deflating like a pricked balloon. He frowned for the first time, heaved a labored breath, and let out a huge sigh.

"Emily, let me be perfectly frank. These are powerful people. What I mean is that these are the kind of people you don't want to mess with. You are *bothering* these people and they do not like to be bothered. Is that clear?"

"No," Emily asserted demonstratively, "It's not clear at all. In fact, it sounds like a veiled threat, if you'll pardon the accusation."

"I'm not threatening you, or anybody else. I just meant that if you let this thing die, I will not have to take any action against you or Danny."

"Then you are threatening us! What do you mean by 'action'?"

Dean Parsons leaned back in his chair, continuing to wring his hands together in an agitated manner. He glanced out the window, seeming to look for an answer to his dilemma in the poplar trees surrounding the building.

"Emily….let me put it this way….I cannot allow you to violate the civil liberties of one of our faculty members without some punitive action. You're putting yourself and Danny in a potentially wrongful legal position."

Now the Dean was trying a new tactic, thought Emily. Now she was a dangerous violator of the Constitution of the United States. She was also growing more fearful of the Dean, of these "powerful people" and the whole mess she now found herself in. She felt she needed to talk to Danny to decipher this bizarre conversation.

"Dean Parsons, let me get this straight. If Danny and I do not lay off the Byrd story, we will somehow be punished by the college. Is that correct?"

"In a word, yes."

"Well, I need to think this over. It is very surprising, and frankly I'm amazed you would be so callous toward students' concerns. It's very disappointing, to say the least."

"I understand how you feel, but believe me, Emily, it's for your own good. I am saving you a lot of grief."

"Perhaps. Well, I won't take up any more of your time. I will let you know what Danny and I are going to do in a couple days."

"That will be fine. Don't worry, everything will turn out okay."

Emily almost said 'for whom?' but decided to withhold her sarcasm.

"Thank you for coming, Emily. Have a pleasant day."

Emily left Dean Parsons office and tried to find Danny. She called his room and spoke to Jason, who told her he was hanging out at the union. Emily found him there going over his notes for a course in political parties. She told him what had transpired with Dean Parsons.

"He strongly implied that he would get us thrown out of school."

"What did he say about me?" asked Danny.

"Well, not much, really. He didn't like the fact that you went to see Professor Ellis. He thought you were *bothering* her."

"I didn't bother her."

"I know," said Emily, but he thought you did. It sounds very odd, doesn't it?"

"Powerful people?" Danny muttered to himself. Who could he be talking about? Sounds pretty scary to me....wait a minute! How did he know I went to see Ellis? Did you tell him that?"

"No."

"Did you tell *anybody* I went to see Ellis?

"No, I don't think so."

"I'm sure I didn't tell anybody. How could he know?"

"I guess Ellis told him herself."

"Maybe...said Danny, "But she didn't seem the type to bring up my visit with the Dean. I got the feeling she would try to keep my visit a secret."

Emily paused for a second and took a sip of Danny's Coke.

"Wait a second. I did tell someone."

"Who?"

"Dr. Chambers."

"You did?"

"Yes," replied Emily, "I remember saying that you went to see Professor Ellis in the theatre and she wouldn't give you any information."

"Maybe Dr. Chambers did tell the Dean. Hell, maybe it's Chambers behind this whole thing. He's certainly a powerful and influential person. I don't see any other possibility unless it really was Ellis who told him."

"Why don't we just ask Ellis? She'd have no reason to lie."

"Ellis wouldn't give us the time of day."

"Why would Dr. Chambers want us to stop our investigation?" asked Emily "He seems straightforward and fair-minded. I don't get it."

"Let's face it, honey," said Danny, "Nobody has been straight with us yet. It could be Chambers as well as anybody. I'm not sure where we go from here. We can try to talk to Ellis, and—wait! We can talk to Jody Hershberger. She might be able to help us. After all, he's her uncle."

"He's supposed to get back in touch with me soon," said Emily, "We need to find out right away whether or not he is on our side."

"I'll go by Ellis' office tomorrow," said Danny. "Why don't you talk to Jody. By tomorrow we should know something. In the meantime, if Dr. Chambers gets in touch with you, stall him and re-schedule the meeting until we can figure out what's going on."

"Sounds good….Danny?"

"Yes."

"Are we in over our heads? Maybe we should bring someone else into this."

"We're okay. Besides, we don't know who to trust, anyway."

Emily loved her apartment. It was a place where she could relax and be by herself. It was a warm, cozy basement apartment in an old Victorian home owned by Mrs. Rogers, a widower who lived alone upstairs. Both Mrs. Rogers and Emily were both quiet, neat, and private people. Emily was in her living room reading an assignment for modern philosophy, getting bogged down in the syntax of Bertrand Russell. It was early evening and Danny was due in about an hour. Restless, she went over to her work area and began absentmindedly cleaning off her desk, sorting out papers, tossing old notes and receipts into the trash. She was going through some of her old notes on the disappearance of Professor Byrd, trying, once again, to piece together some explanation, or find a clue somewhere in her papers. She looked through the notes taken with her interesting interview with Dr. Mason and contacting MG. She laughed to herself to think MG could be so close to picking Danny's birthday, but so far off on the restaurant question. Glancing down she tried to remember what MG had "said." Rummaging through a series random notes, she came upon the cryptic letters from several months ago: "D," "A," "N," "S," "C," "O," "K," "P," "R," "O," "B." She stared, mesmerized by the letters. Like trying to speak awkwardly in a foreign language, Emily sounded out the words slowly: "Dan's…cok………probe……Dan's…… coke…………prob….ably……………Dan's………cook………probate…….. Dan's coke…….prob……lem." Her eyes riveted to the letters. She slumped back into her couch, dumbfounded by her possible finding. She was sick to her stomach and went into the kitchen for a glass of water. Perhaps, she thought, she was overreacting. It doesn't *have* to mean that, of course, she reasoned, but something deep inside made her suspicious that MG was on to something, and Danny was hiding a big secret from her.

Emily went into the kitchen, poured herself a glass of Chardonnay, and returned to the living room to wait for Danny. She knew she had to be careful because MG could certainly have meant something else and she didn't want Danny to think she did not trust him. She hoped she was wrong, but she had the nagging feeling that Danny may have kept a drug problem from her. Maybe it was the reluctance to reveal much about his past, or the fact that he seemed so troubled by things. She could imagine him taking out his anxiety through the use of drugs, or maybe it was his attitude about life, his I-don't-give-a-shit attitude that came through when he was despondent about something. Or, it could just be her own vivid imagination and paranoia. Time seemed to stand still as Emily waited for Danny to arrive. She finished the glass of wine and got another one, wondering how to approach this very touchy subject.

The mountains in the wintertime had a stern and austere quality, haunted with desolation, and the savage sky of wild, torn gray came in so low that its scudding fringes whipped like rags of smoke around the mountain tops of the Blue Ridge. The fierce sky of wintry gray combined with a maniacal wind increased the feeling of isolation and barrenness in the region. The great trees in the distance rose with grim determination; snowcapped, barren, leafless and storm-tossed. The road leading to Emily Patterson's apartment was frost-hardened and rutted as Danny eased his Jetta into the parking spot. Shutting off the car and opening the door, the grim frozen tenacity of winter clung to Danny like an ice blanket as he walked from his car to Emily's apartment. A howling Northeastern wind cut through his body as he covered his head with his parka and wrapped his arms around himself, fighting the blustery weather and the mad-fiend voice of winter. The sidewalk leading to her apartment was ultra-slick from a thin layer of sleet which had fallen throughout the day. Danny was relieved when Emily opened the door and lead him into her apartment.

"Damn, it's cold out there," Danny exclaimed, still rubbing his hands together to revive his circulation.

"I think it's about fifteen degrees," said Emily. "How about something to drink?"

"Got any wine?"

"Chardonnay, okay?"

"Terrific. What have you been doing?" asked Danny as he sat down on the couch next to her.

"Oh, I was studying Bertrand Russell, but I got kinda lost. I just can't seem to be philosophical tonight."

"I have trouble doing that every night," said Danny. "What do you want to do?"

"Emily didn't say anything. She stood up and walked over to her desk, glancing down at the assortment of papers strewn over the top.

"Danny, I want you to look at something."

Danny walked over to the desk and looked down at the scattered papers. "What do you have here? Something on Byrd?"

"Well, I wanted you to look at something I never showed you because it didn't make any sense to me, but now I think that it might mean something, but I'm not sure."

"What is it?"

"It's a message that was given to me by Dr. Mason. You know, his contact, the Indian, MG."

"What does it say?"

"Well, look for yourself."

Emily pulled out her notes with the letters spelling out "dans cok prob" and showed it to him.

At first Danny had no idea what the letters could mean, but within a few seconds he knew that MG was well aware of him—and his past. Danny didn't say anything for what seemed an eternity to Emily.

"It says "Dan's coke problem. The spelling is terrible, but that's the message."

"I assume its not Coca Cola."

"No."

Emily gripped her wine glass so tightly that it almost exploded in her hand. She glared at Danny with penetrating look Danny had never seen. Anger rose up from deep within her, and she fought to keep her composure.

"Christ, Danny, how long have you been doing cocaine?"

"I'm not doing coke—not now—it's in my past," Danny stammered. "I haven't done drugs in over four years."

"Damn it! Don't you think that was something you might have mentioned to me before? Now that we're on the subject is there any other surprises I don't know about?"

"I did time. They gave me two years for dealing cocaine. That's where I got my first two years of college—in jail. I'm sorry, I should have told you, but I was afraid you'd leave me."

"Oh, and keeping secrets from somebody is supposed to make them want to be around you? That was a shitty thing to do. I trusted you." Enraged, Emily took her wine glass and hurled it into the fireplace, shattering the crystal glass into a hundred pieces.

"I'm sorry, really! Don't get upset—"

"Don't get upset? I am *very* upset. I can't even think right."

"I never go near the stuff any more. I love you and I don't want to mess up what we have now."

"You're doing a pretty damn good job."

"Emily, please. I had a problem, but its gone. Its in my past—before I met you."

"Why didn't you tell me?"

"I thought you would not go out with a former coke-head. I thought you'd dump me."

"Well, now the thought has certainly entered my mind."

"Please, Emily. Give me one more chance. I swear I'll never do drugs again, or lie to you about anything. I'm really sorry."

"I can't believe you didn't tell me about this. You hid drug use and two years of your life from me. I need time to think about this."

"Do you want me to leave?"

"Yes."

Danny reluctantly went to the closet and retrieved his coat. He knew that there was not much more to say, and talking about it now would probably make it worse. He slowly put on his coat and braced himself for an exit into the cold night. As he stood in Emily's doorway, he paused before leaving. Right now, he wished he could turn back the clock to a day last semester when he had many opportunities to tell Emily all about his past. Opening the door to a frozen blast of wintry wind, Danny said, "I'm sorry, Emily, really."

"Good night, Danny."

MARCH MADNESS: MARCH 3-14

"So, Where are you going Spring Break?"
  "You asked me that five minutes ago."
  "So?"
  "I told you—Florida."
  "Where in Florida?"
  "Miami. I think."
  "Whatever."
  "What's in Miami?"
  "The beach. Gorgeous guys. What else?"
  "My body's not ready for public display."
  "God, I'm fat."
  "I think my grandmother lives somewhere in Florida."
  "This lunch sucks."
  "So does my body."
  "Is that Jody Hershberger?"
  "Who cares?"
  "She can't act."
  "I heard she went out with Chad Dutton."
  "Chad Dutton is gay."
  "No way!"
  "Really. He slept with Franklin Bosserman."
  "We're gonna have so much fun."
  "Where?"
  "Spring Break."
  "Can we talk about something else?"
  "Does anybody know a diet that works?"
  "My boyfriend wants to come with me."
  "Where?"
  "To Panama City."
  "No Way!"
  "What did you tell him?"
  "I wanted to be with the girls."
  "That's a laugh!"
  "I need a bathing suit."
  "I need a body."
  "I need to lose ten pounds."

"I was thin once."

"Get the fuck."

"Franklin Bosserman is gay?"

"I've got some diet pills."

"We're gonna have so much fun."

"Where?"

"Spring Break."

"There's vomit girl!"

"I thought she died."

"Where's she going Spring Break?"

"I heard she's going to model in New York."

"Does Ritalin make you lose weight?"

"Two piece or one piece?"

"Yeah, this lunch sucks."

"Piece of what?"

"My bathing suit."

"My thighs are…"

"Where are you going Spring Break?"

"…Too big…"

"We're gonna have a blast."

"Where?"

"What about my tattoo?"

"That hideous thing on your back?"

"Don't wear a bathing suit."

"Maybe I can have it removed."

"I can't wait to show off my belly button ring."

"I'd rather die than try on a bathing suit—

"When does Spring Break start?"

"Where are you going?"

"Florida."

"Ohmygod, there's Constance Bellamy."

"Speaking of fat."

"She hates us."

"I hate her."

"She said she liked the print on my sofa."

"Bitch."

"It's painful."

"What?"

"Tattoo removal."
"Isn't that Amy Toeffler?"
"I hate her."
"She gave Franklin Bosserman a blow job in his Range Rover."
"I thought he was gay."
"How much does a Range Rover cost?"
"He must be bi."
"Let's go shopping."
"God, what for?"
"A bathing suit."
"Can I lose twenty pounds first?"
"Come on, let's go."
"Okay, but I want dessert."

HERPES!
GONORRHEA!
CHLAMYDIA!
AIDS!

A hoard of sweaty wingnuts were shouting different diseases in my ear, giving me a major headache, until I spotted Wade Lowinsky hitting on a cheesy freshman in an okay-looking fuck-me mini-shirt. She had too-small tits, but Wade was staring down her blouse anyway. Moving through a myriad of drunken bodies dressed in drab-green hospital gowns with stethoscopes dangling stupidly around their necks, I worked my way toward Wade (who looked like Jason Sparrow, but not as cute). I was about to move in for the kill (no pun intended) when this total dork intern wannabe barges into my face, carrying a bed pan filled with purple Kool-Aid mixed with grain alcohol.

"Hey, Red!" *he blurted,* "Have some punch!" It will kill your herpes!"
"Thanks," *I said, taking a sip,* "…but don't call me Red, okay?"

This stupid-as-shit guy really threw my game off for some reason and I decided to retreat somewhere to collect my thoughts. I weaved my way through the wasted throng of medical animals, thrusting my boobs out, hoping to catch some hot guy's attention. I finally located a mirror next to a ripped poster of the Dallas Cowboy cheerleaders. I noticed one of the cheerleaders died her hair the same color as me, but it didn't bother me. After checking out my lipstick which was smeared to hell, I carefully blotted my luscious red lips with a tissue from my pocketbook. Soon, they returned to perfection. Thank goodness I didn't go up to Chad looking like a stupid-as-shit clown with bad makeup.

I looked in the mirror and adjusted the "I have herpes" badge on my sweater. How ironic. Herpes? Hell, herpes is child's play compared to what I have. I turned away from the mirror, then glanced back over my shoulder to see if I missed a flaw in my appearance. I didn't.

I hated the idea of fighting the crowd, but I had no choice. Spring Fling always brings out all the library losers who don't know shit about partying. Bumping and shoving my way across the room, I suddenly felt someone putting their hand on my left breast. I jerked the hand away from me, whirling around, hoping it would be Chad, but unfortunately I was facing a yuppie-looking guy with neat hair, very white teeth, and an "I have AIDS" button on the lapel of his hospital gown.

"HEY!" He yelled in my ear, *Where are you going?"*
I smacked him across the face as hard as I could.
"It's none of your business, asshole!" *I screamed.*

He clutched his face for a second, then gave me a smirky look.

"Oh, a feisty redhead!! I like those!!!"

Gee, this guy is really original. I wonder how many times I've been called a feisty redhead. I glared at him.

"Fuck off, okay."

"Hey! Don't go away mad! Let me tell you a joke."

This is why I hate men. They always get on my nerves.

"Are you always an asshole, or is this just a part-time job?"

Wingnut ignored my question. I should ask him if he wants to be dead in six months.

"How do doctors tell the difference between new-born babies?" *he persisted.*

"What? Is this a joke?"

"Yeah, it's a joke. Come on, don't be so stuck up. You got a stick up your ass, or something?"

This guy may have been getting on my nerves, but he's kinda cute in a preppy way, and besides, he was paying major attention to me. I love playing the bitch game, knowing I can still get the guy, no matter how awful I act. I decided to flirt with him for another minute. Chad must be wondering where I am by now.

"I'm not stuck up," *I lied.* "I just don't like your manners. You're rude."

"Sorry," *he said, apologetically,*….well…."

"Well what?"

"You know…the joke."

"Oh, I don't know. How do they tell the difference?"

He paused dramatically.

"Well, the doctor takes them out, turns them upside down, and slaps them on the ass. The one's whose dicks fall off are the dumb ones."

"YOU'RE A FUCKIN' ASSHOLE!!!," *I screamed.*

I ran past the asshole, barging into assorted "medical students." I mean, what did I expect from a theme party. I hate theme parties. When we came in everybody got a "disease" button to wear, and we had to go to the appropriate "doctor" for a "cure." Of course, the "cure" turned out to be some ass-kicking drink made with pure grain alcohol or 80 proof rum. We were not allowed out of the "hospital" until we had sampled several health stations and pronounced healthy enough to go upstairs where the party was really happening. All of this bullshit from supposedly normal college students. It was dumb as shit, but it did give me a chance to circulate and hang out with guys who wanted to sleep with me. Every since I was twelve years old, I never met a man who didn't want to sleep with me.

In the midst of watching a fraternity geek being turned upside down while sucking beer from a keg, I spotted Georgie Spajek, whose hips are too large for her skirt, trying to pick up a football-looking guy.

"Hi, Georgie," *I said,* "Have you seen Chad Dutton? He asked me to meet him here."

Georgie looked mildly annoyed, as if I was interested in her steroid gorilla piece of meat.

"No, Jody. I haven't seen him. Maybe he's gone upstairs already."

"Oh, maybe he has. Thanks."

All of a sudden, I began to feel ill and slightly dizzy. Maybe I shouldn't try to pick up Chad tonight. Maybe I'll just let him live, although I can't think of any reason why Chad should be allowed to live. He's the biggest trash dick on campus. Hoping to avoid embarrassment, I moved cautiously toward the rear exit, feeling wobbly and disoriented, I needed some fresh air.

As I walked toward the door, I inhaled a sickening sweet odor causing me to feel nauseous. Where was that vile stench coming from? What is that? Toxic sludge? Is vomit girl around here? In my delirium, I wondered how much weight I would lose if I threw up. Forcing my way through the crowd I lurched out the doorway onto the porch. I noticed a beat up brown couch in the corner. As I made my way toward the couch, I began losing consciousness.

Before I passed out I remember wondering if I had ever fucked anybody on a brown couch.

And yet, I did not completely lose consciousness; I slipped into the throes of a night-time fit, that terrible mid-point between wakefulness and sleep, my body moving restlessly on the couch, momentarily aroused to reality by a slight sound on the porch, students mumbling in the background, whispering, "What up with her? Is she dead? Who cares?" *Was the wind howling in the night, or is that the sound of my heart beating? It must be the wind blowing through the trees, causing the Chinese chimes to ring in my ears and puncture my mind. I tossed to one side, hoping a change in position would grant me needed sleep, a respite from the agony of the night-time sweats. Perhaps, I should get up and go back to the party. Maybe I need a strong drink. But the thought of getting up made me nauseous and I didn't like the idea of any light penetrating the blackness of the night. I heard the muffled sounds of Madonna emanating from a car driving near the house...was it an old one?* "...We are living in a material world..." *Maybe I heard nothing, or maybe it was a delivery truck. I couldn't be sure. I did hear the monotonous, persistent sound of a loose window shutter clanking against the side of the house, creating a tedious drum beat in the night. Beat...beat...beat...down the bumpy stairs. Thump. And thump again. Was I dreaming? I tried to sit up on the couch, but my feet were immobile and numb. My mind told my body to move, but body said no way. I was stuck as shit.*

Then, just my luck, Dracula came to suck the blood out of me and transform me into a vampire. At least I thought it was the Prince of Darkness. Or maybe not. I felt hands crawling over me, feeling me in very weird places. The fingers moved gently, but steadily up my thigh toward my genital area. I'm not sure what is happening, but I distinctly feel a body begin to come into my space. For some reason, I know it is a male; it smells animalistic, primitive, like a hungry tiger stalking its prey in the jungle. Is it Jason? Has he come for me? Dreadful thoughts race across my mind like I'm also being attacked by vampires, or werewolves, or maybe one of those crazy serial killers on the loose these days. Wasn't there a horrible mutilation or gruesome kidnapping of a young girl somewhere, some place tonight? The body who is moving over me is, I think, unloosing my bra strap, and massaging my breasts. I tried to open my eyes, but they are sealed shut, so I moved my hand to feel his face, but It's like I'm made of rubber. Is that you, Jason? The porch suddenly changed form and the screens surrounding the porch faded away and were replaced by a large white screen. Grotesque creatures flashed before me, mutated images writhing and squealing in agonizing unison. I think, maybe, a horror show was playing. Halloween? Michael Myers? Who was sucking on my left tit and kissing me rudely on the lips with just a little too much force? Was it Jason, or a phony substitute? Jason, you don't have to force me. I want you...

I vaguely saw an old medieval castle shrouded in fog, perched precariously at the edge of a steep, jagged cliff overlooking a pounding ocean spewing waves onto the rocks below. I heard the high-pitched whiny sounds of bloody bats flying about and I saw the silhouette of a lone wolf baying at the moon....or maybe it was this man on top of me whom I still did not know, but he was taking off my skirt, loosening the black leather belt with the gold loops, jerking the belt from my waist with brute force. This guy was strong. Why doesn't he wake me up? A rickety horse-drawn carriage clamored up the cobblestone lane toward the castle. The driver was dressed in a dark brown raincoat; a large brimmed hat shielded his eyes and identity. He slapped vigorously at the reins and commanded the horses to yield—like I want this person—Jason—(???) who is on top of me now removing my Victoria Secret black lace panties, and clutching my crotch, rubbing his hands around and around my pussy, like I'm supposed to be excited? Where is everyone? Why don't they come and put a stop to this? Maybe it is Jason, though. From the carriage the small gaunt man dressed in a black waist coat, stepped down, carrying a cylindrical object. He took the object and put it to his mouth and began playing an eerie tune I did not recognize. Was it coming from the party? Is the party still going on? He stood stone-like on the steps of the castle, as the mysterious driver drove away. No one appeared at the door to let the stranger in, but to my hor-

ror, a chorus of hideous rats stormed out of the castle from all directions. At the same time I could feel the stranger on top of me breathing heavily. He put his face very close to my left ear and began murmuring in a soft voice, "Jody, I want you so bad, I can't stand it." I could feel his face press against mine and I could smell his aftershave, he was so close. I think he was a Halston man. I think it was Jason. The rats continued to storm out of the castle by the hundreds, perhaps thousands, trying to find the source of the song—the man in the black waist coat. The traveling troubadour assembled all the rats in the front courtyard of the castle. He didn't seem particularly distressed at the notion of being surrounded by a multitude of dangerous looking vermin. In fact, the rats were remarkably calm and businesslike. "I love you, Jody. I want your body so bad. Give it to me…Give it to me." The repulsive rats formed a neat, military line, apparently waiting instructions from their leader. God, what a loathsome sight. And I tried to get my bearings and wake up from this nightmare, but I couldn't regain consciousness. Did somebody put something in my drink? I bet it was that creepy yuppie with the bad joke. I struggled to get this dude, or Jason, off me because I wanted to know who was fucking me without my permission. If it was Jason, I wanted him to stop because I think I am in love with Jason and I want him to live. But I don't like the attack mode of this dude, anyway.

But I do not come out of this nightmare and I'm transported back into the dream from hell where I peer closely at the crowd of rats and it seems as if each one has a name tattooed or printed on their backs, but I can make out the names, but it seems each rat bears the name of a person, like a dog tag on a soldier. I looked, and the rats are very composed, even stoic, just hangin' out at the courtyard, like teenagers at the mall with nothing to do.

Suddenly the wind began to pick up, but I can't tell if it's the winds of Cannonville or the winds inside my dream. As trees rustle gently in the breeze, the rats lift their pointy noses to sniff the air; their heads turning slowly back and forth, waving in concert with syncopated rhythms of wind, trees and leaves swirling and free falling in a ballet of nature's movement. It was a sprightly, crisp wind and I couldn't help but notice a peculiar odor coming from the screen. I couldn't be sure, but I swear it was sweet-smelling, like maple syrup. And the strange man with the flute and black waist coat began playing a different tune, a smooth melodic entrancing solo which somehow induced a macabre dance of rats, as they swayed to and fro in the gentle, sugary wind. And the sound of the flute and the wind combined to form a fairly pleasant mood among the rats, and indeed, they seemed harmless enough. I almost forgot that I was in a nightmare and being raped—or was I?

I tried to gauge my senses which were completely disoriented. I tried again to open my eyes and move my body. I got half a lid open and tried to focus on the body on top of me. He was not very heavy, really, but he was all hands, feeling me everywhere, and I concentrated enough to know that his hands were inside me now. He is sticking his fingers inside my vagina and trying to locate my clitoris, I think. I tried to move a little, to get some leverage, but he's much stronger than me, and I can't really do anything about this. He's sucking on my right boob, while he feels me up all over, then finds my vagina again and starts finger-fucking harder and harder and rubbing his face against my tits and then he finds my ass and rubs that in a circular motion, finding my anus and finger-fucking my ass with one hand while rubbing my pussy with the other. I tried again to open my eyes, but everything is just a blur…and then…I begin…to lose…it…once… more…

…and suddenly the whole mood of the room/nightmare changes. The flutist changed his tune to a rousing, marching song, like the fife and drum corps in the Revolutionary War painting and he began moving from out of the courtyard, down a narrow dirt path along a row of hedges. The rats followed him in mechanical fashion, just like in the fairy tale. Maybe he was a good person ridding the castle of all the rats and vermin. Maybe not. I guess this trail is going to lead down to a river where the obedient rats will march and drown themselves and the dream would be over. But instead, the rats were lead to a series of warehouse-like buildings, all marked with specific, but strange names, like Flea-Market, Dog Pound, and Blood and Guts. And the rats began to move inside the buildings, instinctively knowing which house to enter. The Pied Piper waited until all the rats were inside, then sat down on a tree stump, playing another tune, this one sounding like a funeral dirge, a lament for lost souls.

Then the Piper turned to me and the nightmare and the reality of being raped began to merge even more together until the Piper faded completely and I could feel myself coming out of the dream. The man on top of me was more distinct. I was beginning to regain my senses enough to see that he had dark hair, like Jason, and fine, straight teeth, like Jason, but I couldn't be sure. The man on top of me began to get more violent. He pried open my legs and jumped directly on top of me, smothering me for a second. It was hard to breathe and I told him to stop, at least I tried to tell him to stop, but it was no use. My legs were powerless to prevent him from entering me with his penis which was very large and, of course, painful as he thrust and thrust inside me while he took his hands and covered my mouth as I tried to yell for somebody to help me. NO!! NO!!! NO!!! I screamed, but he held my mouth tight—so I bit his hand and then he slapped me across the face and called me something—bitch???—I couldn't tell because I was so fucked up and I hope this is not Jason because I can't believe he would do this to me—or would he? I mean, do I really know him? Then the bastard punched me hard in the face and I passed out momentarily…but I was awakened shortly by his voice saying something to me like, "Move, motherfucker!!"—and I didn't know what to do, so I tried once again to scream, but I quickly felt the hand slap me again, so I decided just to give up because I thought he was going to kill me for sure.

Traffic was heavier than usual on the way to downtown Cannonville, as Danny maneuvered the Jetta into the left lane, and gunned the engine to escape a slow moving Federal Express truck.. He was going to see Mr. Jones.

Danny had called Emily many times over the last month, but she was clearly not in the mood to talk to him. She said she needed time to think about their relationship. Meanwhile, Danny was sending her a red rose every day and sent her a note apologizing once more for not telling her about his past. Valentine's Day came and went without the two lovers making up. He knew he should have told her right away, but the years of doing drugs surreptitiously and hiding so much about his life from every one was a hard habit to break. Among the many problems drugs posed for Danny was the fact that you had to keep so much to yourself, never revealing any bit of information that might be used against you at a later date. It was part of the regime of the drug culture. Never tell anyone more than they needed to know. A friend here now could be testifying against you tomorrow, so you had to cover your tracks, so the least said the better. No last names. No addresses. No home phones. The fewer details about your life, the better. It was a obligatory part of the scene and Danny survived in this environment by keeping the world at bay. He built a solid emotional and psychological fortress around him and created an identity necessary to survive the continuous risks, paranoia, back-stabbing and violence imbedded in his drug lifestyle and prison experience. Without using guile, dishonesty, false identity, razor-sharp cunning, and a hustler's shrewdness, Danny Alderman would have been eaten alive in this world. The transition back to a normal existence was not just a matter of giving up friends like Frankie Beauchamp, but it meant changing his whole outlook on life, and above all, trusting people. In Danny's previous world, self-disclosure was tantamount to disaster because it meant you were weak; any display of emotions, feelings and insecurities could get you in real trouble. Danny had no trouble playing the tough street guy, but now that he was back in the legitimate world those traits were revealed for what they were—a phony, hyped-up masculinity created to obscure a false sense of security. All that, of course, backfired in his face. No street-smarts in the world was going to work in getting his girlfriend back. The very skills he mastered for so long in his drug society were coming back to haunt him in a very serious manner. She wanted no part of the old Danny, and even though it was true that Danny wanted to escape his past, the steady behavior modification of living in a seedy underworld weighed on Danny's being like the ghosts of dead ancestors. Danny was determined to change and he knew that he needed Emily to make the transition. At this point, however, he could only wait and hope she would get in touch with him.

Traffic had slowed down considerably as Danny turned left on Beverley Street and headed south on Coalter Road. The cold spell of the last few days had abated and the valley was experiencing an early March warming trend. Parking his car in the usual parking lot of the correctional center, Danny made his way into the office of Mr. Jones. As he entered the office, he found his probation officer standing by the window, watering his plants.

"Good morning. I never thought of you as a plant enthusiast."

"Well, that goes to show what you know—which isn't much." Mr. Jones turned toward Danny and placed the watering can on a shelf by the window. "How's everything?"

"I came to say you were right. Now you can say 'I told you so.'"

"About what?"

"Emily. She found out."

"And now you're out in the cold, so to speak."

"I'm in Siberia."

"Is she speaking to you?"

"No, not really. She said she may call me, but I'm not holding my breath."

"That's too bad. I assume you've apologized."

"About a hundred times. I'm sending her a red rose everyday."

"Good idea. A little expensive, but a good idea."

"That's what a grandfather's trust fund will do for you."

"How's everything else?"

Danny gave him an update on the Byrd mystery, his school work, and more about his relationship with Emily. His old dealing buddy, Frankie Beauchamp did not come back from Florida, but he did call Danny last week and asked him to drive to Florida over Spring Break to play some golf and escape the inclement Virginia weather. Danny was tempted, but declined the offer. He knew it would only lead to more trouble. Besides, he needed special permission to leave the state and he didn't think Mr. Jones was in the mood to give him permission to visit Frankie Beauchamp.

"What about your visit to the high school?"

"I don't know what they thought about me," said Danny. "I tried to tell them how easy it is to go in the wrong direction. It's like one day you're sneaking a cigarette in the back yard and the next day you're snorting white powder up your nose.

"Did they ask you any questions?"

"A few. I think they were surprised that I was so straight looking."

"What do you mean?"

"I don't know….I think they have this image of a drug addict as someone hovering in a burned out inner city alley, sticking a dirty needle in his arm."

"They're suburban kids. That's not surprising."

"Yeah," said Danny, "I think they thought that—hey, he probably came from the same background as me. Maybe he knows what he's talking about."

"Did they ask you about yourself?"

"Yes. They were curious about how I got started. I talked for a long time about myself. In fact, I told them things I haven't told anyone. It's easier for me to talk about myself in front of a group of complete strangers than any of my friends or relatives—and, of course, Emily. Anyway, I told them what it was like growing up in an upper-middle class family that was normal, but pretty uptight. I told them that it was hard to relax around my parents and my two brothers and sister. I mean…I've told you this before. I was the fourth one to come along and my brothers and sister were a hard act to follow. Dad was the dean at Winton College and I grew up in an extremely bright family."

"You're bright, too."

"Hey! My dad got a perfect score on the English section of the SAT's. A perfect score! I couldn't beat that if I tried. I get along with my older brothers, but they were more like my dad. James is now a Professor of Religion at Drake University and William is studying artificial intelligence in a think tank outside of Charlottesville. See what I mean? It was just like….what the hell can I do? My sister Jane is working on a Ph.D. in history at Wake Forest in North Carolina. I really don't have an aptitude for advanced scholastic work.

"I told those kids that when you're under pressure and you feel you may not be the best at something like sports, school, having good looks, or whatever—just don't let it get you down. And the answer doesn't lie in drugs. Certain drugs—like cocaine—make you feel that you are on top of the world, but it's a false sense of well being because you always crash, plus it can ruin your life if you get busted. Look at me, for God's sake."

"Danny," said Mr. Jones sympathetically, "You haven't ruined your life. You're just starting your comeback."

"Well, I told them that in a way. I told them that no matter how things get, they can overcome it. It was kind of a pep talk, but I don't know if I got through to them."

"Don't worry," said Mr. Jones, "You're not going to change too many kids by giving them a speech. Maybe you can get through to one or two. In this business, you look for little victories. We lose most of the troubled kids to drugs and street crime."

"I know. I'm not exactly Mr. Motivational. But I enjoyed talking to them. I may not know much about religion or artificial intelligence, but I know all about the drug culture. I was a full-time member."

"I thought you would do a good job. You underestimate yourself."

"Poor self image?"

"I told you, I'm not a psychiatrist. I think you tried too hard to live in the footsteps of your siblings and when you found out you were not like them, you rebelled in the opposite direction. Let's just say you overreacted."

"That's a good way to put it. I overreacted. I guess I was jealous of them, really."

"Maybe so, but you're making a good comeback. You'll do okay. It's not too late."

"Hey! I'll have a diploma in a couple months. Who would have guessed that four years ago?"

"Not me—that's for sure," said Mr. Jones. "Anything else?"

"Yes, there is one thing. I'm going back to the high school. The guidance counselor and I are going to work out a program for the rest of the year.

"Good going. Keep this up and you may even be a law abiding citizen some day."

"Don't laugh. It could happen."

"I hope Emily calls."

"Thanks."

Danny drove back to his apartment, wanting to check his answer machine before attending his American Presidents class. As he came into his apartment, he went straight to the machine, but no one had called.

Momentarily, Jason emerged from the bedroom, looking haggard and hung over.

"Jesus, you look like sin dipped in misery."

"Ouch…my hair hurts."

"Morning after the night before?"

Danny turned on CNN and there was more news about the O. J. Simpson trial which was currently mesmerizing the nation. Jason went over to the coffee pot and began brewing his morning coffee.

"So, lover, boy. Where'd you go last night?"

"You're not going to believe it. I went to Spring Fling at Phi Delt. It was wild. They had a medical theme. When you walked in they gave you a disease like herpes or gonorrhea and you had to get well by getting your medicine from a doctor. Of course, the medicine was pure grain and Kool-Aid."

"Jesus, I can't drink that stuff."

"Tell me about it, 'O wise one. Guess who was there?"

"Who?"

"Jody Hershberger."

"Uh oh, so you hooked up."

"You're not going to believe it."

"What?"

"I get to the party, right. It's real late, around two o'clock. Stuart Lemon comes up to me and asks me if I know some crazy chick named Jody Hershberger. I say, yes, in fact I am going to ask her out. He looks at me like I'm completely out of my mind. So I say Stuart, what's up? He tells me that Jody came to the party looking for some dude named Chad and Chad never showed up, so she starting hitting on guys and asking them if they would like a rendezvous with a princess on the back porch. Well, it seems my dream date gang-banged five guys before I came to the party."

"You gonna be kidding, like one right after the other?"

"I talked to Everett Barnes, who was one of the guys. He was still at the party, bragging about his adventures with the psycho gang-banger."

"Why did he say she was psycho?"

"Get this. Everett is the second one in line at the time and some dude he didn't know gets finished, so Everett jumps on top of Jody and starts fucking her brains out. Guess what she says to him after he fucks her?"

"What?"

"I love you, Jason."

"What?"

"Yeah, in fact every guy who fucked her said the same thing. She would tell them she was a princess, call each of them Jason, then screw their brains out."

"Do you think she was talking about you?"

"I know she was."

"How do you know?"

"Everett said before he left her that she was mumbling something about two sparrows sharing their love for one another and flying away together. I don't get it. Why you? You've never even gone out with her."

"Beats the shit outta me. I think it's weird that some chick is calling my name while she's gang-banging five guys. It's *really* weird. I wasn't even there to partake in the goodies."

"If you say so…"

"Don't worry, old roomy, Jason is not *that* stupid. I'm not going anywhere near that girl. She's probably got AIDS by now."

"No, shit…I'm amazed. She seems like such a nice girl."

"I think she has problems you and I haven't even thought about."

Suddenly, the phone rang. Danny went over and picked it up.

"Danny?"

Danny's heart jumped three beats. It was Emily.

"Oh, hi. How's it going?

"Great. How are you?"

"Good…good."

"Listen, I was wondering if you would like to hear a folk singer playing in the union tonight. He does a lot of Dylan…and I thought you might be interested."

"Sure. What time?"

"I'll meet you there at 8 o'clock, okay?"

"Sure."

"Bye Danny."

"Bye."

"Who was that?" asked Jason.

"It was Emily. She wants to see me."

Danny was more than a bit anxious about his meeting with Emily. He did not know what to expect, but he took some cold comfort in the fact that she called. He spotted Emily right away in their favorite booth by the pool tables. Well, that's a good sign, he reasoned. She picked our old booth. Maybe there's hope for me yet.

"Hi"

"Hi, Danny, good to see you."

"It's good to see you, too. Seems like a long time."

She appeared relaxed and glad to see him. She was sipping a glass of red wine.

"Hey, that looks like a good idea. Merlot?"

"Yes, Californian. Remember we had some at Professor Wilson's house?"

"Same stuff?"

"Yes."

Danny looked toward the stage area and the folk singer was just beginning to set up. He looked a bit older than the last performer, but he was dressed similarly in black jeans, a red plaid shirt, brown corduroy vest, and cowboy boots. Although the stage was dimly lit, he was sporting a pair of sunglasses. Danny felt he should try once more to explain himself.

"Emily, I'm glad you called. You know I've been wanting to talk to you."

"The same here."

"I just want to know that I'm very sorry—"

"Listen, Danny," Emily suddenly interrupted, "I don't want you to say you're sorry. You've already done that, and I don't think you will be doing that sort of thing again. I didn't ask you here to put you through some kind of religious absolution."

The waitress came over to the booth and Danny ordered a glass of wine for himself and another one for Emily.

"Okay, why did you ask me here?"

"I've been thinking about what you did and whether I could—or should—forgive you. But then I thought about my own self. I tried to be honest and ask myself if I was entirely honest with you, and I wasn't."

"What do you mean?"

"Well, I may look like goodie-two-shoes, but I wasn't exactly a paragon of virtue in high school. I smoked pot, for one thing—more than once—and I *did* inhale."

"That's hardly up there with dealing cocaine."

"That's not the point. I didn't tell you. There's probably a lot of things I didn't tell you. I realized you can't be totally honest with someone even if you tried."

The folk singer began his first number and, indeed, it was a Bob Dylan song from the *Blood on the Tracks* album called "You're a Big Girl Now."

"What about us?" asked Danny, "I want us to get back together. I want to put this fight behind us and move on as couple. We had too much to throw away."

"That's the same conclusion I arrived at," said Emily. "After the initial hurt, I realized that you really did do it because you were afraid of losing me. I know you love me and that's enough for me."

"Me too. Have we officially made up?"

"Yes, except I have one request."

"What?"

"Stop sending me a red rose every day. You'll be broke in two weeks."

Jody, Chad and Franklin had it all planned. They would travel to Panama City, Florida over Spring Break in Franklin's Range Rover. They figured they could make the trip in 18 hours, sharing expenses. Franklin said he knew a buddy of his that could put them up in his apartment for a week. Jody was anxious to get away from her two roommates and relished the thought of partying at the beach, catching some "rays," checking out MTV's beach party, and all the hot, hardbody guys who descended on the Florida beaches every spring. Franklin also asked Chad Dutton to come along to help out with expenses. Jody had no idea Chad was coming when she told Franklin that she would go. She remembered seeing Chad at a few parties and was attracted to him and she wondered vaguely if they had ever hooked up. She knew she supposed to meet him at a party once, but had gotten too drunk to keep the date. She hoped Chad was not mad at her for not showing up. Chad was surprised to find out Jody Hershberger was coming along. He had never met her, but heard that she was a good actress. Chad was supposed to go to New York for Spring Break to be with his boyfriend James who was a struggling actor. James' plans, however, suddenly changed when he had to fly to Los Angeles for an audition in a new television comedy based loosely on the *Friends* concept. Franklin's motive for asking Chad was not only financial. Franklin, who was bisexual, had a terrible crush on Chad and hoped that they could hook up during the trip.

On Wednesday afternoon Franklin picked them both up at the union and they began their odyssey by pulling out of the union on to Frederick street, heading directly for Interstate 64 East. Franklin slipped a tape of REM's *Murmur* into the cassette player and the three students sat back and relaxed as Franklin set the cruise control at 70 miles per hour. Chad sat in the passenger seat and Jody lay stretched out in the back of the forest green Range Rover.

As they approached the interstate by-pass at Richmond and dusk was settling, Chad asked the other two passengers if they wanted to get high and Franklin and Jody both said "yes," so Chad pulled out a bag of marijuana and a pipe and began to stuff the pipe with the Columbian pot that James had sent him through the mail. Chad passed the pipe to the other two riders and they all took deep exaggerated hits. Franklin turned up the tape as the song "Talk About Passion" was playing and they all remained silent for a few minutes. Then Chad asked Jody if she was going to be in a play this spring and Jody lied and said she had gotten the part in *Gentlemen Prefer Blondes*, but the truth was that they had not even held auditions yet. So, Jody asked Chad about what he was majoring in and Chad said he couldn't remember, laughing like it was a joke, but in reality Chad had no idea what he was majoring in because, really, he just wanted to move to LA with James and kept hoping that James could get this part, so they could find a quaint little bungalow in LA, just for the two of them. Franklin eased the Range Rover into the left lane and gunned the engine to 85 miles an hour as they cruised past Petersburg on the outskirts of Richmond, heading south on Interstate 95.

Franklin, very stoned now, told Chad that the pot was really "far out" and immediately wondered why he used such a worn out phrase, but neither Chad nor Jody noticed that Franklin's hipness needed some vast improvement. Jody agreed that the pot was definitely "out there" and Chad said he got it from his "friend" James. Then Jody, for the first time, wondered if Chad was gay because of the way he said the word "friend." She felt it sounded like more-than-friend, but she couldn't be sure and wondered how she might find out if Chad was gay or not. Or maybe he was bi because she vaguely remembered him hitting on her at the Dress-Like-You-Work-on-Wall-Street Party, the same party where she also flirted with Jason Sparrow. Maybe she did go home with Chad that night, but she couldn't be sure. Then Franklin asked Jody if she knew Amy Toeffler and Jody said "of course" because she was her roommate and Franklin said he didn't know that, but he went out with her last semester and he said they had a great time. Jody wondered why Amy didn't mention to Franklin that she was her roommate. "You had a good time with Amy?" asked Jody because it seemed so unlikely that a cute, smart guy like Franklin could possibly have a good time with such an airhead like Amy.

"Yes, we went to a movie," said Franklin. "I think it was *Die Hard II*, then we went out for pizza," not mentioning the fact that Amy gave him the greatest blowjob of his life (except for a Jamaican dude on Spring Break last year).

Jody figured Amy must have given Franklin a great blow job; otherwise, it didn't make sense because going out for pizza with Amy was tantamount to a root canal and she knew Franklin would not say he had a great time based on a Bruce Willis movie and a conversation at a pizza joint with Amy.

After two hours on the road Franklin asked if anybody was hungry and Chad said he could use a bite so they pulled over and got a couple hamburgers at McDonalds. Jody tried to eat a whole hamburger, but she had no appetite because of her sickness and she went into the rest room to take her medication for her disease. Franklin also went into the men's room to take his medication, following by Chad who also needed to take medication. Then they all climbed back into the Range Rover, only this time Chad and Jody sat together in the back. Chad and Jody were sitting close together and Chad asked Jody if she wanted a Xanex and Jody said "Yes," so Chad pulled out a bottle of pills and asked Franklin if he wanted a couple and Franklin said, "Okay, why not?" and Chad quickly dispensed Xanex to the other two. Jody asked Chad where he got the pills and Chad told Jody that he was bi-polar manic depressive and he used to take Lithium, but had a bad reaction, like an overdose, and Xanex was much better. Jody said she was mostly manic, but not bi-polar, and needed to get her Ritalin prescription refilled. Franklin added that he was more depressive than manic, but he had also been diagnosed as having a generalized anxiety disorder. He said he originally was given Prozac, but now was he was taking a new drug called Navane. Jody said she thought Navane was an anti-psychotic drug and Franklin said that might be true because he didn't trust his psychiatrist who was currently having sex with his sister. That got Chad's attention and he asked Franklin how his psychiatrist could be having sex with his sister and Franklin told him that his sister took him to a psychiatrist and the three of them met to discuss Franklin's psychiatric problems. After the three of them concluded that Franklin was probably sexually confused because he was sexually abused by a Methodist minister, the psychiatrist and Franklin's sister decided to meet alone to further discuss Franklin's problems. An hour later Franklin's sister came out of the psychiatrist office completely disheveled and Franklin asked her what happened and she said she just had the best sex of her life and "Don't tell dad."

As the threesome rambled down the highway and darkness descended upon eastern Virginia, Chad asked if anyone wanted another Xanax and they both said "Yes" and then Chad said he had some ecstasy and wondered if anyone wanted to have one. Jody said she loved X and Franklin said that sounded like a good idea to him, so they each popped another Xanax, smoked another bowl, and downed a hit of ecstasy. Franklin said he thought it might be a good idea to fill up the cooler with Coor's light, so he decided to stop and get some beer at a little convenience store in Emporium, Virginia. As he pulled into *Rita's Stop and Shop*, Chad said he was much too stoned to go inside and Jody felt that she couldn't handle "local people" right now, so Chad and Jody stayed in the car as Franklin went inside to get the beer. Jody thought that this would be a good time for Chad to hit on her and she was surprised that he had not made his move earlier.

Undaunted, she pulled a Marlboro Light out of her pocket book and in her best phony Southern accent purred like a kitten to Chad, "Dah….ling, can you give a poor Southern girl a light?"

Chad, who hated cigarettes, reached in his pocket and lit her cigarette from the lighter he used to smoke marijuana. Jody gave Chad her most seductive look, but for some reason her feminine wiles were not working on Chad. Jody thought that maybe Chad was too stoned to think about having sex in a Range Rover, although at this minute she couldn't think of anything she'd rather do. As Franklin approached the Range Rover, Chad glanced out the window and, for the first time, concluded that Franklin was cute and he'd like to sleep with him before the trip was over. When Franklin came back to the vehicle he asked if anyone else wanted to drive and Chad said he would take over. Jody was disappointed that Chad was going to drive because she was convinced that they should sleep together before the trip was over. Franklin hopped into the back seat and Chad pulled out of *Rita's*, driving back onto the highway.

The three stoned travelers cruised quickly past the quaint, sleepy towns of North Carolina; towns with names like Wilson, Fremont, Smithfield and Dunn. Jody was beginning to feel woozy and horny as the ecstasy kicked in and her senses heightened and colors seemed brighter. Silver flashes of light from oncoming cars exploded across the windshield like giant silver arrows and the funky sounds of Al Green's "Let's Stay Together" pulsated rhythmic vibrations that Jody could feel in the night. Jody and Franklin swayed together to the beat of the music until she could feel Franklin's thigh slightly touching hers. As the intensity of the music increased, so did the leg motions of Jody and Franklin until their legs were wrapped around each other, their bodies edging closer together. Jody whispered to Franklin that she was glad he asked her to come along. Franklin could feel the steamy sexual vibes from Jody, but wasn't sure whether he wanted to sleep with Jody or Chad. He quickly concluded that it was both of them; but for the moment, it was Jody who was commanding his attention.

As the ecstasy began to create physical and sensual rushes in all the passengers, the Range Rover transformed into a pulsating sexual machine that desperately needed some action. Jody moved closer to Franklin, putting her arms around him as Chad put in a new tape of *Marvin Gaye's Greatest Hits* which made the scene feel even more sex-driven. Then Franklin leaned over and kissed Jody on the lips and Jody felt a sexual rush like never before and reached down and grabbed Franklin's hand and led it slowly between her thighs which were sweaty and moist from the excitement. Franklin began rubbing Jody's vagina in a circular motion and Jody reached down between Franklin's legs and began to squeeze and gently stoke his penis. Franklin hit the latch on the side of the Range Rover and the seat collapsed to form a mobile bed for the two impassioned travelers. Chad heard the sound of the seat collapse and glanced back to see what was going on. He was not surprised to catch a glimpse of Franklin's ass arched high into the air, and Jody's legs splayed out on both sides of Franklin's gyrating torso. Chad laughed to himself and felt jealous because he wasn't part of the action. Besides, he liked the look of Franklin's ass.

The Range Rover continued its journey southward, passing Florence, South Carolina, heading rapidly into the lowlands of Georgia. An hour passed and Chad had not heard a word from Jody or Franklin. He assumed they had fallen asleep, although he could not imagine falling asleep on ecstasy. Finally, he heard low murmuring sounds from behind him, barely able to discern bits of conversation. He heard occasional random phrases like, "*It feels good there*" "*....Your hair is…*" "*Is that…Halston…?*"

"Hey, are you alive back there?" asked Chad. Jody and Franklin both giggled like a school children saying, "Nobody here, but us chickens!!!" Then more peals of laughter and Chad said, "What's going on back there?" and Franklin said, "Why don't you come back and find out?" So Chad said, "Okay" and drove the Range Rover off the exit of the Interstate, made a left hand turn off the ramp, then pulled off to a side road in the middle of nowhere, South Carolina. Chad jumped in the back, finding to his delight that Franklin and Jody had no clothes on. Immediately, he ripped off his clothes with a frenetic Franklin energetically helping him, and as the clothes fell away, Franklin reached over and kissed Chad on the mouth as Jody crawled up Chad's legs, searching for his penis which was now erect and waiting achingly for Jody to make her appearance. Franklin continued to French kiss Chad who found Jody's breasts and began to feel her up, and Franklin found Jody's anus and put his middle finger up her ass as Chad stopped kissing Franklin and turned him around and slipped his penis into Franklin's ass while Jody began to suck on Franklin's penis. Franklin almost came, but before he did so, Jody took Franklin's penis out of her mouth and shoved it into Chad's mouth. Chad said, "please don't come yet" and continued to suck Franklin as Jody began to suck off Chad, then turned around and Chad began to fuck Jody in the ass while he was still sucking Franklin off. Then Franklin came and watched Chad fucking Jody in the ass for a few minutes before pulling Jody out of Chad and offering his own ass to Chad and to which Chad gleefully obliged. Then Jody, who was watching Chad fuck Franklin, broke them apart and put herself between them and then Chad started fucking Jody in the front while Franklin mounted her in the back and the three of them rocked the Range Rover for several minutes until Chad screamed that he was coming and Franklin said, "Me too" and they both came in Jody at exactly the same time, as Jody squealed with pleasure as she reached an orgasm from both ends, as all three of them collapsed into a sweaty heap of exhaustion…

The three of them lay entwined together for an hour, unable to make the slightest move to resume their journey. It was Jody who first showed a sign of life by saying that she was thirsty and asked if there was any bottled water in the Range Rover. Franklin said "Yes, I'll get you some" and struggled to the front of the vehicle and retrieved a bottle of *Deer Park* spring water for Jody. Chad mumbled that his foot had fallen asleep and his mouth was also dry. The three passengers were still peaking on the ecstasy and formed a small circle, passing the bottle of water to each other, grateful for the quenching of their thirst. The love-bonding effects of the drugs and the lust fulfillment produced a strong, if artificial, camaraderie between the young travelers. No one knew quite what to say about anything, especially any mention of just what took place in their lives. They were not sure whether to be happy, ashamed, thrilled, complacent, or just plain exhausted. Franklin finally broke the silence by saying that he really liked both of them and he was glad they came along and he had no idea that they were all going to have sex together, but he said he was glad they did because he really cared about them as persons and hoped that having sex would not mess up the rest of the trip or the friendship that he wanted to form with both of them.

Chad said that he agreed and boy, did he have a good time and wasn't this X the "bomb?"—meaning that it was good shit, of course, and yes, he agreed that they should all be great friends, but maybe not lovers because he was gay and had a boyfriend who was an actor in New York and told Jody and Franklin that he hoped James got the acting job in LA so they could move into a modest bungalow in the city. Jody, at this moment, was in love because the ecstasy was really kicking in and she felt more love within her for these two people than anyone in her whole life. But Jody was so oblivious to what true love was like compared to the faked-up fervor of ecstasy that she made the mistake of thinking that these feelings were authentic and meaningful. Chad and Franklin were also under the lotus-like spell of a drug that created instant bonding and love, but feelings resembling instant gratification rather than lasting affection. Perhaps, this is why in the darkness of the night, following her rarified intimacy, and gushing with emotion, Jody made her confession.

She felt so close to these two people and believed she had to tell them her terrible secret, so they could at least know she was an honest person who loved them very much and did not want them to be hurt. She wanted to tell them how much they meant to her and she never wanted to do anything to hurt them like she did with all those other men who didn't mean a thing to her.

"I have something to tell you both," said Jody. "I hope you won't get mad or even kill me, but I have a confession to make."

Chad and Franklin both asked what she was talking about and Jody just sort of blurted it out, sobbing uncontrollably, that she was HIV positive and hoped that they would find it in their hearts to forgive her for not telling them. Chad and Franklin were stunned. It took a few moments for Jody's words to sink in. Chad and Franklin stared at each other. Unexpectedly, Franklin began to cry profusely, sobbing incoherently, waving his arms, totally out of control. Chad reached over to comfort him and Jody, too, reached out to try and settle Franklin down, but he was out of his mind with pain, crying and screaming at the same time, suddenly shouting, "OHMYGOD, ME TOO, ME TOO!!!!!"

"What do you mean?" asked Chad. Franklin, with his hands in his head, shaking uncontrollably, cried out into the night, "I have AIDS, too! I'm a dead man. We're all dead!"

Chad drew back in horror, unable to believe what he was hearing; aghast and now retreating back into the Range Rover huddling in a corner, shivering, like he was freezing to death. Franklin and Jody rushed up to comfort Chad who was crying and shaking even more than Franklin earlier.

"Please, Chad forgive us," said Jody, "We're so sorry. Please, Chad forgive us," They kept repeating. Then Chad starting laughing hysterically for some reason and Jody and Franklin just sat there looking at Chad laughing out of his mind, like he had just seen the funniest show on earth. "OMYGOD, IS RIGHT!!!! THIS IS PERFECT!!!!

"What do you mean?" asked Franklin.

"ME, TOO!!! I'VE GOT AIDS, TOO!!! CAN YOU BELIEVE IT? WE'RE ALL GOING TO DIE!!! ALL THREE OF US!!!!

It took Chad several minutes to calm down and for the three of them to come to grips with what had transpired. They sat huddled together like three little children who were lost in the woods and were waiting for their parents. They all cried softly and held each other tightly, feeling as close as they could come to love and compassion for each other. In the end, they realized that there was nothing they could do about the situation, except literally and figuratively take their medicine and hope for the best.

It took a while for the ecstasy to wear off, but in the meantime, the three young people embraced inside the Range Rover and for a little while they felt protected from the outside world and thought that maybe things might turn out to be okay after all. With these positive thoughts in mind, each of them gradually lost consciousness, falling asleep together in each other's arms.

It was close to sunrise when Franklin woke up and found himself nestled between Jody and Chad. With a labored effort, he managed to extricate himself from the tight sleeping quarters, and climbed gingerly out of the Range Rover. Rubbing the sleep from his eyes, he opened the front door, started the engine, and eased the vehicle out from a gravel road beside an abandoned farm house. He made a right hand turn, spotted the blue and red sign for the Interstate, and nursing a mighty hangover, drove the Range Rover south as the other two passengers slept contentedly in the back of the vehicle.

One week after Spring Break Emily and Danny were in the apartment waiting for Jason. It had been a while since the last "psycho tape" and Danny had pretty much forgotten about it. But another one had shown up yesterday and the three students were set to hear the latest installment. Emily and Danny had listened to the first two tapes very carefully and reached the following conclusions: They couldn't help but feel the tapes were somehow connected to the year-long events at the college and Byrd's disappearance. Everyone agreed there was a strange atmosphere on campus that no one could quite put a label on. Emily, in particular, suspected the tapes might be from Byrd, although she admitted she didn't have much to go on. There was the combined secrecy surrounding the arrival of the tapes and Byrd's disappearance. Also, there was the matter of suspecting that Byrd had AIDS, and Emily and Danny were well aware that the AIDS epidemic was currently being likened to a plague.

Jason came running into the room, energetic and wild as usual, heading straight for the refrigerator.

"How about some beers?" yelled Jason. "You don't want to hear the psycho tape without a cold one, do you?"

"No way!" Emily chanted..

Jason twisted the tabs off three Budweisers and proceeded to listen to the latest installment of what were now dubbed "the psycho tapes:"

".......and as I proclaimed at the beginning of this tale, it was a most unusual time to witness. Is the Red Death set upon the land? I know not; yet I fear. Woefully, I could not understand the general notion or temper of the ones infected; namely that they did not take the least care or make any scruple of contaminating others. Bill Ferris, a sophomore, who knows he is contaminated because his pale white face turned a ghastly purple spent the night in Patty Broughton's room, even though he is supposed to be Jill Satterfield's boy friend. Patty, who will soon be infested, was seen earlier in

the library reading the Wall Street Journal, planning for a future she will never experience.

And besides those who were so frightened as to die on the spot, there were great numbers frightened to other extremes, some blasted out of their senses; some out of memory:

Jackie Augerbright forgot to go home for Christmas.

Mary Zukowitz forgot to dress herself on Tuesday morning.

Patty Harrison forgot she was blinded by the plague.

I say I could see before me a vision of several pits in another ground near the Church and football field when the distemper began to spread to other parts of the college, especially when I saw the dead carts began to go out. But now, the plague was raging in full-force in a dreadful manner, and the number of burials on campus was larger than any other part of the country.

There was a strict order to prevent people coming to those pits for it was dangerous and a bad omen. But after some time, that order was more necessary, for the people who were infected near the end, and clearly delirious, would run haphazardly into those pits, wrapped in college blankets or rugs, and throw themselves in, and as they said, commune with the dead. Some threw themselves in, but they were not quite dead, and they would just lie there on top of the pile. And it was surprising that so many did not know that they were dead, both in body and spirit. Bernie Slater walked up to me on the softball field and tried to convince me that he was alive. And I almost laughed because I was there when the dead carts picked him up after he collapsed in front of the college gymnasium. Bernie Slater had been dead for a long time. He was transparent and you could see the dead cells eating his vital organs. Some were, indeed, in relatively good physical health, but spiritually dead, thus major plague carriers. The rampant selfishness and disregard for the plight of others was particularly striking....

.....and yet, when looking casually, they appeared to be such normal creatures.....

I must say that it was a time of cheap investment in love and friendship among the students. Personal lives of students were devastated beyond belief. The consciousness raising gurus were at play in the devil's field. They told the people not to make large investments in love or friendship and avoid dependence on others. How strange...the cure becomes the disease...

I could not detect the purpose all these futile actions about me, It was as if people thought there wasn't enough love and the good things in life to go around. Of course, everyone pretended there was no crisis, but they were fooling themselves.

Denial was rampant.

Perhaps, this was the reason they all began to look alike. I was having greater diffi-culty distinguishing the individual identity of the students. Sometimes, I couldn't tell if they were male or female. I would see a group of youths walking across the campus and think I was seeing triple or quadruple. Perhaps, I was. I do not know if it has anything to do with the plague. Maybe, they were reducing themselves to interchange-able objects for some reason.

This may serve a little to describe the dreadful condition of the day, although it is impossible to say anything that is able to give a true idea of it to those who did not see it. Other than this; that it was very very dreadful, and no such tongue can tell.....

It is the beginning of early spring, yet the weather is temperate, variable, and cool enough, and the people still have hopes. That which encourage them was, that the whole campus is more or less healthy, the seven dormitories losing but twelve students in the past few weeks, buried in the Black Ditch, and I began to hope that since it was chiefly among the older ones in the Southern dorms, it might not go any further. I con-tinued in these hopes for a few days, but it was but for a few, for the students were no more to be deceived thus. They searched the houses and found that the plague was really spread in every way, and many died of it every day. So now all my extenuations were abated, and it was no more to be concealed; nay it quickly appeared that the infection had spread itself beyond all hopes of abatement.

One day, being at that part of the campus on some special business, curiosity led me to observe things more than usually, and indeed, I walked a great way where I had no business. I went to the inner courtyard, and there the street was full of people, but they would not mingle with anyone from a known dormitory which carried the disease, or meet with smells and scents from frat houses that might be tainted.

Everybody was at peace; there was no occasion for lawyers; besides, it was in the time of the annual spring frolic, and some had left for the plague-infected southern lands. Whole rows of houses were closed up, many inhabitants fled, and only a security man or two remained.

But I must go back to the beginning of this surprising time. While the fears of the people were young, they were increased strangely by several odd incidents, which put together, it was really a wonder the whole country did not rise up and leave for another continent. And from the west, a fiery, blazing comet appeared, and flew directly over the bath houses and parlors of the afflicted.

.........and lo, it was an ill time to be sick in.

And the people bowed and prayed to the materialists of the day, and bought and sold each other in the market place, thus creating the Second Plague. How weary and tiresome it is listening to the slow droning of self-induced chatter; the mindless, mir-ror-laden conversation, dangling in the ancient fiery dynamo of night.

I think it was in the middle of March, seeing a second crowd of people in the street. I joined with them to once again satisfy my curiosity, and found them staring up into the air to see what a woman told them that appeared plain to her, which was an angel clothed in white, with a burning sword in his hand, waving it or brandishing it over his head. And I felt a deep sense of déjà vu as if surely I had seen such a vision before. And suddenly, I remembered England and the terrible plague set upon the land and the journal I had written so long ago. And sure, enough, the plague has returned in a similar form, another place and time; plagues of plagues, when will it ever cease?

I remember living in England when the plague was raging with great fury and the dead carts were operating at record paces, unable to fully clear out the streets of the dead by morning.

Time is running out.

I have never witnessed such hopelessness. There were pockets of spiritual healers and dedicated servers of humanity in London town, but this modern plague is more insidious, and without much hope of recovery. And I continued to think about my enormous burden. I remember every detail, every revulsion of the senses, every lifeless body stacked in the empty courtyards of St. Giles. I heard a thousand cries of pain bursting through centuries of civilization. My body was born in England, I will die in the merry weather.

I must tell you that I suspect the worst. The Red Death—taunting me with her morbid accusations. I fear she may be spreading the terrible plague to others—.

The tape ended,

"Jesus," said Jason, "I need a shot of tequila."

Danny and Emily were silent. Danny went into the refrigerator and got three more beers.

"I'm mystified," said Emily, "It doesn't make sense, but then again it *does* make sense."

"What do you mean?" asked Danny.

"Well, first of all," said Emily, "The language is consistent throughout and so is the tone of the message."

"What message?" asked Jason.

"It's about the impending plague," said Emily, "The one that's going to happen, or is already happening. I'm not sure."

"There's no plague on this campus," asserted Jason, "And what the hell is the Red Death?"

"Are you sure there is no plague?" asked Emily. "You and Danny both said you thought the tape may be from Byrd. Maybe he's talking about AIDS."

"Come on!" cried Jason, "Who the hell has AIDS except for that weirdo in theatre?"

"Jason, That's the point. We don't know. There could be students who are HIV positive, and we wouldn't know."

"I doubt if there's a plague".

"Emily's right," said Danny. "We don't know for sure."

Jason was extremely skeptical of the tapes and did not see them as anything but a student prank. He frowned and shook his head.

Okay," said Jason, "What about dead carts and burials? Are you gonna tell me they're for real?"

"No," responded Emily, "but it could be symbolism for the severity of the problem. If this is Byrd, he could be trying to alert us by using hyperbole. After all, he is in theatre. He may like a touch of the dramatic."

"It's dramatic, alright, Dramatic crap!"

"What's this about England?" Danny asked. "What would England have to do with us? Is Byrd from England? Didn't something like that happen over there?"

"It did," said Emily. "Don't you remember the Bubonic Plague? It wiped out half of England."

"Yeah," said Jason, not withholding his sarcasm, "Three hundred years ago."

"So, what," said Emily, "Maybe there are similarities. Maybe Byrd is trying to tell us there are similarities between then and now."

Danny, who had been pacing the room trying to figure out the tape, was torn between Emily who thought the tape was significant and Jason who thought it was gibberish.

"Alright," Danny said patiently, "He said something about a journal in England, something about keeping a journal."

"Oh, sure," said Jason, "The guy is three hundred years old and he's still alive. Maybe he's a vampire."

"Play back that part," suggested Emily.

Danny turned the tape player back on and found the part where the voice uttered:

"......*and suddenly I remembered England and the terrible plague set upon the land and the journal I had written so long ago....*"

"I think there is a book about the plague in England," said Danny, "But I can't remember the title or author. I think it is a kind of diary or journal by someone who lived through it."

"Suppose you do find the book," offered Jason, "Do you think this guy wrote it?"

"Of course not," countered Emily, "But it might give us some clues."

"Well," we're certainly clueless," added Jason.

"Tell you what," said Danny, "I'll go to the library tomorrow and check out all the books on plagues in England."

"You might check out any references to a red death," said Emily.

"Oh, yes," said Danny, "The dire warning."

"Maybe it's the Poe connection," suggested Emily. "*The Masque of the Red Death.*"

"Yeah," joked Jason, "Maybe it's death from bad lobster!"

"Or the red beans in the cafeteria!" chimed in Danny.

"Very funny," said Emily.

"Okay," said Danny, "We'll try to be serious for a moment. Is there anything else I should check out?"

"What about the second plague," asked Jason.

"I think that one's pretty clear," said Emily.

"What do you mean?" Danny asked.

"Well," said Emily, "I think he feels our students, or maybe all students, have the plague of selfishness, or narcissism. They are too concerned with their own lives and not the welfare of others. They are also too materialistic, always thinking about money."

"This is too much for me," said Jason. Let's deal with one plague at a time, shall we?"

"Alright, said Danny, "I'll go to the library tomorrow and check out the England connection.

Emily rewound the tape, playing a section over again.

"What is this about 'he was born in England and will die in the merry weather?' I wonder what that means?" asked Emily.

"Maybe he means warm weather, like Florida," suggested Danny.

"Maybe he means some girl named Mary Wether," offered Jason.

"What would *that* mean?" asked Danny.

"I haven't the foggiest idea," admitted Jason.

"Well, boys," I think this is enough detective work for one night, don't you?" asserted Emily, "Let's go out for a pizza, okay?"

"Sounds good to me," said Jason, "But I'm currently financially embarrassed."

"You been 'financially embarrassed' your whole life," said Danny.

"So?

"So," said Emily, "I guess Danny's buying."

"Me, why me?"

"Because Jason and I are both financially embarrassed."

"I think there is more than one conspiracy going on around here," said Danny.

"You know," said Jason, "I think I'll get a large one with lots of extras."

"Me, too," said Emily.

There were only a few students studying in the library when Danny entered to do his research on the English plague. He wasn't sure what direction he was going, so he decided to contact Mrs. Franklin who helped him find some references for a paper on political theory last semester. He walked through the main lobby and asked one of the students at the check-out desk where he might find Mrs. Franklin.

"I think she is in the main office putting some books on reserve," the student answered. "You can go on back."

Danny walked passed the check-out desk, through the side door, and found Mrs., Franklin in a large office standing beside a row of books on a shelf. She was labeling a book with a book marker.

"Hi, Mrs. Franklin."

She looked up and smiled warmly. Danny remembered her as one of the nicest, most helpful persons on campus.

"Oh, hi, Danny. How are you doing? Can I help you with something?"

I need to know about books on a couple topics, but not for a research paper. It's more like, well…like a news story."

"Oh…"

"About why professor Byrd did not come back. But these topics are going to seem little strange. I mean, I don't know if they are even connected to Professor Byrd."

Danny was going to tell Mrs. Franklin about the tapes, but he felt too foolish. He figured she would think he might be going crazy.

"Just tell me what they are," said Mrs. Franklin, patiently, "Maybe I can help."

"Okay. Do you know any books or stories about a red death, besides the Poe story?"

"I don't know any off-hand, but why don't we go to the card catalogue and find out."

Mrs. Franklin and Danny exited a side door. Danny followed Mrs. Franklin to an old worn mahogany card catalogue in the middle of the main floor. They were still under the ancient system of using a card catalogue with author and subject categories.

"We're upgrading our system soon to our own public access catalogue," explained Mrs. Franklin.

Mrs. Franklin opened the drawer of the subject section labeled "DAR" to "FAB" and flipped through a few cards until she came to "death." She muttered a few references underneath her breath that did not seem to be much help, including *Masque of the Red Death*, by Edgar Allen Poe. Having found nothing, she turned to the section labeled "Red."

"Danny," said Mrs. Franklin, "There's "Red Cross," "red deer," "red river," and "red guards," but no "red death." I'm sorry, but there doesn't seem to be much under that topic. Anything else?"

"Are there any books about plagues," Danny asked.

"Sure, said Mrs. Franklin, "Do you have a particular plague in mind, or an historical period?"

"Not really," said Danny. "How about a plague in England?"

"There is the bubonic plague that spread through England in the seventeenth century. We can look at the plague as an historical medical problem, and, of course, there's the Defoe book."

"Defoe book? I thought he wrote *Robinson Crusoe?*"

"He did. But he also wrote *The Journal of the Plague Year*. It's a powerful study of how people in London dealt with the plague."

"Mrs. Franklin, I think I just hit pay dirt."

"Is that the book you need?"

"It *has* to be. Can you give me the number?"

"Of course."

"Thanks, Mrs. Franklin," Danny gushed, "You've been a big help, believe me!"

Danny bounded up to the fourth floor and after a few minutes of wandering around the book stacks, he found a dusty ancient copy of Defoe's book. Danny figured this had to be what the voice on the tape was talking about, although he couldn't figure out how a three hundred year old book would help them find a professor in the latter part of the twentieth century. Nevertheless, he was extremely excited and couldn't wait to tell Emily and Jason about his discovery.

He hurried back down the stairs and was on his way out when he remembered that he needed to check the locales of the hospices in the state. He once again approached Mrs. Franklin. He hoped she did not think he was being a pest.

"Mrs. Franklin, Do you know where I could find the names and location of the hospices in Virginia?"

"I think you'll find that in the directory of medical services. It's in the reference section."

After a few minutes of searching in the reference section, Danny came across a huge thick book entitled, "Associative Medical Services of Virginia." He flipped through the pages until he came to a list of hospices. He was writing down the names in alphabetical order, not paying much attention, until he saw directly under *"Lindstrum Hospital and Hospice"* the implausible name: *Merryweather Hospital and Hospice, Fairfax, Virginia."*

Danny arranged to meet Emily in their favorite booth in the union. He was watching two guys play a strenuous game of ping pong when Emily came through the door. She sat down in the booth opposite him and he told her about his discovery.

"I can't believe it," Emily said. "It's got to be more than a coincidence. Have you called the hospice yet?"

"Yes, that was the first thing I did after I left the library. I asked if they had a patient named Byrd and the lady told me no. Of course, she might not be telling the truth. If Dr. Byrd is there with AIDS, he probably doesn't want the general public to know about it. We'll make the trip and see for ourselves."

"When can we leave?"

"I think this weekend would be good."

"He's got to be there," said Emily. "I knew he was trying to tell us something important."

"I think that voice may be more than just Byrd. I think we were also listening to Daniel Defoe."

"What do you mean?"

"My guess is that Professor Byrd is in the advanced stages of AIDS and he's practically out of his mind. He probably thinks he *is* Daniel Defoe, at least part of the time."

"That would explain the strange language and flights from reality."

"Yeah."

Danny produced a copy of Defoe's book from his book bag.

"I've read this book, Emily. Every thing fits. Byrd was practically begging us to read this book."

"Why?" Asked Emily. "What for?"

"It's one man's chronicle of a terrible plague ravaging London in 1665. Byrd was telling us to read this book to understand AIDS."

"I knew there was a connection."

"It's amazing," Danny continued, "Everything I read in this book reminds me of how people are responding to the AIDS epidemic. Everyone is scared. Some refuse to admit there is a problem. There is an incredible amount of hysteria connected with the disease. People avoid anyone who's got the disease, and the people who get AIDS suffer and deteriorate as if they had a plague."

Emily hesitated for a moment. This was beginning to overwhelm her.

"Danny, this is so confusing and scary. Why did that tape come to you? We're only two people. What are we supposed to do about peoples' ignorance about AIDS?"

"I don't know. But maybe Byrd has the answer to that too."

"Do you think he will really see us?"

"I don't know. He's certainly very secretive."

"Well," said Emily, "I think we should go this weekend. I just need to do one thing first."

"What's that?"

"I need to talk to Jody Hershberger."

Emily wasn't sure why, but she felt it was better to meet Jody Hershberger on her own turf, so she called the theater to find out when she would be working. She knew theatre majors put in about twenty hours a week helping out in the department as part of their requirements for the major. Emily was not certain, but she had a hunch that Jody could fill her in on the activities of her uncle. She got through to the department and talked to Professor Ellis who politely told her that Jody would be in the theatre at three o'clock that afternoon.

Emily walked down the steps of the theatre, through a small foyer that apparently served as the lobby during performances. She entered a "black box" theatre, almost completely empty except for several folding chairs stacked along the sides, and a small table containing an assortment of bulky lights in the middle of the room. No one seemed to be around. She checked her watch and it was almost 3:30.

"Hello!" Emily called out.

No answer. The atmosphere was spooky with the lights dimmed way down, and thick, black curtains enveloped the entire theatre, giving it a cave-like quality.

"Hello!" Emily shouted again.

"Yes?"

The voice startled Emily because she couldn't make out where it was coming from.

"Hello?" Emily repeated to no one in particular.

She looked in the corner near another table of lights and noticed a ladder for the first time. Two thin legs extended from beneath a shaft of light above the ladder.

"Can you reach me that blue light?" the voice asked in a pleasant tone.

"Sure."

Emily reached over and retrieved a large blue light and lifted it toward two arms descending from the top of the ladder. As the arms moved forward to grab the light, gradually, a freckled-faced, redhead in cut-offs with her hair tied in pigtails, emerged into her line of vision. It was Jody Hershberger.

"Thanks," she said, as she fastened the light to a metal beam, adjusted the color, and climbed slowly and carefully down the stairs.

"Whew! That's hard work! A girl could get killed. Thanks for the help. Can I help you?"

"Yes, my name is Emily Patterson. You're Jody Hershberger, aren't you?"

"That's me. Welcome to show business!"

"We talked on the phone once. I asked you how to get in touch with your uncle."

"Oh, yes, I remember the phone call. You're not from David Letterman? Shucks!"

"I'm afraid not, but I heard you're very good."

"Boy, you must want something *really* bad. Flattery will get you everywhere."

"No, really. I think you're a fine actress. I've seen you several times."

"Thanks, would you like a Coke?"

"Sure."

They two women walked through one of the black curtains and entered the theatre's dressing room which was lined with mirrors and littered with gaudy costumes, shiny jewelry, make-up kits, and several closets bursting with theatre paraphernalia. Jody went over and dropped two coins into a drink machine and produced two Cokes.

"Thanks. It's kind of hot in here," said Emily.

"It's *always* hot in here. They forgot to add air conditioning in this room."

Emily took a sip of her Coke, glancing around the room. She looked out the window and saw two burly men carrying a large sofa past the window.

"Well, what can I do for you? Do you want to know more about my uncle?"

"Yes. I'm writing a feature article on him for the school paper."

"Uncle Chuck is a great man. He loves this college."

"I know. I talked to him once. He seems like a real nice man."

"He is."

"Can you tell me more about him? His interests, his hobbies, things like that."

"Sure," said Jody, sitting back in one of the chairs in front of the mirrors. "Uncle Chuck has been connected with the school for a long time. He went here for undergraduate school, then came backing the 70's to work in development, fund raising, stuff like that. He made the school a lot of money when it was in financial trouble, but I don't know very much about the details."

"What does he do now?"

"He's on the board of trustees. I really don't know what he does. He was an economics major and he's really smart about things like that."

"What about his hobbies? What does he do in his spare time?"

"I think he travels a lot. He's not on campus all that much. I know he went to Germany last year."

"Anything else?"

"He collects pigs."

"Pigs?"

"Not real pigs! You know…all kinds of ceramic pieces shaped like pigs…pictures…clay models…that sort of thing."

"How about his children?"

"They never had any. It's a shame because I think he really wanted them."

"Didn't your aunt want any children?"

Jody frowned slightly. "I don't think she ever knew what she wanted, besides working for Big Brothers and Big Sisters."

"I'm sorry," said Emily, "It's none of my business. I just wanted to know more about his personal life for the article. I don't mean to pry."

"That's alright," said Jody, "He's not unhappy or anything. I didn't mean to leave that impression."

"Can you tell me anything else that might be helpful for the article?"

"Well," said Jody, "I guess you've got his resume and all the degrees and awards he's gotten. Do you know he was given a community service award from the governor?"

"Yes, I saw that on the resume sheet that they gave me in his office. It's very impressive."

"He's a great man, believe me.. This college would be nowhere without him."

"I'm sure you are right. Anything else?"

"No, not really. He's the kindest man I ever met. He's done a lot of work for the community, helping local kids, sponsoring all kinds of sporting events, that sort of thing. I think he's very active in the Little League."

"Thanks, Jody, you've been a big help—and thanks for the Coke!"

"Don't mention it. Tell them over at the paper to give me a good review for the next play. I could use some favorable publicity!"

"I'll see what I can do."

RED DEATH RE DUX: APRIL 12-28

Danny and Emily were driving up route 29 toward Fairfax, anticipating a meeting with the mysterious Dr. Byrd. It was a dazzling mid-April spring day in the Shenandoah Valley, and as they reveled in the beauty of the countryside, they were both feeling apprehensive about the prospect of finally meeting the mysterious Professor Byrd, and remained uncharacteristically silent throughout most of the trip. Dr. Chambers had still not contacted Emily. They had both concluded that Dr. Chambers may have something to do with this mystery, but were not sure about his precise involvement. Danny had contacted Professor Ellis and asked her if she mentioned anything to the Dean about their meeting. She told Danny that she considered the meeting a private encounter between a professor and a student and she was not in the habit of revealing that kind of information. For some reason Danny believed her. Emily was satisfied that Jody did not know much about her uncle's business, but she got the impression that his marriage may not be ideal. Emily was considering talking to Mrs. Chambers.

After driving for about two hours, the couple finally arrived at the hospice. They turned off the highway and proceeded down a winding, maple tree-lined road that led up to an imposing iron gate archway marking the entrance to a large, expansive estate-like complex. A sign next to the gateway read:

Merryweather Hospital and Hospice

Commonwealth of Virginia

Est. 1958

Danny eased the car slowly toward a military-style check point station with a small open window, a swinging gate, and a nondescript man dressed in a gray uniform, holding a clipboard.

"May I Help you?" he asked.

"Yes, said Danny, "We're here to see a patient."

"Who would you like to see?"

"Joseph Byrd."

"Just a minute."

The man went back inside his office and they could see him making a phone call. Momentarily, he came back to the car and handed them a piece of paper.

"Here's a two hour pass. Go to the information center in Gerrard Building—third one on your left. Ask for Dr. Thompson."

"Thanks."

"This place looks like its right out of a Franz Kafka novel," said Emily.

"It does look like a military installation, doesn't it?"

The couple drove past the sentry, turned to the left, passing two officious, red brick buildings. There were a few patients loitering freely about the grounds, idly basking in the warm sunshine. The landscape was meticulously well kept, the grass was neatly cut and the trees finely pruned. Several wrought iron benches were placed along the side of the road and Danny noticed the obligatory gazebo clustered between two gigantic oak trees. Danny parked the car in the parking lot of the building designated the Malcolm E. Gerrard Visitor and Information Center.

"This place gives me the creeps," said Emily.

"Me, too."

They got out of the car, walked up to the entrance, and slipped through a revolving door. Inside, they found themselves lost in a small unlit lobby painted in drab hospital colors of pale pink and green. Odd pieces of uncomfortable looking furniture were scattered about, an unsuccessful attempt to provide a touch of intimacy about the place. The tables and chairs managed to look both worn out and unused at the same time. The room was dark, but the couple gradually adjusted to the light and located an obese, scraggly-haired old woman reading a National Enquirer magazine. Apparently, she was the nurse on duty.

"Excuse me, may we speak to Dr. Thompson?" asked Danny.

The nurse barely looked up from an article which was revealing to her at that moment that Don Johnson had four gay boy friends in Brazil. She picked up a phone and in a barely audible voice spoke to someone on the other end.

"Have a seat," she ordered, motioning to a small table and chairs adjacent to the front desk. Emily and Danny sat down and waited. Within a few minutes, they were greeted by an attractive, well dressed woman in her fifties.

"I'm Dr. Thompson. You wanted to see Dr. Byrd?"

"Yes," Danny answered.

"Please, come with me."

They followed the woman down a long corridor, leading to her office. They passed a secretary typing at her desk, and Dr. Thompson closed the door behind them.

"Please sit down," she said.

The young visitors sat down in the two chairs in front of her desk.

"I'm afraid I have some bad news for you....Joseph Byrd died two days ago."

The news stunned Emily and Danny. Neither one of them were prepared for this kind of shock.

"What happened?" asked Emily.

Dr. Thompson ignored her question.

"Are either of you related to Dr. Byrd?"

"No," said Emily, "We're students at Wattford College, where Dr. Byrd taught."

"I see."

"We're very sorry to hear about Professor Byrd," said Emily. "We were hoping to see him before he passed away.

Dr. Thompson leaned forward, looking directly at Emily.

"He was a very courageous man, a fine person. You should be very proud of him. He was a tough fighter, right to the end."

There was a moment of silence, which Danny broke.

"Can you tell us anything about how he died? Frankly, Dr. Thompson we thought he had AIDS and he came here because he got fired and he didn't want anyone to know he had AIDS."

Dr. Thompson remained expressionless.

"I'm sorry," she said, "I can't divulge that information. It's confidential."

Well," said Danny, seeing no other alternative, "I guess we need to go. Thank you for your help, and we're really sorry to hear about Professor Byrd."

"I understand."

"Can we see his room?" Emily asked.

"I'm afraid not. It's against policy."

"Can you tell us who visited him?" She persisted.

"I'm sorry. This is a private institution."

Having given up for the time being, the couple left the office, walked past the lobby and out the door.

"Well, I guess it's a dead end—no pun intended, said Danny.

Danny glanced at Emily, recognizing the determined look on her face that he had seen many times. She wasn't satisfied with the encounter with Dr. Thompson.

"Maybe I'm insensitive, but I can't see why it's so controversial. Its no crime to die of a disease. Why was Dr. Byrd so secretive? Why did he come up here to die in this God-forsaken place without any friends or relatives by his side?"

"I don't know," said Danny, obviously as frustrated as Emily. "All I know is the guy's entitled to his privacy, and he certainly got it here. This is the Hilton of privacy."

Just as they were about to get into the car, Emily stopped in her tracks, and stared into the distance, as if looking for guidance in the clouds.

"Let's go for a walk," she said.

"What?"

"Let's walk around the grounds. Maybe we can learn something."

"Sure."

They strolled aimlessly around the Gerrard building, past two utility buildings, and eventually made their way to the gazebo.

"This is a beautiful spot," said Emily, "But I wonder why they always choose to put a gazebo in private sanitariums. It must be required assignments for architecture schools."

They sat for a while, soaking up the late afternoon sun. They were about to leave when they were confronted by a thin wiry man in overalls who mysteriously appeared from behind a small clump of trees.

"Pardon me, but do any of you young folk have a cigarette?"

"No, I'm sorry," said Emily.

"Good for you—they're killers anyway. Are you folks visiting anybody?"

"Well, said Emily, "We came to see our teacher, but unfortunately he died two days ago."

"Oh, really?" the man declared, "I'm sorry to hear that….Did you say two days ago?"

"Yes."

"It must have been Joe Byrd, huh?"

"Yes," said Emily, "Did you know him?"

"Sure. We were on the same ward—nice fellow."

"You were on the same ward," Emily repeated.

"Yes, I'm afraid Joe and I were in the same boat—so to speak."

"I'm sorry," said Emily, "I don't know what you mean."

"I said we were in the same ward."

"I still don't understand," said Emily.

"Honey, don't you know where you are?" the man asked incredulously.

"Yes, of course. We're at a hospital—hospice."

"Honey, you're at AIDS death door. Don't you know that? Practically, everybody who dies here, dies of AIDS."

Emily looked at the man as if seeing him for the first time. The man was awfully thin, and concluded that he might have AIDS. Looking closer, she noticed a couple of lesions on his arm.

"I'm sorry," said Emily, "I didn't know. Everyone is so secretive around here."

"I know. We're like a leper colony, or worse. They put us here to die. It's horrible."

"Did you know Professor Byrd very well?" asked Emily.

"Joe? Sure, I knew him pretty good. He bunked right near me. He was a nice man. He suffered a great deal, especially toward the end."

"I don't mean to pry," said Emily, "But did he ever say anything about his situation, like why he left Wattford College?"

"Look, I don't know nuthin' about that. In the past couple weeks, all I ever heard was ranting and raving. He was hallucinating toward the end. He didn't make a lick of sense. I felt sorry for him."

"What did he say?" asked Emily.

"Just crazy stuff."

"What kind of crazy stuff?"

"Are you a reporter or something? He just rambled about…I don't know…He must have had some hang-up about red-heads."

"Red-heads?"

"He just kept saying something about red-headed death…red death…something like that…."

"Red-*headed*," repeated Emily, "Are you sure he said *red-headed*?"

"Honey, he said it a thousand times. Of course, I'm sure. Now, if you'll excuse me, I have to go."

The man walked away. Danny felt uncomfortable because he did not like trying to get information from someone who had just lost a friend. Undaunted, Emily ran after the man.

"Wait a minute! One more question! Did Professor Byrd have a tape recorder?"

The man stopped abruptly, turned toward Emily, still obviously irritated. "Please, girl, go home!"

"Please! It's important! Please tell us!"

"Okay, but you're getting on my nerves. Yes, he would make tapes for his mother, the poor soul."

"For his mother?" How do you know?"

"Because I saw him give them to her."

"In a brown manila envelop?" asked Emily.

"Yes, what difference does that make?"

"Sir, I think it makes a *big* difference."

The man turned around again and trotted briskly toward the main building, this time determined to escape these irritating people.

"Well, I guess that clears that up," said Emily.

Neither of them said anything until they arrived back at the car.

"Danny," she said, "Who do we know that is red-headed, connected with the theatre, and has been ill lately?"

Danny turned and looked at her in a frozen silence.

"I think Jody Hershberger is the red head, and the red death."

Constance walked into the room, glanced at the mirror, and noticed her lipstick was much too bright. Damn, she thought, while turning on a light, I look like a clown glowing in the dark. The television was on, but nobody was watching it. She recognized the program as a re-run of *The Love Boat*. She concluded that Amy must be working out in her room and that Jody was sleeping. Jody had been doing a lot of sleeping lately and Constance was beginning to worry about her. She really felt bad for her because all she did was sleep, and she ate practically nothing. She also was beginning to look really bad. Constance figured she was down to around ninety pounds. It was the first time in a long time that Constance felt sorry for both her roommates. She felt sorry for Jody because of her health. She was beginning to realize the limitations of wanting to be an actress. She thought that if actors did not make it in the entertainment business, they would think they were nothing. Jody, in particular, never expressed much of an interest in anything else. What will she do if she doesn't act? She is totally unprepared for the real world. Constance felt her weight was connected to the fact that she didn't get cast in the Marilyn Monroe part in *Gentlemen Prefer Blondes*. Jody fully expected to get that role and that made her even more depressed. Constance also felt sorry for Amy. She banked her whole existence on looking good and keeping her body finely tuned. What's going to happen when her face and body begin to age and she develops wrinkles and flabby muscles? She never got into the intellectual life of the college. After fours years of college all she's got to show for it are firm thighs and a boy friend. Amy and Chipper had begun to make wedding plans for after graduation, so Amy's future was pretty well set: she will wind up a bored housewife, watching her soaps, reading her dumb books, and working out on her *Buns of Steel* video when she's fifty years old. The phone rang.

"Hello?"

"Jody?"

"No, this is Constance."

"Constance, this is Emily Patterson. We met at the poetry party."

"Yes, of course. Danny Alderman's friend."

"Yes. I was wondering if Danny and I could talk to you about something...something important....maybe we could meet in the union."

"Sure."

"How about three o'clock today."

"Is this for a Sound Bite?"

"No. It's something else."

Constance did not know what to expect, but she knew it had to be serious. These two people would not call her out for something frivolous. She felt slightly nervous and hoped that it did not involve anything with her relationship with Tom Wilson. Maybe the school was going to put a stop to it. She was seated across from Danny and Emily. It was Emily who spoke first.

"Constance, Danny and I have been working on a story about the school, specifically why Professor Byrd was fired. We think that we have found out some information that is very sensitive in nature and we want your assurance that what we say will not be repeated."

"Of course."

"Let me cut to the chase. We know for a fact that Professor Byrd died of AIDS about a week ago. He died in a hospice in Fairfax. He was HIV positive for the last few years, and anybody who slept with him could have contracted the AIDS virus."

"Wait a minute!" yelled Constance, "You don't think I have AIDS do you?"

"No—No—asserted Emily emphatically, "We're not suggesting that at all."

"Go on..."

"Well...we do know that he was a professor in the theater department. and that he was gay. But, we also have reason to believe he was bi-sexual and may have slept with a female student."

Constance was extremely uncomfortable with the flow of this conversation. *Who were these people? What have they been doing for the past year? Prying into peoples' private lives?*

"I'm sorry," said Constance, "I don't see what this has to do with me."

"Constance...we have a strong suspicion that the girl is Jody Hershberger."

For the first time in her life, Constance Stewart was speechless.

"Constance....?"

"I need a shot of Jack Daniels."

Time seemed to freeze until Constance's shot of Jack Daniels arrived. After slugging the shot and chasing it with a huge gulp of beer, Constance manage to get a question out.

"What makes you say such a terrible thing?"

Danny was content to let Emily explain the situation to Constance. What the hell, he thought, she's doing a good job, much better than I could.

"Professor Byrd sent Danny a series of tapes," Emily began…"Audio tapes. They were sent anonymously, but we have strong reason to believe it was Professor Byrd. They were Professor Byrd playing his last role, a modern day Daniel Defoe."

"You lost me," said Constance.

"Daniel Defoe wrote *The Journal of the Plague Year* in the seventeenth century. It was a chronicle of the bubonic plague in England."

"I've heard of it. Didn't he write *Robinson Crusoe?*"

"Yes," said Emily. Anyway, the tapes are pretty weird, but he does talk about a new plague like AIDS and warns of a red death on campus."

"I don't get it."

When we went to visit Professor Byrd a man told us that toward the end of his life Professor Byrd was screaming about a red-headed death spreading the virus on purpose."

"Oh, come on!" Constance shouted, "There must be twenty-five red-heads on campus. Why do you suspect Jody?"

"Well," said Emily, "She is a theatre major."

"SO WHAT!!" Constance interrupted, "THEY ALL DYE THEIR HAIR RED!"

"I'm sorry, Constance. We feel badly about this. We thought you might be able to give us some information to help us deny or confirm these suspicions."

Constance was sickened, but she realized she would have to tell the truth about Jody's recent behavior and physical signs of deterioration.

"Well," Constance began haltingly, "Let me be honest with you. I don't know what to think, but I do know this. Jody has told everybody for the past few months that she has mono. She's tired all the time and always has symptoms of the flu. She also takes medicine every four hours for what she says are kidney problems. I guess you could say she has symptoms of the AIDS virus, although I certainly never thought of it before…..She just doesn't seem the type. As far as promiscuity is concerned….well….let me be honest….Jody has dated a lot of guys and stayed overnight in the dorms and apartments on many occasions. I heard the rumors….."

Constance's voice trailed off into the distance. She couldn't believe what she was saying. It sounded too fantastic to believe. Jody with AIDS? And yet, as the information began to sink it, it sounded more plausible. She suddenly felt sick to her stomach, struggling to maintain her composure.

"What are you going to do?" Constance asked.

"We don't know," said Emily. "We're still not totally convinced, although the evidence would dictate that we do something. Obviously, we need to be careful. This could ruin a person—or persons."

"It could also ruin innocent lives if she's not stopped," said Danny.

"That why we wanted to talk to you Constance," said Emily. "We didn't know what else to do. We're not in the habit of trying to ruin peoples' reputations."

Constance thought for a moment.

"Let me see if I can find out more information," said Constance.

"What do you mean?" asked Danny.

"I'll snoop around in her room. It's beyond tacky, I know, but I might find a prescription, a doctor's note, or something."

A penis is a thing to behold, really. There must be a ghastly creature inside every one—a miniature little bastard who gets on your nerves, fucks you like a locomotive, then shrivels up and quits on you, like bad deodorant on a blind date. I am sucking this guy off—or should I say, I am sucking off the little bastard, and I completely forget there is a human being attached to this thing. When Big Bastard spoke, I jumped out of my skin, as if me and Little Bastard were caught with our hands in the cookie jar.

"Oh………Jody, that feels soooo…..good."

"What?"

"Lower………..lower………"

What is this guy? A director? Is he giving me directions? I remove my luscious lips from his slim,y pulsating penis and slide upward toward his face. I have completely forgotten what it looks like. I remember his penis a lot more than his face. Who is this guy? Why am I sucking him off? It's dark as shit, but I feel his flat stomach and hairless chest with my fingers and lift myself up, knees bent, back arched, thrusting my legs forward until I am on top of him. Feeling much better, but still confused, I grab Little Bastard by the shaft and rub him against my pussy in a circular motion. More moans from Little Bastard's friend. Something like, Oh, Jody…….stick it in—something like that. Who cares?

No points for original lines in this play, but I'm willing to perform my part. Come to think of it, he's got his lines down pretty good. I hate it when I'm stuck with amateur actors who fuck up their lines. At least this guy is a pro.

"Oh, Jody, that feels sooooo………good."

"Do you like that?" *I ask while gently stroking it up and down.*

"Yes, give me more………give me more…."

"More what? More what?

"Fuck me, Jody………fuck me………"

"More what? More what?

"Fuck me………."

"GODDAMNIT!!! YOU BLEW YOUR FUCKIN' LINES!!!!!! I THOUGHT YOU WERE A PROFESSIONAL!!!!!!!!!"

"What???………"

"THAT'S NOT THE LINES, YOU IMBECILE!!!"

"Huh?"

"DON'T ACT STUPID!!! YOU SHOULD HAVE BEEN IN REHEARSAL ALL WEEK!!!"

"Rehearsals? What are you talking about? We're not in a play, for chrissakes."

"Well, obviously you're not," *I said mockingly.*

It's just my luck, being stuck in this lousy play with a lousy as shit actor. Gently removing myself from his chest, I roll over to the other side of the bed. Sighing deeply, I have to break the bad news to him.

"You blew your lines, Brando."

"I don't get it," *Big Bastard says,* "Do you want to play a game like we're in a play or movie?"

"This is no game, Marlon. Believe me, this is no game."

"Well, then, what are you talking about?"

I look at his face, really, for first time. He's just a skinny kid with a smooth baby face, hazel eyes, and closely cropped blonde hair. He could be a surfer dude riding the magnificent waves at Malibu. But no, he's here with me in Virginia, playing with death herself. Perhaps, he's a freshman; he looks about seventeen years old. Too bad he won't make it to twenty-five.

"I think I need to recast your part. I'll talk to the director tomorrow."

"What?"

"I hate to tell you this, but you're fired."

"Jody, are you alright?"

"I beg you're pardon?"

"You're not making any sense. Did I do something wrong? Are you mad at me for some reason?"

"What's your name?"

"Kevin."

"Well, Kevin, it's like this. In life, you're either right for the part, or not right for the part. It's that simple. I personally picked you out for this role tonight, and I'm sorry, but you are not right for the part. You're too young and immature, and unfortunately you don't know your lines."

"Oh, yeah, since when is picking up a chick at a fraternity party a performance. This is real life, not a play. Are you nuts?"

"Perhaps."

"Look," *said Big Bastard,* "Why don't you just leave."

"Don't worry, the curtain has dropped on this debacle. But I want to ask you something…something personal."

"We just had sex. You can ask me something personal."

"I want to know how you felt when you were inside me. How did you feel when you were pounding away at me without any regard for my feelings? Were you only thinking about yourself?"

"Honey, you've seen too many Oprah shows."

"How old are you?"

"Nineteen."

"You weren't thinking about me at all, were you?"

"Hey, I think you have a great body. I was turned on by your body. How could I feel anything about you? I don't even know you."

I glance away from this geek for a second, feeling around under the covers for my panties and bra. Where the hell was I? It smelled like a nasty dorm reeking with foul odors of sweat, stale beer, and peanuts.

"I just wanted to know if there was a connection between your dick and your mind, that's all."

"Man, you're one sick pup."

"And you, Kevin, are going to be sicker than me."

"What the hell are you talking about? You don't have a disease do you?"

"Of course not, stupid. I just mean you shouldn't go around sleeping with strange girls. It's not good for your...ah...development as a person."

"Great."

"I just have one more request before I leave."

"What's that?"

"Help me find my dress so I can get the hell out of here."

Amy and Stuart were sitting in the union going over more ideas for their interactive magazine on the web. Over the past few months, she had met with Stuart several times and he had finally convinced her that she had something to offer. Amy had written down some of the things she thought college students might need from an on-line magazine. Stuart created a web-site called *collegelife.com* and was in the process of adding Amy's ideas to the site. They decided to name the magazine *Contemporary College Life*. Stuart did not have a girlfriend and would have asked her out long ago, but felt he did not have a chance with her. Amy still dated Chipper and other guys on the side, but she was beginning to slow down her involvement with other men. She thought it was time to settle down with someone in a sincere relationship. For the past three years, she always thought it would be Chipper and those other guys were just college flings. But she was growing more discontented with Chipper's attitudes and his total interest in sports. She told him about her ideas for the magazine and he said she was stupid for even attempting such a "hare-brained" scheme. He also said Stuart was only in it for a "piece of ass."

"I think student s need better prices on their books," said Amy. "That's real important,plus they need information about concerts, plays, that kind of thing."

"I know a guy who can write great album reviews," said Stuart.

"Maybe we could offer an advice column, especially for freshmen who are trying to get adjusted."

"Maybe you should do it."

"I think Constance would be better than me. She's a good writer."

Chipper entered the union and approached the couple. He was dressed in tattered blue jeans and a *Green Bay Packers* sweatshirt. A *New York Yankees* baseball cap was perched backwards on his head.

"Well, if it isn't the magazine moguls. How sweet."

"Chipper, you know Stuart. We're putting together the magazine."

"Stuart. How's it going? Mind if I sit down?"

"Well?"

"Thanks. What are you working on?"

"Ideas for the first issue." Said Amy.

"I have an idea."

"What?"

"You two can kiss my ass."

"Don't act stupid," said Amy.

"We're just going over ideas," said Stuart.

"Yeah, ideas about sucking and fucking."

"Chipper, don't be an ass. You're making a fool out of yourself."

"Listen, maybe I better leave. You two probably need to talk."

"Oh, don't' leave, Stuart. I want to know all about this project. I may order a subscription. How much does it cost?"

"Chipper, why don't you just go away."

"Let's go Amy. I want to talk to you."

"I'm not going anywhere"

"Oh, yes you are—"

Chipper reached over the booth, grabbed Amy by the shoulder, lifted her out of the booth, and dragged her ten feet, kicking and screaming. Stuart bounded from the booth and ran up to stop them.

"Hey! Let go of her!"

Chipper, who was much bigger than Stuart, turned around and pounded Stuart in the face with his fist. Stuart went flying across the room, blood spurting profusely from his face.

"Chipper!" yelled Amy. "What the hell are you doing?"

"Taking my girlfriend back, that's what!"

"Let go of me! Are you out of your mind?"

"You're my girlfriend and I'm not going to let you cheat on me with that computer geek."

"I'm not cheating! We're just working together on a magazine!"

Danny and Jason entered the union and saw Stuart lying on the floor bleeding, dazed and confused. They spotted Chipper dragging Amy toward the door.

"Hey! What's going on?" screamed Jason.

"None of your fucking business," said Chipper, pushing Jason aside.

"Let go of me!" screamed Amy.

"Hey, Chipper, cool it," said Danny.

"Fuck you, Alderman."

Jason and Danny turned and faced Chipper, preventing him from leaving with Amy.

"Get out of my way, assholes."

"You know Chipper, I never did like you," said Jason as he swung and landed a mighty blow to Chipper's face. Chipper reeled back from the impact, letting go of Amy. Chipper staggered, but did not fall. He recovered and came toward Jason with a sneer on his lips and murderous hatred in his heart. Chipper drew back his right hand and was about to deliver a shot to Jason, but Jason was much too quick for him. Jason darted to his left, dodged the blow, and came up with an uppercut to Chipper's jaw. He fell like a giant oak onto the floor of the union, out cold.

"Nice shot," said Danny.

"I never did like that punk," repeated Jason.

Amy was upset, but quickly regained her composure. "Thanks Jason— Danny....I'm sorry about all of this."

"Let's see about this other guy," said Jason.

The three of them went over to Stuart. Jason and Danny hoisted him up and sat him down in a nearby booth.

"Hey, fellow. Take it easy," said Danny.

"I'm alright," said Stuart. "I don't think anything is broken."

Amy sat down next to Stuart and offered him a cloth for his bleeding nose. "Thanks."

Chipper was regaining consciousness on the other side of the union.

"You guys are dead meat!" he yelled.

"Oh, yeah?" said Jason. "You want some more of me?"

"Fuck you," scowled Chipper, as he limped out of the building.

"That guy is a wusse," said Jason. "Thinks he's hot shit, picking on people that are smaller than him."

"He's a coward," said Danny.

"That does it," said Jason. "I'm drinking!"

"Hey," said Amy. "Thanks, you guys. You came just in time."

"Don't mention it," said Danny.

Emily found Mrs. Chambers at her favorite bar stool in the elegant lounge of the Boar's Head Country Club. She was alone, staring vacantly at a row of whiskey bottles, sipping a mixed drink. The easy listening, cool jazzy sounds of a Frank Sinatra tape drifted effortlessly from a set of speakers behind the bar.

"Pardon me, are you Mrs. Chambers?"

"Yes, dear. Who wants to know?"

"I'm Emily Patterson, a student at Wattford College. Can I talk to you for a minute?"

"Do I look busy?"

"I'm writing a newspaper article about your husband. I was wondering if you could tell me some personal stories or anecdotes to make it more interesting."

"You have beautiful hair. Natural?"

"Yes. Thank you."

Mrs. Chambers stared back into her drink. Emily thought for a moment she had forgotten she was there.

I've got you under my skin

I've got you deep in the heart of me

So deep in my heart

That you're really a part of me......

Mrs. Chambers...?"

"You want stories? You mean the kind that describe the great man and his kindness toward strangers?"

"Actually, I didn't have anything specific in mind. You could just tell me something about his personal likes and dislikes."

"He dislikes me."

"I beg your pardon?"

"He's a shit. You know that? A real shit."

Mrs. Chambers leaned further into her drink, as if she wanted to fall in.

But why should I try to resist

   When baby I know so well

      That I've got you under my skin……

"So, you want to know about the great Chuck Chambers?"

"Listen, if you'd rather do this some other time….?"

"No, this is a perfect time. Your timing could not be better."

"Well, if you could just tell me one story…?"

"How much time do you have?"

"I have all night."

"Let me see…one story. Okay, Emily, relax. Here's one for the books:

"Once upon a time there was a young couple and they were very much in love. They both attended the same small college in a little town in Virginia. He was an outstanding athlete, a promising undergraduate economics major, and the cutest hunk on campus. Do they still use the word 'hunk?'"

"Yes."

"Anyway, she was a beautiful, wholesome cheerleader who adored and worshipped him. They were a perfect couple, envied by everyone on campus. After graduation, she followed her Knight in Shining Armor to the University of Virginia. He enrolled as a graduate student in the Economics Department and she went to work as an elementary school teacher…"

Mrs. Chambers paused for a moment, carefully took another sip of her drink, and nodded to the waiter.

"Hal," she said to the waiter.

He brought her another drink.

"How am I doing so far?"

"It's a good story," Emily said.

"Well, I'm sorry my dear, but that's about all the good stuff…for the next thirty years, anyway. Now…where was I?"

"You were at the University of Virginia…"

"Oh, yes, of course."

"As the months went by something went wrong with their marriage. In the beginning it was hard to put your finger on it. Things just didn't seem right. Perhaps, it was a small thing like forgetting to call her if he was going to be late. Or maybe it was a big issue, like never making time to do things together. He would study all the time and begin to spend more and more time with his friends in the Economics Department. They had fights about money. There never seemed to be enough. She was not making much money teaching, and he was barely bringing in three hundred dollars a month as a teaching assistant for two courses. He began to spend more money on his socializing, leaving her out of the picture. Gradually, their conversations practically ceased. You see the Knight was growing tired of his cheerleader wife, and the wife was beginning to notice a few rust spots in the armor. He was learning all kinds of new ideas, studying sophisticated Macro-Economics and she was just teaching little kids how to learn their ABC's. He was becoming an intellectual and she was becoming a small town, frumpy school teacher and housewife. The Vietnam War was raging and the Knight was becoming more conservative and patriotic, even though he avoided the draft by going to college and getting married. He began to preach against pointed-headed liberals, anarchists and cowards who wouldn't support their country. He joined the University chapter of the Young Republicans. She had very little interest in politics and preferred to read old Victorian novels like Pride and Prejudice. They grew further and further apart until they barely spoke to each other except to communicate the bare essentials of living. What time do you want to eat, dear? What time will you be home? Did you pay the electric bill?

Mrs. Chambers carefully removed a pack of cigarettes from her purse, extracted one, and patiently tapped the end of a cigarette into her silver lighter. She did not seem to be in a hurry to finish her story. Finally, after a few seconds of packing her cigarette, she lit it up, taking a deep drag.

Strangers in the night, exchanging glances

Wondering in the night

What were the chances…

"Do you smoke?" she asked.

"No…no thank you."

"Of course. You don't look the type. Were you ever a cheerleader?"

"No."

"Too mindless, huh? Too much playing second fiddle to the boys?"

"No, ma'am. I just wasn't very coordinated."

"I see…"

Emily was somewhat surprised that Mrs. Chambers' behavior was composed and her speech barely suggested that she might be drinking heavily. She felt she spoke like one of her fourth grade teachers, very poised and careful about pronunciation. There were, however, tell-tale signs that she was drinking. She slouched slightly forward in her chair, folding her arms over her lap for support. The slouching, coupled with the tendency for her head to droop into the direction of her drink, made her look like a tired patron of a bar, which of course is what she was. At times, she looked permanently attached to this spot, as if she was eternally condemned to play the part of a broken down middle-aged alcoholic housewife. Yet, at the same time, Emily had no doubt that there was a lucid and quick mind behind all the alcohol.

"Don't call me ma'am, okay?"

"Oh, yes…I'm sorry."

"It's Dolores."

"Dolores, please go on with the story…if you want to."

"Of course I want to. I've never had so much fun in my life. Are you writing all this down?"

"Yes, ma—I mean, Dolores."

"Good, but it doesn't matter. It's already written, if you want it."

"I'm sorry, I don't know what you mean."

"I have kept a diary of my life. The sordid affairs of Ellsworth Chambers."

"Are you saying that you would give me the diary of your marriage?"

"Certainly, but let me proceed. You can decide later if you want the fine details. Where were we?"

"You were growing apart. He was becoming more political."

Doesn't like crap games with Barons or Earls

Won't go to Harlem in ermine and pearls

Won't dish the dirt with the rest of the girls…

"Time went on and he was working on the final stages of his dissertation. I rarely saw him—I mean, she rarely saw him. He was either in the library or in a bar with his friends. She couldn't stand his friends. All they would do was get drunk, talk economics, and rail against the protesters against the war; how the were tearing the coun-

try apart. Then she met Henry Faulkner. He was a graduate student in Political Science—a genius. She met him at one of the faculty get-togethers. He was totally unlike Ellsworth. Henry was a real intellectual. They began going out surreptitiously, and eventually she began sleeping with him. He was the kindest man she ever met. Henry was a left-wing radical who routinely protested the war and was a member of Students for a Democratic Society, a radical group led by Tom Hayden, who married Jane Fonda, of all people. Naturally, Ellsworth hated Henry. There was a lot of hate in those days. I don't know why they called us the 'Love Generation.' That makes about as much sense as the 'Pepsi Generation.' Anyway, the former cheerleader found herself pregnant by Henry. She knew it was Henry's because she hadn't slept with her husband in three months. She did not know what to do. She panicked. Henry wanted the young woman to leave her husband and have the baby. Henry really loved her very much. But she was young and stupid. She didn't believe in divorce. So, she went to New York and paid some butcher in a back alley a thousand dollars to give her an abortion. He botched the job and made her infertile.."

"End of story, Emily, except for a few messy details. You see that's why Chuck and I never had any kids. He found out about the affair, the abortion and my infertility. I had to tell him eventually. He really wanted kids very badly. You know, a little Chuckie junior to take to the baseball games. Of course, he never forgave me. When he found out I slept with a radical student protester, he went berserk. So you see, honey, that's why ole Chuck Chambers is so conservative. Liberals have ruined his life in more ways than one."

Mrs. Chambers stopped talking, glanced around the room as if she was coming out of a dream, and ordered another drink.

Don't you know that it's worth

Every treasure on earth

To be young at heart

For as rich as you are

It's much better by far

To be young at heart......

"So, you see, Emily," Mrs. Chambers continued, "My life is a mess. I'm married to the biggest bastard in Virginia, probably the world, and everybody thinks he's a big hero. The only think he ever loved was that little twit niece of ours, Jody. He dotes on her like a long lost daughter. He blames me for everything. If it wasn't for my work with Big Brothers and Big Sisters, I would have given up a long time ago."

"Mrs. Chambers—I mean Dolores—I do have one question. Do you know if your husband had anything to do with the firing of Professor Byrd in the theatre department?"

"Yes. Chuck fired him. He contracted AIDS and he had to go. That was part of the plan."

"Plan?"

"Emily, don't you know by now? Chuck Chambers is trying to turn Wattford into a right-wing totalitarian institution. He's dangerous."

"You mean he's behind all these conservative actions taken lately?"

"You bet he is. And I bet you'd like to see that diary now, wouldn't you?"

"Dolores, it's up to you. That's you personal diary. However, if you want to give it to me, I'll certainly take it. Is there a lot of information about your husband's dealings at the college?"

"Honey, it's all in there."

Constance walked into the apartment, heading straight for Jody's room. She felt guilty about going in there without her permission, but she knew she could not be concerned about privacy. She had been thinking about what Emily and Danny had told her and she admitted to herself that she really did think that Jody had the HIV virus. In fact, she was surprised she did not suspect it before. She had been steadily losing weight and always had symptoms of a cold. She also still wore a beeper on her wrist to remind her to take her "kidney" medicine. She had not noticed any lesions on her body, but those could be covered up with make-up. Sadly, she did not have any trouble believing that Jody would sleep with guys and purposefully give them AIDS. Constance also recognized that Jody's personality had been going through some drastic changes in the past month. It was not just the mood swings between manic and depression, but she would zone out at times and stared into space as if she were drugged. She noticed that she was losing her ability to concentrate and caught Jody several times mumbling to herself. Constance dismissed all these warnings because, after all, Jody was an actress. She might be rehearsing a part or just being theatrical.

Constance rummaged around her room, looking into closets, drawers, and under the bed. Jody's room was a mess: Clothes, magazines, shoes, jeans, books, sweaters, and socks were piled everywhere in total disarray. She couldn't even tell what color comforter she had on the bed because it was filled to the maximum with bundles of clothes. She glanced in a couple of her dressers and did not see anything incriminating, except for a cheesy pair of silk panties from Victoria's secret. She was beginning to think that she wasn't going to find anything. Moving stealthily into the bathroom, she opened the medicine cabinet, but it contained on the usual stuff: aspirin, Midol, cough syrup, toothpaste, nail clipper, and band aids. She looked behind the shower curtain, although she had no idea what prompted her to look there. She did not think she would hide drugs in the shower. As she was going out the door, she took a quick look down at the trash basket in the corner. Underneath several torn up, make-up stained tissues, she found a prescription bottle. She turned the bottle over, checking out the label, thinking it might be AZT, but it read, "Flexeril." She did know what flexeril was, but somehow she did not think it had anything to do with AIDS.

Going into the bedroom, Constance was growing more discouraged, guilty, and uneasy about searching Jody's room. She might come in any minute. Constance sat down at Jody's desk which was littered with dirty ashtrays, textbooks, floppy discs, notebooks, and romance novels. Lifting a few books from beneath a pile, she absentmindedly scanned a few of the titles. Jody had terrible taste in literature. How could anybody read a book called *Lust for Love?* She pulled the desk back from the wall to see if anything was behind it, and heard something hit the floor. Awkwardly, she starting crawling on her hands and knees, arching her neck and spine, straining to fit into the tiny space. Stretching her left hand, she managed to retrieve the fallen object. It was a plain black notebook. Constance dusted it off and looked at the title on the cover: *The Last Official Journal of Jody, the Princess.* Quickly scanning the journal, it did not take long for Constance to feel sick to her stomach. She had never read such horrible trash. She promptly concluded that this was the voice of a lunatic. Suddenly, she felt nervous and apprehensive. The journal made her afraid of Jody. Obviously, the real Jody was a violent, sadistic person. Slipping the journal back into its original position, she hastily left the room.

The apartment was strangely quiet. The television was not even on. Constance sat down on the living room couch, staring into space, feeling completely immobile, almost catatonic. Her feelings were so mixed up. She felt a combination of anger, dismay, disgust, helplessness, betrayal, resentment, and pity, all at the same time. She realized that she was living with a mad woman, a woman criminally insane, and she didn't know it. She wondered how she could have been so naïve and how Jody have fooled her so completely. Constance thought she was a perceptive person, but concluded that she was a fool. Of course, Constance realized she was not the only one. Jody truly turned in one of her finest performances at the expense of a lot of ignorant, innocent men.

Constance also felt pangs of sympathy. She knew Jody must be going through hell, and she was obviously severely mentally ill. She wondered why she did not let her and Amy know; they could have given her some moral support. Then again, she also realized that the two of them were not that good in times of crisis. They were, after all, shallow people. Constance knew that deep in her soul.

She still could not bring herself to imagine Jody deteriorating and dying. She was so ignorant that she really did not think college kids could get AIDS. Jody was the first one she had heard about in Virginia.

She began to cry profusely and she felt terrible, like she was drowning in her own tears. She was not even crying for Jody, but for all the suffering, sad and lonely people in the world. It seemed, at that moment, the only way of responding to the sad human condition. She wept for a long time. She was slowly coming to realize that she had been a horrible phony the whole year, possibly her whole life. She had been denying her true feelings and ignoring the emotional needs of everyone around her, including Tom Wilson. No amount of sugarcoating could hide the fact that Constance at this very moment considered herself to be a worthless, selfish college brat who only thought about herself.

She was determined to change all that. Perhaps, with time, she could improve as a human being, but she did not have much practice at sincerity, but she wanted to give it a try. She was going to start with Tom Wilson. Maybe, she thought, I can begin living for someone else instead of just thinking about myself.

She snapped out of her trance. This was no time for introspection. If she was going to be a more responsible person, she had better start with the current problem. Rising from the couch, she left the apartment, resolved to find Emily and Danny with one thing on her mind:

Jody Hershberger has got to be stopped.

DENOUEMENT: MAY 5-19

"……and if that wasn't bad enough, in comes this dodo with some cock and bull story about Jody having AIDS. My niece having a homo disease. How ridicules can you get? Now I have a hundred reporters outside my office wanting to know why I fired that queer bait Byrd. I mean, who really cares? It must have been those two students who tipped them off. I'll get them for sure, this time…..Uh…..Dolores….pass the black-eyed peas, plu…..ease! So, they're throwing a microphone in my face asking a lot of questions about my supposedly right-wing conservative agenda, bribing the Dean of the College, and threatening to have two innocent students thrown out of school. Innocent, my ass. I high-tailed it out of there without answering one single question. Let them talk to my boatload of lawyers! 'No comment' is all I have to say.!……Dolores, pass the black-eyed peas, for God's sake!….Anyway, it's the damn liberal press snooping around my business…..DOLORES!!!! WHAT ARE YOU? DRUNK—OR DEAF?"…..I bet that little piss-ant Parsons is spilling his guts right now. Dolores, what gives with you? You haven't said a word all night. Been down to the club all day?"

"Yes."

"You'd better watch out, they're gonna permanently screw you to that bar stool if you're not careful. Never mind, I'll get the damn peas myself."

Dolores watched him closely. She saw him grab the bowl of peas, shoving them on his plate; his grim, determined dog-eyes darting back and forth, like a caged animal.

"I wonder how those bastards found out. They knew everything. How did they know all about my plans? They even knew details about our marriage, the snooping bastards."

The animal moved about with a troubled countenance, his kingdom toppling in ruins, yet fighting with obstinate fury for wounded pride.

"I'll get that whole damn team of Cohen, Cohen, and Cohen on their ass. They don't know who they're dealing with. They're violating my civil liberties…that's what they're doing. They will never get way with this."

Afraid and worried, the wounded creature tugged at his collar, sweating profusely, attempting to breathe easier.

"Dolores, you could at least say something. My God, I could be ruined. Your niece is dying, for God's sake. Don't you care?"

"I told them."

"What?"

"I told them."

"Who? What?"

"Everything. I gave them my diary. It's all there."

"You mean those two reporters?"

"Yes."

"Are you out of your mind?"

"Yes."

"Dolores, you're a stinking, drunken lunatic, do you hear?"

The surging animal's blood began to boil, fire flaming out his nostrils. Dog-eyes staring…cornered, rat-like, he felt threatened without his defenses. He must strike out at something. It's his nature.

"Dolores, I'll kill you…"

The first blow landed squarely on the victim's face, a huge purple bruise immediately weld up around her eyes. Lying down in a prone position, and covering her face as best she could, the victim was pummeled with pelting blows from the animal's horrific charge. Her frail body withstood the relentless pounding.

"YOU STUPID BITCH!"

Worried no more, she felt the hammer-like fists crush her body. Bones began to crumble. Gradually, a kind of contented numbness overcame her. He has already killed her many years before, so there was nothing more to declare.

"YOU WRECKED MY LIFE!!! YOU STUPID WHORE!!!"

Curled in a fetal position, covering her face, the animal is frustrated that he could only land blows to her ribs and stomach. More bones, tiny and larger, crumble and collapse. She almost passed out, lying silently until his energy slowly dissipated.

"THIRTY YEARS I PUT UP WITH YOUR SHIT!!!"

Growing weary of beating his victim, the brute finally slowed down his assault, and returned to the head of the table. He grabbed a piece of chicken and took out a huge bite.

"You deserved that, you wretched slut."

Moaning slightly, the victim's hands clutched her stomach where most of the punches had landed. She attempted to rise up, but the pain was too much for her. She slumped back onto the kitchen floor. Her time was coming, but it would have to wait a few minutes.

"I want you to call those two students and tell them it was all a pack of lies, do you hear me? Lord knows what you told them. You tell them you are a broken down alcoholic who has lost touch with reality."

Groping for support, the victim latched onto a chair, pulled herself up, and gingerly sat back in her seat. The pocketbook was dangling from the arm of the chair.

"Dolores, I don't know who the hell you think you are…"

Reaching into her pocketbook, she felt the comfort of cold steel against her bruised wrist. The metal object makes her feel more secure, powerful.

"You deserved that, you know. Now tell me what you told them."

Although one eye was almost closed, she could still see the terror in his eyes, as she pulled her equalizer from its hiding place. He may have said something at the end, she couldn't be sure. But she waited a few seconds, savoring the moment, so that in time she would not forget this wonderful feeling. It was her finest hour.

With one slight, but determined movement of her finger, she was a victim no more.

Old stone walls crawling with honeysuckle curved into neat lines of black and white fences along dirt lanes sunken with centuries of weather-beaten use. In the distance, cows and horses speckled florid emerald fields among the red barns, silver silos, and white farmhouses. The quiet serenity of spring had finally arrived in the Shenandoah valley chasing the harsh hill-earth in favor of softened, thawed, rich patches of woodland. A great tree of birds rejoicing the arrival of spring sang their warm throated notes to the assembled crowd at Foxfield races. The countryside was bursting with a plethora of wild flowers, stunning collections of dogwoods, spectacular flame azaleas and spring blossoms of violets, chickweeds, and blood roots in the quiet oak glades of Albemarle county. Amidst the mossy stone walls, gravel lanes and sloping green lawns gathered a great multitude of people eager and ready to watch the great running of the thoroughbreds at Foxfield stables. There was nothing on earth like the coming of spring in the central part of Virginia. All around the participants was the sound of nature recovering from the barren lostness of winter. An early contingent of excitable robins flew over a tree hung with wisteria vines; the meadows were ringing with bird calls from every variety, like the velvety sounds of scarlet tanagers and hooded warblers. Adjacent to the wood-frame stables, unnoticed by the growing throng of horse bettors, small wooded animals came out to loiter by the fresh water marshes dotted by beaver ponds, teeming with renewed birdlife.

Hundreds of anxious would-be winners lined the wooden rail encircling the well-groomed race track, while hundreds more sat in their expensive box seats like sophisticated aristocrats from the Old South, sipping mint juleps and discussing anachronistic politics and tawdry affairs; while in the grassy fields a massive hoard of already-drunk, tail-gating college students were gulping down gallons of beer and watermelon shooters; while along the edges of the fence, beautiful young maidens smiled coquettishly in pastel sun dresses, and twirling multi-colored fans beaming with innocent eyes toward the neatly Docker-clad, blue-button-down boys from the local military academy and fraternity houses at the University of Virginia. Nowhere else in America could such a variety of people assemble for social intercourse; yet here at Foxfield races the well-bred snooty Republicans blended with the stoned, Deadhead marijuana smokers; independent environmental "GreenPeace" advocates shared a bar with Missy and Skip, who just arrived by limousine from their society debutant ball; a greasy, multi-tattooed biker named Boris from Oakland could place a bet alongside Mrs. J. Winston Piersall, III, one of the influential patrons of the arts in Charlottesville. It was, indeed, a cosmopolitan atmosphere, an atmosphere in which a slightly drunk Jason Sparrow did not mind resorting to one of the things he told everybody not to do at a party. He told a joke.

"Okay, so this guy walks into a psychiatrist's office and tells him he's having a strange dream over and over. Tell me about it, says the psychiatrist. Well, he says, in the dream I am either a tepee or a wigwam. What do you think, doc? Well, first of all, says the psychiatrist, you need to relax. You're two tents."

"Ohhhhhh…..that is the *worst* joke of the century….ouch."

The three students were enjoying themselves at Foxfield, but also trying to piece together the strange, incredible sequence of events of the last couple weeks. So much had changed in so short a time, all their heads were still spinning. Somehow, through the crisis, Wattford College managed to survive. Mrs. Chambers was currently awaiting trial for murder, but considering her physical condition, the likelihood of an acquittal or light sentence seemed probable. Her attorney was arguing for self-defense. Emily visited her in jail and found her quite content and extremely composed, not worried at all about the upcoming trial. After reading her journal, Jody was not surprised to find her happier now. Her husband was obviously torturous to live with.

The board of trustees formed a special council to look into the affairs of Dr. Chambers and issued several statements to the college community indicating that the college did not endorse any of his "radical views." They also hired an interim President of the College until a full search committee could find a replacement for Dr. Cronin. He was not found guilty of any wrongdoing, but he was fired for letting all this happen on his watch. Through it all, Danny and Emily were asked to attend several meetings at the request of the board and told them all they knew. They were also questioned by the police investigating the murder of Dr. Chambers. Emily said she never got so much attention in her life. Dean Parsons resigned under pressure and they hired a new person in the Dean of Students Office. There was a tremendous shake-up at the college, but Danny and Emily and most of the others seemed to have weathered the storm.

"Hey, Emily," cried Jason, "Are you and Danny going to the Commencement Ball?"

"Yes," Emily answered, "Can you believe Danny's going to wear a tux?"

"What do you mean?" asked Danny. "Don't you think I'm Mr. GQ?"

"I think you're Mr. Low IQ," interjected Jason.

"And that, ladies and gentlemen, from someone who took six years to graduate from college! They will probably give you a twenty-one gun salute when you walk down the isle to pick up your diploma."

"I'm expecting the governor and Colin Powell to be here for the occasion," countered Jason. "Hey, who are you betting on in the third race?"

"I like *Gypsy Dancer*," said Emily.

"That dog?" responded Jason. "He won't even finish!"

"I think he'll run good on a fast track."

"I'm putting my money on *Dirty Low Down*."

"One thing still bothers me about all this mess," said Danny. "Why didn't Byrd just call us on the phone and tell us about Jody instead of having his mother deliver those off-the-wall tapes?" He could have saved some guys a lot of worry and grief, or worse."

"I thought about that," said Emily, "And I've come to the conclusion that Professor Byrd did not know Jody was HIV positive until much later. I asked the people at Merryweather and they told me that Jody had come to visit him one time in February. We received the last tape two weeks ago. Remember, there was no mention of a red death until the last tape."

"Do you think Jody told Byrd that she was giving guys AIDS on purpose?" asked Jason.

"I'd say she probably did," Emily said. "It does make sense. Why else would she go for only one visit? All we know is that right after the visit, we get the first warning from Byrd that the red death is contaminating people."

"So," said Danny, "Why didn't he call us then instead of making an obscure reference to it in a tape."

"Professor Byrd was very concerned about anyone finding him," Emily continued, "I'm not sure why. Perhaps, he was ashamed, or maybe he knew he was losing his body, and his mind, and didn't want anyone to see him in that condition. Mrs. Chambers' diary said that Dr. Chambers threatened to withdraw the insurance payments if he went public. Maybe it was a matter of money."

"Maybe he wanted to milk his last performance to the hilt," suggested Danny. "I think he really got into playing the role of Defoe. He probably couldn't resist making the last tape."

"He still deserves a lot of credit, though," said Emily. "Without the tapes, it may have taken us a while to catch on to Jody and her uncle."

"Yeah," said Jason, "How lucky do I feel? If it wasn't for that medical party, I'd be a dead duck. It's bizarre."

"Like I said before," said Danny, "I think she really liked you and didn't want to infect you."

"Well, for once in my life I got lucky. There are plenty of guys on campus who are sweating it out right now."

"I feel sorry for them," Emily said. "Jody was taking advantage of so many men. It's unfair."

"It sure says a lot for safe sex," said Danny.

"Yeah," said Jason, "From now on, I'm going to abstain from sex until I get married."

"We'll see how long you keep that promise," joked Danny.

"I still can't believe it," said Emily. "Did you hear that *Hard Copy* is sending a crew to cover the trial of Mrs. Chambers. It's all over the national news services."

"I got a call from *The National Enquirer*" said Danny. "They wanted to know all about Jody Hershberger."

"What did you tell them?" asked Jason.

"Nothing. That's all we need is for the media to turn this thing into a circus. It's already a big enough circus without trash TV and the tabloids taking over the story."

"Where is Jody?" asked Jason.

"I know she left school," Emily said. "I was talking to Constance Stewart and she said that Jody disappeared from sight. By the way, she's engaged to Professor Wilson."

"You're kidding," said Danny.

"No, in fact, she said we would be getting an invitation for the wedding in the mail."

"What about Amy Toeffler?" asked Danny.

"She's dating Stuart Pennington."

"The computer guy?"

"Yes, they're starting a magazine on the Internet."

"Well, they don't call it commencement for nothing," said Danny.

"What do you mean?" asked Emily.

"Commencement means beginning. That's what it is for the three of us. It's not over for the good guys. It's just beginning."

"I'll drink to that," said Jason, lifting his beer mug high into the air.

Danny and Emily did likewise, hoisting their beers in the air, and all proclaiming in unison:

"TO GRADUATION!!! TO GRADUATION!!!"

There were runners on second and third base for the Cannonville Little League Tigers as Larry Ramsey slashed a wicked line drive off the third baseman's glove, sprinted down to first base, and streaked for second base as the left fielder chased down the ball and threw it to third base.

"Way to go, Larry!" shouted Wilson. "That's two RBIs in one swing!"

"Alright!" screamed Constance. "That's the way to do it!"

"What's an RBI?" asked Sally.

"An RBI is a run batted in," explained Wilson. "That means Larry knocked in two runs with his hit."

Constance, Professor Wilson, and Sally Benjamin were sitting in the sun-bleached stands watching a Little League baseball game. Wilson had asked Constance to come and see Joey play, and Constance had brought along her new little sister, Sally. Sally, who came from a very poor family, had never seen a baseball game. She was thrilled to be there.

"Are they going to win?" asked Sally.

"I hope so," said Constance. "But they still have four more innings to go."

Lucy Satterfield popped out to the shortstop to end the inning. The score was: Tigers 6, Cardinals 3.

"I like baseball," said Sally. "Did you ever play baseball, Constance?"

"Well, I played a little softball in my time, but not baseball."

"These days lots of girls play in the Little League," said Wilson.

"I want to play," said Sally.

"We can go out and practice if you want to," said Constance. "I can still throw the ball."

The Cardinals mounted a rally in the fourth inning, scoring three runs on a bases-loaded double by the center fielder. Joey, playing left field, made the third out by flagging down a deep line drive to left-center. The score was tied.

"How about some hotdogs?" asked Wilson.

The two girls nodded and Wilson went to the concession stand to get hotdogs for everyone.

"I like Mr. Wilson, don't you?" said Sally.

"Yes. I like him very much. He's a doctor you know."

"I thought he was a teacher."

"He is. Teachers can be doctors too, doctors of philosophy."

"Gee, he must be smart. Are you going to get married?"

"Yes. In a few months."

"Are you going to stay in Cannonville?"

"Yes. I'll be here for a long time."

"I'm glad."

Wilson came back from the concession stand cradling three hotdogs and drinks for everybody.

"What's a baseball game without hotdogs?" asked Wilson, dispensing them to the two girls.

In the fifth inning, the Tigers threatened a rally when Stevie Bumgarner singled to right and LaShawn Rivers walked. But Louie Furman stuck out and Ritchie Evans grounded into a double play. The score remained tied.

"I want to be a baseball player when I grow up," said Sally.

"You better practice a lot," said Wilson.

"What are you going to be when you grow up Constance?" asked Sally.

"Do I have to grow up?"

"Doesn't everybody?" asked Sally.

"No, they don't. Unfortunately, not everyone grows up...I think I want to work for Big Brothers and Big Sisters. They have some paying jobs in the organization. What do you think of that?"

"Will I see you again?"

"You will see me all the time."

"That's great...then we can practice baseball?"

'You bet."

In the top of the seventh inning, the Cardinals scored three runs on four singles, a double, and an error by the second baseman, Calvin Jones. The score going into the Tigers last bat was: Cardinals 9, Tigers 6.

"It looks pretty bleak for the home team," said Wilson. "They need a big rally to won.'

"I want to be a pitcher," said Sally. "That's looks like fun."

"Do you want to go to Dairy Queen for ice cream afterwards?" asked Constance.

"Can we? I love ice cream!"

In the bottom of the seventh inning, Ritchie Evans walked to lead off the inning. Brooks Eisenstadt struck out. Butch Cowers lofted a flair into the right field that barely escaped the grasp of Todd Michelson. With runners on the first and second, Suzie Cramer popped out to the catcher. Following a walk to Shelia Jones, Joey came up with the bases loaded, two out, trailing 9 to 6. The first pitch was a slow curve, barely missing the outside corner. Ball one. The second pitch was a wicked fastball that Joey ripped for a foul tip. The third pitch was a high fast ball out of the strike zone. With the count two balls, one strike, the pitcher wound up and threw a fast ball right down the middle of the plate. Joey swung with all his might and crushed the pitch deep into left field. The left fielder ran back toward the wall, and made a gallant effort to catch it. But the ball sailed over the fence for a home run.

The fans burst into a frenzy of excitement as Joey rounded the plate and headed home for the game winning homer. Wilson, Constance, and Sally were beside themselves with joy. As he touched home plate, his teammates hoisted Joey on their shoulders and carried him off the field.

Running up to Wilson, Constance and Sally, Joey screamed, "We won! We Won!"

Jumping up and down and hugging Joey, Wilson exclaimed to everyone: "Our hero! Let's celebrate with some ice cream!! What do you say!!"

"Welcome parents, alumnae, students, and friends to the one hundred and thirty first commencement ceremonies of Wattford College…"

Thus, began the annual commencement speech by Senator John Warner. Sitting in the back row with the rest of the graduates, donning a cap and gown, Emily still found it hard to believe that this day had come. She was filled with giddy excitement and just a little bit apprehensive about the future. She glanced over at Danny in the third row and he winked back at her. She thought he looked cute in a cap and gown.

Danny did his last Sound Bite one week ago. The subject was "What are you going to do after graduation?" It was a good subject for the couple who had discussed the issue at length. The decided they cared about each other too much to live apart. Danny said that when two people love each other, they organize their lives to be with each other. It was that simple for the two young people. After graduation, they would move to Washington, DC. Danny had made a contact with the Washington Post and was going work for them as a reporter. Emily was accepted into graduate school at American University in the philosophy department. Danny was also going to work part-time as a drug counselor for inner city kids. Emily reflected on the events of the past months as she was half listening to the speech. She thought about the fact that there was a big scare among the students about AIDS after the Jody Hershberger revelation. They had several seminars and conferences on the subject, but Emily wondered if students were really going to change. All the men on campus quickly went to the clinic to be tested. The last thing Emily heard was that Jody was in pretty bad shape. Ironically, they put her in the same hospice where Professor Byrd died. She knew that nobody could ever figure out why she did such a thing. Emily remember her conversation with her in the theatre and she seemed so normal then. But, she reasoned, I guess she was acting.

The sun was beginning to peek through the billowy cumulus clouds racing across the sky, and it was turning out to be a beautiful warm day at the end of May. Emily was feeling better as the ceremonies went along. She paid little attention to the speech, preferring to daydream about the future and past. Every once in a while she would hear a cliché like "prepare for the great challenges ahead" or "the road will not be easy." Well, she thought, the road certainly wasn't easy this year, but she felt a strong sense of accomplishment in finally resolving the Byrd issue. It seemed to her like ages ago that he passed away in that awful place.

The speaker was finishing up his speech and as he spoke the last words, all the students hurled their caps into the air, shouting and screaming their lungs out.

Emily looked at Danny. He smiled and gave her another wink. She blew him a kiss as she was reaching into the sky to retrieve her cap.

It was graduation day at last.

If I just lie here very quiet and composed like Norman Bates at the end of Psycho, they will know I wouldn't hurt a fly. In fact, that's all I do. I'm not as stupid as they think I am. They think I'm vegetating here, counting the tubes in my body, but I'm really playing the best role of my illustrious career. I should get an academy award for my performance. If they think they can defeat me, they are the ones who are crazy.

Carefully, I lifted my hand to my cheek, and, with my tired finger nail, picked a red and purple scab off my beautiful face and flicked it into the air. C'est la vie!!! I hope that foul, fuckin' fat nurse doesn't come in today. She's a wicked as shit old crone who ought to be shot. Maybe I'll shoot her myself as soon as I get out of here. There must be something to do besides lie here waiting to get well. I wonder why no one visits me.

Uncle Chuck, or some dude acting his part, came by yesterday, or was it the day before? Uncle Chuck tells me that we're going on a long ocean voyage to retrace the path of Ulysses. That should be fun. I wonder where my tits are. I'm sleeping in a dirty as shit hospital gown that's not my size. It's embarrassing. I can't see my tits any more. I look down and see my toes, but there isn't anything where my tits used to be. I make a mental note to ask the nurse about this new discovery.

Some guy tried to hit on me yesterday, but I blew him off. He told me I was an adoring princess and he was my Prince Charming who was going to carry me away to a fairy land where everything was wonderful and pure. I said, "Get the fuck outta here, Peter Pan!" He wasn't my type at all, but I could get his attention any time I wanted it.

I wonder what year it is. Did the Millennium come?

A kiss on the cheek may be quite continental, but diamonds are a girl's best friend. I can't remember the last time I sat up in bed. I think it was Thursday. No one will give me a mirror around here and it's driving me nuts. They must be jealous of my good looks. I need a mirror to live. I wonder why Jason hasn't visited me. I don't care if he did rape me, I still love him. I assume he will come and rescue me out of this place.

I can't believe they took away my journal. That's okay. I can always start another one. Some asshole acting as a psychiatrist asked me the other day why I gave all those boys the AIDS virus. Ha! Who wrote your crummy script? I laughed in his bad-acting, B-movie face. No one understands me—not even Jason who loves me very much. Actually, it was the only sensible thing to do. The part was, you know....so ordinary. The play needed a better script, so I had to expand its meaning and significance. Sound and fury, signifying, what? Who wants to see a play where nothing happens, but the rotting of a beautiful body. I will just rely on the kindness of strangers. It needed spicing up! A new twist! So, our young heroine is not only suffering from the fatal disease, but seeks out the terrible destroyers of pure virgins and saves mankind from their wicked ways. Get out of here you little no-neck monsters. Ha! I'm a smart as shit genius. It's not as if I did any thing wrong. I mean, let's face it, these guys were scum. I should be getting an humanitarian award for my services. Mother Teresa came to see me the other day and I asked her if she didn't mind sharing the Nobel Peace prize with me. She was nice to me and I asked her what I should wear to the ceremonies when they give me the award. Come to think of it, I wonder where my clothes are; these hospital gowns are stupid as shit.

I saw that scary serpent the other night—the one who was in Byrd's room when I came to visit him. We played a few hands of Pinochle, but one of his arms fell off right in the middle of the game and, well, it was embarrassing really, and we had to quit. I asked him why he looked like the Angel of Death and he told me he had a rough childhood in Muncie, Indiana. And I said, no shit, living in Muncie could turn anybody into a monstrous, hideous beast.

Uh oh, here comes the Big Nurse. She can't fool me. I'm on to her game. Central casting must be desperate to cast an unknown with no experience for this important part. She told me the other day that nobody wants to visit me because I am an infectious leper whom everybody despises. Who told her she could go off script? She can't even get her lines right. "Excuse me, miss," I said, "but it's not infectious leper whom everybody despises, but a wonderful actress whom everybody adores." "Oh, yes," she said, "How could I have messed up my lines that bad?" "Because you stink!" I told her, without the least bit of caring.

Don't worry. Today, I'll just lie here real quiet and peaceful. I won't give them any trouble. They will realize that I am a completely harmless person.

After all, I wouldn't hurt a fly.

EPILOGUE:
HOMECOMING
SOIREE
PHI DELT
FRATERNITY HOUSE
WATTFORD COLLEGE
FALL SEMESTER
1996

LAURA

I rolled over on this guy, not on purpose of course, but he was passed-the-fuck-out, and I wanted to go back to the party, so I leaned over his massive, hairy chest, struggling to get out of bed, but I must have aroused him into consciousness because he heaved and sighed like a beached walrus and made a gross snorting noise of some kind that sounded vaguely like a pig belching, and when he actually spoke, muttering something stupid like "Do you have to go to the bathroom?" I lied and said, "yes," and I rolled over him, inadvertently smelling his funky armpit as I managed to prop my hands on the side of the bed and swing my legs around and plant them on the floor. I glanced down at tonight's love connection and I felt sick to my stomach, almost as if I was going to throw up. Maybe it was the fact that his hairy belly stuck out from beneath his dirty T-shirt. I realized that he was too fat for me. How did I wind up sleeping with such an out-of-shape guy? Maybe I was losing my touch. Just before sneaking out the door I looked on the night table and noticed an unopened pack of condoms under the lamp. I only have a vague memory of fucking this guy, but I swear he told me he put a condom on.

I couldn't care less about the football game or the homecoming festivities, but I wanted to get to know some of the PHI DELT guys. Everyone says they're the coolest fraternity. I walked downstairs, hoping nobody would notice that I came out of the fat dork's room. Someone was playing REM (or was it U2?) and everyone was dancing and moshing real wild-like, bumping into each other and throwing themselves into a mosh pit of sweaty hormonal bodies. I couldn't dig it. In the midst of party bodies flying everywhere into the night, Heather Fletcher (who weighs 435 pounds) stumbled up to me and offered me a sip of her grape juice and grain and I said "No thanks" and noticed Kyle Barrow (who I slept with last year) in the corner hitting on a nowhere chick in painted on red slacks. I heard that Kyle might have AIDS because he fucked Jody Hershberger, but he looks too cute to have AIDS, and besides, I'd go to bed with him anyway—if he used a condom.

In the midst of a lot of confusion, some guy named Jubu asked me to smoke a joint of Colombian and I said, "Okay" and we went up to his room which turned out to be right next to the room I just came from and Jubu said something about the guy in the next room being gay and I wondered if he meant the guy I just left, but I don't care anyway. "Does he have a fat stomach?" I asked, immediately feeling lousy for asking such a stupid question. Jubu looked at me kinda perplexed, drunk, swaying, (probably stoned already) and just mumbled something I couldn't make out.

I walked into his room and of course it was decorated with the obligatory Deadhead poster and a picture of Michael Jordan, his tongue hanging out, legs splayed, dunking a basketball. I wondered how anyone could sleep with a black guy. In the dark, stumbling, I stepped on a baseball glove and picked it up and put it on my hand, although I wasn't quite sure if I had it on right. "Wanna have a catch?" I said to Jubu, although he was busy rummaging through a closet trying to locate a bong. Right away, I wished I had not come into this cave-world of pasty-faced people. I was hoping it would be mostly ZETE guys, but there were these dumb trashed out Theta wannabes in there who didn't belong at all. Some totally bleached out cheesy girl in a bright red fuckme mini-skirt and a Florida gator's T-shirt (who weighs 573 pounds) and whom I saw fucking Carter Mason, III in his kitchen last week came up to me and said, "Hello" and I said, "Nice outfit." Turning around toward the stereo, hoping to avoid eye contact with anyone, I couldn't help but notice a creepy freshman (who weighs 671 pounds) sleeping, passed out, on a dirty brown couch with her suck–face mouth open in a disgustingly grotesque manner. She didn't belong at all.

I went up to Sarah Tobias, who is actually pretty cool, and I asked her if she knew any gossip, especially about the freshmen whom we all hate. Sarah, who once fucked a guy and ate a sandwich at the same time, told me she heard that Jody Hershberger (whom we really all hated) is sick and crazy in some private hospital and weighs about 32 pounds. "No shit" I said, trying to remember why I am so jealous of Jody Hershberger, Then I remembered she was real cute and I'm glad she got AIDS or whatever...

I began to feel nauseated, so I walked out onto the balcony to get some fresh air. I strolled over to the railing and gazed out into the sky. It was a beautiful evening. It feels almost good. My eyes drifted down to the parking lot below and I heard a rustling sound in the bushes near the dempster dumpster. I spotted a couple of naked fratpeople fucking their brains out, trying to be quiet, although I heard things like...."fuck me...suck me..."

I watched them for a couple minutes and nothing very interesting happened except when she lit a cigarette and blew smoke in his face I thought that was a classic.

All of a sudden, I felt dizzy and a bit sick, and I staggered back into the party room. A sickening, sweet, smell permeated the party room. It seemed to be following me around. I went over to the brown couch and sat down, and I could feel my head swimming around and around as I tried to regain my composure. But the grotesque faces of all the people at the party began to encircle me and I felt very claustrophobic, but I couldn't seem to speak, so I just sat there thinking about myself as a black cloud swirled overhead and engulfed me.

Alone, I passed out into the night.

0-595-31876-2

Made in the USA
Middletown, DE
14 August 2022